DARK GAME

A LANCE BRODY NOVEL (BOOK 1)

MICHAEL ROBERTSON, JR.

ISBN: 9781521481714

While DARK GAME is the first full-length novel of the Lance Brody series, Lance's story begins a bit earlier. But don't worry, you can still read this novel in its entirety and fully enjoy it.

However, a 100-page prequel novella titled DARK BEGINNINGS is also available, and will answer additional questions you may have about Lance and his journey, and also explore a bit of his past, where he came from ... and who he's running from.

DARK BEGINNINGS can be read before, after, or even during any of the Lance Brody novels. Whichever you choose, I hope you enjoy.

-Michael Robertson Jr

HIS MOTHER HAD ALWAYS TOLD HIM THAT A FRESH SLICE OF
pie and a hot cup of tea were all any good soul needed to
temporarily forget their problems. The type of pie and the flavor
of tea were of no consequence. Fresh and hot, that was all that
mattered.

For the first twenty-two years of his life, Lance Brody had
shared many an evening in his family home's kitchen, crowded
around the small table with his mother, eating her fresh pies and
discussing the way of things. He'd never acquired the taste for
tea, however, and preferred coffee for their long discussions.
Black. His mother hated coffee, but his substitution of another
hot beverage in place of the tea—instead of something from a
bottle—seemed to satisfy her.

Alcohol was strictly forbidden in the house. If there was a
familial reason for this, Pamela Brody had never told Lance.
Nor was religion to blame; the only time Lance's mother ever
prayed was when the Bulls were in a tight one with whichever
NBA opponent they were competing against, and those prayers
were directed at unseen basketball gods who inevitably cared
little about an individual's libations. She had no affiliation with

the team, nor the city of Chicago. When Lance had finally asked her why she had chosen the Bulls as her team, she'd simply replied that she liked their mascot. He was funny. Her love of basketball in general was a mystery to Lance, as she'd never played the sport herself, but it was the only organized activity she'd ever encouraged him to participate in throughout his entire upbringing. But the alcohol—she said it poisoned the mind and the body, and Lance could see no argument against that. He'd never tasted a drop of the stuff.

Not even on the night she'd died, when no pie seemed big enough and no coffee black enough to alleviate the pain.

He hadn't cried, not then, and not for most of his life. Crying was something his mother had been strangely against. Strange because of how much she'd stressed being at peace with oneself and understanding and trusting your feelings. She hadn't said this the way a condescending therapist might to an uncooperative husband, but in a way that suggested self-strength and confidence. It was what *you* felt inside, who *you* were that mattered in life. "Embrace yourself, Lance. Only then can you fully embrace others." He might have been eight when she'd first offered up this token of wisdom. A typical conversation to have with a second-grader. Typical was something his mother had never come close to achieving. She had been extraordinary. Not in the same ways Lance was extraordinary—wouldn't *that* have been helpful?—but in a way that allowed him the trust and confidence in her to share his world with her and have her love him and help him and stand by his side as he grew and developed in every way you could imagine, and in ways you couldn't.

But now she was dead and Lance was completely alone, stepping off a bus two hundred and thirty-seven miles away from home with the previous night's horrific events still burning fresh in his tired mind.

He had no plan. Hadn't had time for a plan. The bus was the first one headed out of his town, and he didn't care much where it was going. He'd had to leave, been forced to run.

Now he was here.

He was hungry.

Food was as good of a start to a plan as he could think of.

He didn't need to wait for the bus driver to haul his luggage from one of the holding bins along the bottom of the bus. Everything he'd been able to take with him from home was stuffed into his backpack—an expensive thing gifted to him by the owner of a local sporting goods store years ago, when Lance had helped him with a problem—and the backpack had remained in the seat next to him for the bus's entire trip. He adjusted the straps over his shoulders, turned and thanked the bus driver for getting them all to their destination safely—an act that was met with a confused expression and a mumbled reply that might have been "You're welcome"—and then headed across the street, through a large and mostly empty parking lot, and stopped briefly on the sidewalk.

He breathed in deeply and closed his eyes. Exhaled and opened them. Turned right and started walking, the soles of his basketball sneakers making gentle scraping sounds against the concrete. A warm breeze blew into his face, and a warmer sun was just rising above the horizon at his back. He walked with the traffic, the occasional vehicle slowly passing by on his left. The drivers all looked bored. Looked like they'd rather be anywhere else. It was Thursday morning, so Lance imagined that might surely be the case if they were all headed to a nine-to-five so they could pay the mortgage. *Well, that's one thing I don't have to worry about.*

He kept walking.

A mile later, after passing a small strip-mall and a McDonald's, he found what he'd been looking for. The momentary flit

3

of happiness the sight caused him was so brief it might not have happened at all, just a teasing scent carried off by the wind before it could even be enjoyed.

Lance felt something pushing it away.

The diner was called Annabelle's Apron and looked like it might have been built before Nixon resigned. A rough shoebox of a place with a shiny aluminum front and lots of windows. The roofline looked to be sagging a bit, and there was no telling whether the bright neon signage atop it actually still had any juice left, but there were a few faces on the other side of the glass windows, and all of them were forking food or sipping coffee. Lance stepped off the curb, allowed a pickup truck to back out of a parking space, and then crossed the lot and pulled open the door.

The interior of Annabelle's Apron looked, sounded, and—most importantly—smelled exactly as Lance had hoped. Directly ahead was the long counter with a matching row of stools. A few folks seated there, elbows resting atop the counter as they read the morning paper while they ate. The windows were lined from end to end with booths, the upholstery a bright blue—robin's egg, that's what his mother would have called it—and the tabletops showed their age, full of cracks and streaks and blemishes. The battle scars of thousands of meals, tens of thousands of cups of coffee and tea and glasses of orange juice and soda pop. The air hummed and chimed with the noise of the kitchen crew working hard, glimpsed sporadically through the open window behind the counter. Two waitresses went to and fro from table to kitchen to table. Smiles plastered on and only a faint sheen of sweat on their brows so far. Hushed conversation and soft-playing country music from a lone overhead speaker were occasionally punctuated by the yelling of a young child in the rearmost booth—a location surely chosen as a strategy by its not-our-first-rodeo parents.

And all of this was accompanied by the smells of bacon and eggs and butter and coffee and biscuits.

Lance had been standing at the door for too long, and the woman behind the counter called out as she refilled a patron's coffee, "Sit anywhere you'd like, sweetie. Be right witcha."

He looked over his shoulder, back to the parking lot and the everything beyond it. Scanned the horizon. The sun was higher now, almost full-form. Then his stomach grumbled and he took a seat at the counter, setting his backpack at his feet and taking the laminated menu from the woman who'd told him to sit. The menu was smudged with grease and dried grape jelly, but the text was readable. Lance ordered four scrambled eggs, bacon, hash browns, and a large stack of pancakes. The woman behind the counter—early sixties, Lance guessed, and with a look of no-nonsense experience creased into her aged brow—looked him up and down one time before asking, "And to drink, sweetie?"

"Coffee, please," Lance said.

She nodded and tore the order ticket from the pad in her hand and turned to post it on the wheel in the window. She spun the ticket into the kitchen, where it was quickly snatched by a fleeting glimpse of a cook's hand, and then she returned with a black plastic coffee mug and poured from a full pot. "Just brewed this one, sweetie. You're its first." She winked and asked if he needed cream or sugar.

"No, thank you," Lance said, doing his best to smile.

"Margie, I'll take some of that," a gentleman—a regular, apparently—called from the end of the counter. The woman—now Margie—put a hand on her hip and said, "You've been tryin' to get some of this for twenty-three years, Hank Peterson. Today's not gonna be no different!" This got a chuckle out of Hank and the two other waitresses, and Margie went off to fill Hank's coffee.

Lance sat in silence, looking down at the counter and

listening to the sounds around him and sipping his coffee as he waited for his food. His mother had always said that diners were some of the greatest places on earth because everything was real —the food and the people. Honest Americans cooking good ol' American comfort food. The potential of diners always excited her, like each one was an individual mystery just waiting to be unraveled.

Margie refilled Lance's coffee.

His food arrived shortly after.

The bars on the stool were a little too high for him to comfortably rest his long legs—at six foot six, this was the type of problem he'd grown accustomed to—and he had to adjust himself repeatedly to keep his legs from falling asleep. But the coffee was strong and the food was delicious, and the general ambiance of the diner did its best to revive his spirits.

Margie cleared his plates when he'd finished. "I wasn't sure you'd be able to eat it all, t'be honest. Large stack usually fills up most folks."

Lance wasn't most folks.

"I don't suppose you'll be wantin' nothin' else?"

Lance was about to say no, but then paused. Said, "Do you serve pie?"

Margie laughed. "You kiddin'?"

"No, ma'am." Lance shrugged and smiled. "I have a high metabolism, I guess."

"We don't set it out till lunch, but I can get you a slice from the back. Apple okay?"

"Is it fresh?" Lance asked, feeling a twinge in his heart.

Margie smiled. "I bake 'em fresh every morning." Then she disappeared into the kitchen and came back a minute later with a large slice of apple pie on a tiny saucer. "That's bigger than a normal serving," she said. "Figured you could handle it."

Lance felt the warmth of the woman's kindness and smiled and nodded. "Yes, ma'am. Thank you very much."

He was halfway through his pie—it was fresh, as promised—when he noticed the woman sitting on the stool next to him. He wasn't sure when she'd arrived, but she was there now and looking directly at him.

"I used to put more cinnamon in it," she said. "I don't know why they cut back on it. It was much better that way if you ask me. I think it's too sweet now."

The woman looked much older than Margie, eighty at best but more likely closer to ninety. She wore a plain brown cotton dress and brown leather shoes, stockings visible on the bit of ankle that showed at the hem. Her hair was gray, but still thick, done up in a tight bun atop her head. Her face was so deeply wrinkled it was as if her skin were modeling clay, and somebody had dragged the tines of a fork up and down its entire surface.

"I don't think it's too sweet," Lance said, then turned to see if Margie was in earshot. "But I do think less sugar and more cinnamon would be an improvement."

The woman nodded once. "Of course it would." Then she was quiet for a while, staring ahead toward the kitchen window. Lance stared ahead with her, waiting. She spoke again, this time a little quieter, sadness creeping into her voice. "I don't know why the thing with the pie bothers me so much. They've kept things pretty much the same around here all these years, but the pie ... I was darn near famous for that pie. People used to come from two counties over for *my* pie, and then one day these floozies decide to up and change the recipe. Who do they think they are?"

Lance considered this, took his last bite. "Well," he said, "the folks that remember *your* pie, they're going to know that *this* pie isn't your fault. In fact, if it was as good as you say, those folks are probably just as disappointed as you."

She looked at him and smiled. Her teeth were yellowed, but mostly intact. "I suppose you're right, son. I suppose you're right. Guess I never thought of it like that." She pointed an arthritis-gnarled finger at him. "You'd have liked my pie. I know it."

"Yes, ma'am. I believe I would have."

Then they were quiet again. Margie cleared Lance's plate away and he declined more coffee. Hank Peterson paid his tab and left his newspaper when he was finished. The man two stools down took it and flipped to the sports section. The family with the loud child had left and been replaced by two high school–aged boys who looked sleepy, and Lance wondered why they weren't in class. Through the kitchen window, he could see one of the two waitresses counting her tips and joking with one of the unseen cooks.

"So," Lance said, turning to look at the woman on the stool next to him, "how bad is it here?"

The woman closed her eyes, almost as if she were fighting back tears. When she opened them, she suddenly looked very tired. "Bad," she said.

Lance nodded. "Yeah ... that's what I was afraid of."

"Are you going to help?"

"I don't know if I can."

"You don't believe that."

Lance placed a twenty on the counter, stood and grabbed his backpack. "No," he said. "But sometimes I wish I did."

He waved goodbye and thanked Margie and then headed for the door. He stopped. On the wall to the left of the door was a photograph in a rough wooden frame, yellowed with age. It was a picture of the woman who'd sat next to him, only in the photograph, she was behind the counter, holding a whole pie in her hands and putting on a small grin for the camera. Beneath the photograph was written:

Annabelle Winters

1905-1990

Lance turned and looked at the barstool where she'd been sitting, now empty. Then he took one last glance at the photo and pushed through the door, out into the world.

LANCE DIDN'T ALWAYS SEE THE DEAD. HIS WORLD WASN'T A nightmare where he walked around all day amongst restless souls and lingering spirits with unfinished business. He didn't check out at the grocery store staring into the faces of demons.

But demons *were* real.

And he did see the dead. Not every day, but frequently. Most were friendly, though often troubled. Others were not so friendly. Annabelle Winters had been of the former variety, despite her pie grievances, and her visit had had a clear meaning that was nothing to do with pastries.

Lance continued west on the sidewalk. The traffic on the road to his left diminished to only single vehicles passing by with large spots of silence in between. He'd apparently left the outskirts of town—where the strip malls and diner had been— and made his way into what passed as downtown. It was a quiet, tranquil setting—old-school, a place where you could imagine Andy Griffith as sheriff, or Hallmark coming to town to film a Christmas special. The street was lined with rows of brick buildings with dull-colored awnings. Above the awnings, large hand-painted sections of the brick exteriors—badly faded by the sun and years of rain—advertised businesses and stores whose proprietors (and revenue) had surely died long ago. He glanced into a few of the windows on his right as he walked, saw a bakery, a small hardware store, a used bookstore, a lawyer's and a CPA's office side by side. A few faces stared back, eyes locked onto him as he passed. He couldn't blame them. He knew that in a town like this, newcomers would be easily spotted. Especially ones as large as he. He tried to smile, hoped he'd succeeded.

He kept walking. Passed more businesses and crossed side streets before downtown finally spat him out onto an intersection of two rural routes that stretched off into land beginning to show signs of residential development and larger industrial buildings. He crossed the main road and headed south. The sidewalk wasn't as well maintained here, and his sneakers kicked up stray rocks and chunks of concrete as he went. Weeds grew through cracks. The sun was getting hot, and his t-shirt began to stick to the small of his back. A half mile later, he stopped. Ahead he could see where the sidewalk finally died and bled into grass, and a memory flashed in his head of his mother reading to him from Shel Silverstein's *Where the Sidewalk Ends*. He enjoyed the image briefly before storing it away.

He stepped off the sidewalk and walked into a crumbling parking lot with only a handful of cars that could be called clunkers at best. He'd found what he'd been looking for.

Another telltale sign of a small town is that a lot of things are named after their owners. Annabelle's Apron was the first example, and now Lance stood in front of Bob's Place. An L-shaped one-story museum of a building whose sign—medium-sized and, again, hand-painted—advertised simply: ROOMS. BAR. The office was at the far end of the longer segment of the L, and the rest of the structure was punctuated with eleven blue doors that had once likely been deep and royal, but now more resembled the light (robin's egg) blue of the diner's tables. A Coke machine hummed at the L's intersection, an ice machine with the words *Out of Order* written across its door standing silently at its side. Window A/C units drooped from next to each room's door, only one of which was buzzing and rattling in the window frame as it worked. Two modern satellite dishes were mounted on the roof above the door to the office.

Lance checked the license plates on the few cars parked in the lot as he headed toward the office. Found all but one to be in-state. The lone exception was from Alaska. Alaskan plates always seemed very foreign, Lance found, considering you had to drive through a whole other country to get from Alaska to the forty-eight.

Large trees loomed from behind the building, the perimeter of what appeared to be deep forest. He grabbed the handle of the office's glass door and pushed. A small bell mounted above the door frame jingled loudly as he did so, and he was instantly overwhelmed with the smell of lemon—some sort of cleaning product that had been applied so heavily he felt like he'd stepped into a bottle of Pine-Sol. He coughed once and his eyes began to water, blurring his vision.

"Oh my goodness, I'm so sorry! I wasn't expecting anyone so early!" a female voice, high and pleasant and young, called from somewhere ahead. Lance used the sleeve of his t-shirt and wiped his eyes, then breathed in heavily through his mouth. When his throat stopped burning and his vision began to clear, he was genuinely surprised at what he saw.

The outside of the building suggested that the office's interior would be run-down at best. At worst, it might have had hourly rates posted on a sign beside a pane of bulletproof glass, which the desk attendant would sit behind and take wads of cash through a sliding metal drawer and immediately forget any faces seen coming or going.

In actuality, the office was immaculate. The floor was a freshly polished (maybe it *was* Pine-Sol) wood whose color matched an elegant front desk that ran along the short left wall. Centered on the right-hand wall, a large television was mounted above an entertainment center with a satellite receiver sitting on top, along with a large tray full of various neatly arranged liquor bottles. Six small glasses and a small ice bucket with tongs filled the rest of surface, nearly sparkling in the overhead lighting. An old but inviting leather couch provided seating. Lance looked at the liquor for moment (*It poisons the mind and the body*) and then over to the front desk, behind which stood a girl whose beauty was as elegant as the office itself. "Is that the bar?" he asked, pointing to the entertainment center.

The girl smiled, a grin that suggested she wanted to laugh, but her professionalism kept it inside. "It is."

Lance made a show of looking around the office—heck, you could go ahead and call it a lobby—and then shrugged. "Not what I imagined."

The girl's smile was still there, but now it was her turn to shrug and say, "I could say the same thing."

"About the bar?"

"About you."

Lance left the door and made his way to the desk. His left sneaker squeaked and nearly slipped out from under him on his first step. He caught his balance before going down, and the girl behind the desk said, "Careful! Again, sorry. I would have put out the wet floor sign, but like I said, I wasn't expecting anybody at this time of morning."

Lance carefully stepped across the floor and then rested his hands on the desk, a gesture he hoped would show that he meant her no harm, wasn't about to pull a gun or blade and demand whatever it was she could offer. Now that he was closer, he could see the girl was his age at the most, maybe a bit younger.

"But I thought you said you were imagining me."

"I'm sorry?"

"A second ago. You said I wasn't what you'd imagined. Why were you imagining me if you weren't expecting me?" *And why are you flirting, Lance?*

Because I've had a really terrible and really long couple of days and it feels good to have a normal conversation with a pretty girl.

He finished justifying himself to himself just in time to hear the girl give off a soft laugh, and watched as her stiff and professional façade crumbled and she visibly relaxed. "I wasn't expecting exactly you, exactly today. I just meant you aren't exactly the type of guest we usually get."

"And what type of guest do you think I am ... exactly?"

She shrugged. "Normal."

Well, that's exactly *where you're wrong, my dear.* "How so?" he asked.

She rolled her eyes. "Look around. Do we look like the type of place nice wholesome folks stop for the night? Families on vacation? Businessmen en route to a conference? No. The folks I give keys to are usually weathered and beaten. Down on their luck and satisfied with the first roof they can find over their head for the night before they wake up and head off to wherever else life plans on shitting on them. They drink, they do drugs—sometimes they deal drugs, and trust me when I say I'm not afraid to call the police if I suspect that's going down. I've got a shotgun under the counter and Daddy taught me how to use it when I was ten."

Lance held her eyes as she spoke. He was entranced by her confidence and honesty.

"Now you," she said, "you've got baggage, I know that.

Otherwise you'd have hitched a ride another twenty miles down Route 19 like everyone else and got a room at the Holiday Inn Express or the Motel 6. But whatever your baggage is, you carry it well. You're clean, you're handsome, and your clothes aren't tattered and falling apart. That logo on your backpack means it cost more than most people who stay here probably make in two weeks' time, so you've either got, or had, a steady job. Or somebody gave it to you—because I don't think you'd steal it. You just don't have the look. And if somebody gave it to you, it means you've got friends. And trust me, the last thing somebody who stays here has is a single friend in the world."

When she finished speaking, she reached back and tightened the hair tie holding her blond ponytail in place and then adjusted the collar of her black dress shirt. She wore matching black dress pants that were sleek and formfitting. Her makeup was light and simple. Blue eyes that pierced. Lance was impressed with her powers of observation. She wasn't completely right about him—and honestly, nobody would ever be. Unless there were others like him, which he deep down believed there had to be, the Surfer and the Reverend having all but proven this—but she'd come close.

Instead of confirming or denying any of her analysis of him, he turned and spread his hands out, gesturing at the immaculate and upscale look of the office. "Then why all this, if your guests are of the class you say they are?"

She responded instantly, and almost defensively. As if she'd been asked this question before and was tired of some underlying accusation. "Because if I have the chance to be a bright spot in their otherwise dark days, it's my responsibility as a respectable human being to be just that. I can make them feel comfortable. I can let them enjoy some nicer things, even if just for an evening. Most of these folks, despite everything I just said about them, at their core, they're still nice people. The rest of the world has just stopped giving them a chance."

Lance was floored at the size of this girl's heart but worried about her potential ignorance to the evil in the world. "And if they're really not nice at their core?" he asked.

She shrugged. "The shotgun, remember?"

Lance said he did remember, and suddenly he felt very tired. The night-long bus ride—which he'd stayed awake for, staring out the window at nothing but passing cars and expanses of field and trees—was finally catching up to him, and the burst of energy the food from the diner had provided was wearing off. Lance explained this to the girl, not wanting to appear rude and bored with talking to her, and he asked if he could have a room. She said it was twenty dollars a night and gave him the key to room one, which was right next door to the office. He gave her a twenty and thanked her. He turned to leave and then stopped.

This girl was extremely honest and seemed to have an adept ability to read people—and maybe situations. "Hey, listen," he said, knowing his question was going to sound weird, but also knowing this was his best chance of making his job a little easier. "You live here? In town, I mean."

She looked at him for a moment, eyes searching for a meaning to his question, before she finally nodded once.

Lance took a breath and said, "Do you think there's anything bad going on? Like ... I don't know," (*Don't say it, Lance. Don't say it.*) "Evil?" Then quickly, "I mean, you know, like ... anything out of the ordinary been happening lately?"

She didn't move, just stared at him for what felt like an hour. Then she finally reached behind the desk and (*Oh God, she's going to pull the shotgun on me*) brought out a newspaper. She held it out to him. "I almost forgot, all guests receive a complimentary paper at check-in." Lance stepped forward and reached for it, and when his hand touched it, she leaned forward and whispered, "Come back here tonight at eight. Daddy works graveyard, so he won't make a surprise visit. We can talk then." Then she stood, straightened her shirt and said, "I hope you enjoy your stay."

Lance took the paper and was still processing the girl's words as he made his way to the door. He turned back. "Hey, what's your name?"

"Leah," she said.

"I'm Lance," he said, then walked through the door and out onto the sidewalk.

He'd taken two steps when he stopped dead and sucked in a quick, deep breath. He staggered back a step. He closed his eyes and concentrated hard as the cold feeling tried to bury itself in his chest. It didn't last long, but the gloomy feeling that accompanied the moment lingered in the air. Lance opened his eyes and looked around at the parking lot, then out to the road. Turned his head up and looked to the sky, still bright and clear.

It knew he was in town. It knew what he was.

[3]

THE ELEGANCE AND UPKEEP FROM THE MOTEL'S OFFICE didn't make its way to the guest rooms, but it was still better than Lance was expecting. Not that he really would have cared either way, but still, being comfortable never hurt.

The room was small, and dark because of the heavy curtain drawn across the window. Some sunlight shining in would have helped to erase the gloomy feel, but Lance planned on sleeping some if he could, and he definitely didn't want any peering eyes looking in on him. A double bed was centered on the left wall, its headboard plain and chipped. The bed was neatly made, and the comforter, though worn and faded and thin, appeared clean enough. The carpet had been vacuumed recently, because the tracks were still visible, and either the small nightstand and TV table had been wiped down in the past few days, or the room was oddly devoid of dust. The television was a small, unimpressive flat-screen—something off the clearance rack at a discount electronics store, or a Black Friday special used to reduce some dead inventory—and beneath it was a basic satellite receiver, an ominous blue circle glowing from its center. The devices looked like something brought back from the future compared to the rest of the room's décor.

Lance gently set his backpack on the bed and checked the bathroom, switching on the light from outside the door and peeking in. The fixtures were old and chipped and had stopped shining years ago, but he could smell disinfectant and bleach and didn't see any visible signs of soap scum or mildew or, well ... urine or feces. It was always good not to see urine or feces. They could dampen a mood really quick.

He used the toilet and then washed his hands, unwrapping the mini bar of soap next to the hot water knob and finding that it had nearly no smell at all. But it would clean—that was soap's job, after all. Smelling nice was just a bonus. He avoided looking at himself in the mirror, not ready to face how terrible he might look after the past couple days.

Hey, Leah said you were handsome.

Yeah, but she also thought I was normal.

He went back to the bedroom and double-checked that the door was locked and then secured the chain. He stole a quick glance out the window, finding only the same parking lot with the same cars, and then pulled the curtain shut tight and lay down on the bed. The pillow was soft and smelled like detergent—something off-brand, bought in bulk for cheap, but better than nothing. He closed his eyes, took two big, heavy breaths, and tried to drift off to sleep.

He couldn't.

How could he?

His past few days had been a whirlwind that had resulted in him having to flee the town where he'd been born and raised, the town he'd loved his whole life. And his mother ... *tragedy* seemed too weak a word. He tried to push out the images of their last few moments together, but it was impossible. With the realization she was gone surfacing once again, and the sadness filling him from the inside out—his own sadness this time, not the looming threat of an outside presence—Lance clasped his hands behind his head and looked around the tiny dark motel room, feeling more alone than he'd ever imagined was possible. Alone and carrying a burden that even now he still didn't fully understand.

He missed her. Loved her.

But still, he did not cry.

He closed his eyes again and tried to focus. Tried to concentrate on the one thing he could right now that would keep his mind busy and dispel—if only temporarily—his sorrow.

The dead didn't show themselves to him for friendly social visits. He'd yet to have one appear and invite him to a barbecue or tell him that his hair looked nice. They came with a purpose. Lance suspected that showing themselves to him required a great deal of energy—whatever great unseen force somehow governed their celestial world—and they would not go to such efforts without sufficient cause. They usually came for two reasons: to warn him, or to ask for help. Though Lance supposed the two usually went hand in hand, as the warnings in turn required him to take action.

Annabelle Winters's appearance was no different.

He'd felt it when he'd gotten off the bus. After he'd crossed the terminal's parking lot and stood on the sidewalk trying to figure out which way he wanted to go, he'd felt that ping of evil. There was no other way to explain it. Evil could not remain undetected by those attuned to the frequencies along which it traveled, and Lance, despite his best wishes, was more attuned than most. There was something bad lurking in this town, something that had taken root and would continue to blacken what it touched until there was no more to feed on, or until somebody stopped it.

Lance sighed heavily on the bed, adjusted the pillow

21

beneath his head. Most of his friends from high school had gone off to college, graduated, and were in the beginning stages of starting a family. Nice jobs in big cities. Friday nights on the town with new friends. Golfing and running 5Ks and spending lazy mornings on the couch with girlfriends and fiancées on the weekends. And here he was, by himself in a dingy motel in a forgotten sleepy town, getting ready to try and "crack the case," as they say, battle the forces of evil, and probably end up getting himself killed in the process.

And nobody would ever know or care.

He sighed again and rolled over onto his side, stared at the locked door and wondered what was outside, what was waiting for him. He longed for golfing and 5Ks. Longed for a taste of normalcy.

Instead, he feared a fresh, unknown evil. Was terrified to look out the window and find a Volkswagen bus the color of a Creamsicle waiting for him.

He glanced at the newspaper he'd set on the nightstand, was about to reach for it and stopped. Through the paper-thin wall behind him came a soft singing. A slow tune that sounded both beautiful and sad, soothing.

Leah, he thought. *She thinks I'm handsome.*

She continued on with the song, this girl who thought he was normal, her voice imperfect but sweet. Lance didn't know how long she went on, because he finally drifted off to sleep.

GO, LANCE. IT'S ONLY WHAT'S RIGHT. I LOVE YOU.

Lance gasped and jumped up from the bed, his mother's last words to him still echoing faintly in his mind as the dream faded and the room took shape before him. He'd dreamed of that night, the one so fresh it was still cooling, the one where he'd lost his mother and had fled. The night that had ultimately brought him here. Bob's Place.

Leah.

He listened, trying to pick up any signs of her. The singing that had lulled him to sleep was gone, as were all other noises from the other side of the wall. The motel room was darker, the sun having shifted across and beyond his window, leaving only a dim strip of gray light to come through the crack between curtain and wall.

Come back here tonight at eight, Leah had told him. *Daddy works graveyard.*

The fact there was still light outside at all told Lance he'd not missed his deadline, but he had no idea how long he'd slept. He unzipped the side pocket of his backpack and retrieved the pay-as-you-go cell phone he'd had for years. A black plastic flip phone, the device had been a gift from his mother. She'd purchased one for herself as well, a matching one that they often had gotten mixed up, and her number was one of only a handful Lance had programmed into his phone's memory. As he flipped open the screen, he suddenly had two very conflicting thoughts collide in terms of what he should do with her stored number. Part of him, the first part to show its face, said to delete it. It was of no use to him anymore and would only be a painful reminder of her absence every time he scrolled past it. The second part, the one a split second slower to reach him but carrying a seemingly more powerful suggestion, told Lance to call the number. Let it ring the four rings that would go unanswered before switching to voicemail and letting Lance hear his mother's voice again.

(Hi! It seems our paths weren't meant to cross right now. I can't wait to talk to you soon!)

Lance's mother hadn't asked people to leave a message. She had always been of the mindset that information reached her when it was meant to reach her, and that if she'd missed somebody's phone call, the conversation—and thus the information—could wait. Lance had told her this was ridiculous—as he'd said of a lot of the things she'd suggested over the years—but the tenet had never seemed to cause any trouble for her or him, so ... what did Lance know?

(I can't wait to talk to you soon!)

Lance would never talk to her again.

Conflicted, and with the wound still open, he did nothing with his mother's number and simply checked the time. It was almost seven o'clock. He knew that he'd been tired—the long sleepless night catching up with him—but he was surprised he'd managed to sleep the whole day. The way he was feeling, he wouldn't have been surprised to discover he'd never get a full night's rest again.

He was hungry, but with only an hour to spare, he decided to investigate the (what he guessed to be) one clue Leah had so subtly given him. He'd been nearly out of the motel's office when he'd questioned her thoughts on any bad happenings in town, and her response had been to hand him a newspaper. She had told him to come back to the office at eight, but she could have done that without the newspaper. Lance glanced at it, sitting neatly on the nightstand next to him. *There's something in there*, he thought. *There's something in there that'll help me.*

He revisited the bathroom, washed his hands, and then turned on the small lamp on the nightstand. The bulb gave off a quick, loud buzz and then died. Lance sighed. He didn't want to switch on the main overhead light. Call it paranoia, but a light that bright would be more visible from the outside. Say, to somebody across the street looking for signs of life in one of Bob's Place's rented rooms. And though he had nothing to go on except that feeling he'd been hit with upon first exiting the motel's office hours ago, Lance was almost positive somebody would, eventually, start looking for him. *Join the club*, he thought.

Lance walked across the room, the outside light fading quickly, and unscrewed one of the three bare bulbs installed in the light fixture above the bathroom sink. He used it to replace the fried bulb in the lamp, then pulled the pillowcase off one of the bed's two pillows and draped it over the lampshade to further dampen the light. Satisfied, he sat with his back against the cheap headboard and picked up the paper. The first thing he noticed was the date. It was from last week. He started reading the first headline.

Forty-five minutes later, he'd finished the paper. He'd read the whole thing, front to back, then neatly refolded each section and reassembled the paper to the extent that it looked as if it'd never been read at all. He stared down at the front page again, his eyes darting all over the headlines and the smaller text beneath each, picking out words and phrases and desperately searching for something he might have missed.

He'd read the entire paper, ads and all, and had seen nothing—felt nothing—about any of the articles that appeared to be cause for alarm. Of course, he knew that the workings of evil would often go undetected. It wasn't as if he'd expected a headline to scream out BAD PERSON DOES BAD THING! PLEASE HELP US, LANCE! But he figured he had a better eye (and a better gut feeling) than most when it came to reading between the lines about these sorts of things. Plus, Leah had given him the paper for a reason. He knew that as well as he knew his name was Lancelot Brody, so the fact that this girl had seen something he hadn't bothered him. Somewhere in these thousands of words on these sheets of paper was a starting point for him, and he was blind to it.

"Oh well," he said out loud to the room, choosing not to dwell on the issue. Because he had another way to get his answer, you see. Lance was gifted, but he wasn't too proud to admit needing help. "I'll just ask her." His voice was groggy and sounded weird bouncing off the motel's walls. He cleared his throat and stood, stretching and giving off a big yawn. He ran his tongue across his teeth and the roof of his mouth, wished he could brush his teeth. He'd have to go shopping soon. He had nothing but what was in his pockets and his backpack, which didn't amount to much in terms of daily living. He didn't even have deodorant or a clean pair of boxer shorts.

He checked the time on his phone. Ten minutes till eight. He went to the bathroom, which was now thirty-three percent gloomier thanks to his lightbulb excavation, and ran the cold water from the tap. He splashed his face and then dried it with the small hand towel. He finally braved a look in the mirror and saw that he wasn't too bad off. He could use a shave, and he had

26

bedhead—both from the bus's seat and the bed's pillow—but otherwise he looked okay. He searched the countertop for a mini bottle of mouthwash but was disappointed. There was only the bar of soap and the hand towel. He supposed Leah and her father (*Daddy works graveyard*) could only stretch the budget but so far.

The two remaining bulbs above the sink flickered, once, twice, then remained fully lit. Lance stopped moving and looked ahead into the mirror, listened. He heard nothing but the weak hum of the bulbs and saw nothing but his own reflection staring back at him.

It's nothing.

He switched off the bathroom light and went back to the bedroom, grabbing his backpack in one hand and the newspaper in the other. He swung the pack's strap over one shoulder and made his way to the door, unlocked the handle and unlatched the chain. He pulled the door open a crack and peered out.

The sun had mostly set, and only the faintest traces of dusk still remained, the night air looking pallid and the deepest of grays. Single bulbs inside cracked plastic domes were mounted above the doorway of each of the motel's rooms, but the light they offered was laughable. Lance could see the glow of light from the office's door falling from his right and it cast long shadows on the sidewalk outside his door and into the parking lot. The lot itself was almost entirely deserted. The car from Alaska had moved on, and only two other vehicles remained, a battered green Ford pickup with a rusted-out bumper and a faded blue Jeep Cherokee with expired tags and a stuffed Garfield the cat clinging to its passenger-side window.

Lance looked through the crack and across the street, where a lone streetlight stood high like a sentinel, its branch-thin pole arching over the road and casting a dome of orange-yellow light.

There was no traffic. Not a single car going either direction, nor any to be heard approaching.

Small town, Lance thought. *Some good, some bad. Just like people.*

He opened the door the remainder of the way and stepped outside. The air had cooled considerably, and he shivered once as his body adjusted to the temperature change. He pulled the door securely shut behind him and patted his pocket to verify he had the key. He turned right, about to take the two steps—two for Lance, three or four for average folks—needed to reach the motel's office and get his question answered.

The streetlight across the road flickered.

The single bulb above his room's door went out entirely with a loud *crack!*

And then a long gust of wind, strong and unexpected and unexplained, *whooshed* across the parking lot like a tidal wave, rocking the two cars on their axles before slamming into Lance. His body was flung backward like he weighed nearly nothing, and his head snapped back, smashing into his room's door with the sound of a heavy knock. Stars peppered his vision before fading, fading along with everything else as the gray evening sky began to allow the blackness to creep in from the sides and swallow everything in sight.

Lance slid down the door and landed hard on his rear, toppled over onto his side.

The newspaper fell from his hand, its pages scattering like buckshot across the parking lot and out into the street and the field beyond.

Then the wind stopped completely and the night was as still as before. Not even a gentle breeze to rustle the leaves remained.

[5]

HE WAS BACK AT ANNABELLE'S APRON. HE SAT ALONE AT THE counter, no other stools occupied and none of the tables either. The music that'd played from the single speaker was no longer humming a tune, and the smell of bacon had been replaced with something rancid, spoiled. Something like rotting meat. The lights were dim, the air was still. He turned in his stool and tried to look out the windows but found nothing except a solid pane of static, like a television channel that refused to tune in correctly. He turned back around, and when his arms slid across the countertop, he saw that he'd smeared a thick layer of dust, creating one arm of an incomplete snow angel. It was if the diner had been deserted for years.

"Don't let a little bump on the head scare you off."

Lance spun back around and found Annabelle Winters sitting in one of the booths by the windows of static. She looked out, as if seeing everything Lance couldn't, and then turned to face him. "It would only come after you if it thought you were a threat."

"What is it?" Lance tried to say, but he was interrupted by a voice coming over the speaker above.

(Lance!)

He looked up, saw a black sky in place of the diner's ceiling tiles.

(Lance!)

He looked back to the booth were Annabelle had been sitting and saw—

Leah grabbed him by the shoulders and did her best to sit him up. "Lance, can you hear me? Are you okay?"

He felt her fingers dig into the meat of his upper arms as she used all her strength to push him forward. His head swam at the change of direction, the parking lot going in and out of focus and the cars doing a little jitterbug on the asphalt. He closed his eyes and took two deep breaths. Opened them. The cars had stopped dancing and his vision was mostly back to normal. But the back of his head was throbbing and he had a headache that produced a sharp stab of pain at the base of his skull with each beat of his heart.

He looked to his right and painfully tilted his head up. Leah, same outfit from earlier, only now he noticed she was wearing black Nike sneakers. Maybe she'd been wearing them all day—a touch Lance liked—or maybe she'd changed out of dressier shoes once she knew peak hours were past and she was ready to slow things down for the day. Lance mentally scolded himself for so easily getting sidetracked. Leah's choice of shoes was officially the least of his concerns at the moment.

"I assume you can hear me?" she said, hands now on her hips.

Lance nodded. "Yes."

"So are you going to answer me? Are you okay, or do I need to call an ambulance?"

Lance took another deep breath and then slowly pushed himself off the sidewalk outside his room and stood. His surroundings did another half jitter but then remained focused.

With him standing at his full six-six height, Leah looked very small so close to him. He took a step back so as to not intimidate her. "Yes. I'm okay." He rolled his head on his shoulders, his neck making one sharp cracking sound. "I've got a headache, but otherwise I think I'm fine."

Leah's stature relaxed a little, and she blew a wisp of loose hair out of her face. "Thank God. I really didn't want to have to bring an ambulance out here. We get a bad enough rap as it is." She leaned to the side and looked at the back of his head. "Yeah, nice goose egg back there. What happened, anyway?"

Lance reached a hand up and gingerly touched the back of his head, felt the lump that'd formed, and then looked across the street. The streetlight was glowing strong. A small coupe drove along the road and then was out of sight. Lance nodded toward the office. "Let's go inside. Then we can talk."

Leah glanced across the street. Something like fear flickered in her eyes and then it was gone. "Okay." She turned and pulled open the door to the office. When they were both inside, she drew the blinds down across the glass and locked the deadbolt.

"What if somebody needs to check in?" Lance asked.

Leah walked to the window next to the door and flicked a switch attached to a small neon sign that advertised NO VACANCY. It burned a dull red behind the set of blinds she then pulled down over it.

"That's false advertising," Lance said. He tried to grin, but found the motion caused more pain in his head.

"Daddy'd be pissed to hell and back if he found out I did that," Leah said. "But what he doesn't know won't hurt him. So long as I get it switched off by morning."

"What if he gets sick on the job, decides to go home early and stops by here to check on things?"

Leah thought about it a moment, then continued, "Daddy

31

hasn't taken a sick day as long as I can remember. I don't expect him to start now."

Lance shrugged.

"Do you need some ice?" Leah was already moving toward the entertainment center with the wet bar on top. She looked around at what she had to work with, shook her head, and then said, "Be right back," and disappeared through the door at the rear of the room. She was back a minute later with a dish towel. She pulled three ice cubes from the stainless-steel bucket beneath the television and wrapped them in the towel. Motioned for Lance to sit. He walked over to the leather couch and slowly eased himself onto it. This time everything in his sight stayed where it was supposed to. *I guess that means no permanent damage done.*

Leah stood in front of him and held out the homemade ice pack. "Might get a little wet, but it's all I've got."

Lance took it. "Thanks." He leaned back into the couch's leather and used his right hand to hold the ice against the back of his head. It was cold—too cold—but felt good all the same. Leah was still standing in front of him, watching his every move. They remained that way, looking at each other in silence for a full minute before she finally said, "Well?"

Lance glanced down to her sneakers. "I like your shoes," he said.

"You wha...?" Leah looked down to her feet, then glanced at Lance's basketball shoes, as if maybe he was making fun of her.

"I like it when girls wear nice-looking sneakers," Lance said, reassuring her. "Makes them seem more laid-back, in my opinion."

She looked at him for another moment, and Lance could see her trying to conjure up some sort of response. She finally settled on, "You were going to tell me what happened?"

Lance shifted in his seat. "Oh, yeah, sure. Can you sit down, please? You're hovering over me and it's making me nervous."

"*I'm* making *you* nervous? I'm a small young girl all by myself with a big stranger of a man."

Lance respected her caution but didn't completely buy it. "If you thought I was dangerous, I wouldn't be here right now. And"—he pulled the ice pack from his head and showed it to her, melting ice dripping onto his cargo shorts—"I wouldn't have this."

Leah didn't move.

"Face it," Lance said, "you've got a special intuition about people. You know I'm one of the good guys. Just like I know that I can trust you."

Then she smiled, and Lance was taken aback by how cute she really was. "How do you know you can trust me?"

Lance wanted to tell her that he could practically feel the good energy that came off her, touch the honesty she had in her heart. "When I asked if you thought anything bad was going on around here, you invited me back, and you gave me that newspaper. Which, I regret to inform you, I lost when I had my accident outside."

Leah didn't respond to his explanation of trust, but she did move and sit on the other end of the couch, leaning against the arm and pulling her knees up to her chin so she could face him. Apparently Bob's Place wasn't strict about no shoes on the furniture. "Which you still haven't told me about. What happened to you out there? All the lights in here dimmed, and then I heard a bulb explode outside. When I looked out, you were on the ground and down for the count."

Lance continued to hold the ice pack to the back of his head, water dripping down the back of his neck and down his shirt. He shivered as the icy droplets snaked down his spine. He tried to figure out how much of the truth he wanted to tell Leah. In his brief time with her, she seemed more levelheaded than most folks, but Lance's hard-to-explain abilities were more than even the most open-minded and trusting types of people could usually accept. In fact, it was those who were, in society's eyes, less deserving of respect and trust that usually found Lance's gifts to be a matter of fact instead of fiction. Few people had ever learned the truth about him, but that small group had been diverse enough for him to be able to form this clear divide of understanding.

Which group did Leah fall into?

If she believed him—either completely, or partially—she could prove to be a valuable asset. He would never expect, nor want her to get involved if things had the potential to be dangerous—which, after the violent gust of wind, he was pretty sure things would be—but she could be helpful in other ways. She was a local, and a local would have the type of knowledge he might need, and would know where to go to find other answers. If she trusted him and they worked together, he might be able to cleanse—*Cleanse? Who are you, that little woman from* Poltergeist?—this town of whatever evil had found its way here more quickly than if he were at it alone, and then he could get back to—

Get back to what, Lance? What exactly are you going to do? Where are you going to go?

—figuring out what his next move would be. Figuring out the rest of his life. His life alone.

If Leah chose not to believe him, she would think he was just a kook. She would remove him from the safe harbor category of "normal" guests she'd so quickly placed him in and drop him right down into the pit of the "typical" guests Bob's Place was accustomed to. She would understand why he was drifting. She would understand why he'd chosen to stay at Bob's Place instead of making his way another twenty miles to the Holiday

Inn. She'd think him a loser. Just another crazy person passing through who'd never amount to anything and should have an eye kept on them at all times. She'd might ask him to leave. Throw him out. And then he'd be all—

Where will I go?

—alone again with just his expensive backpack and his troubled mind and his dead mother's voicemail greeting to keep him company.

She won't do that. She's more like you than not. She's one of the good ones.

The ice was almost completely melted now, the dish towel just a soppy mess with a few small ice chips left over. Lance stood, his vision solid but his headache no better, and placed the wet towel inside one of the small glasses atop the entertainment center. Leah's eyes never left him as he moved. He sat back down and turned to lean against the other arm of the couch, so that the two of them were able to face each other comfortably. He got situated, took a long, heavy breath, and said, "You can ask all the questions you want, but it might be easier if you just let me finish first before you do. Is that okay?"

Leah's brow crinkled, apparently confused at the depths to which the conversation appeared to be diving. But there was no apprehension in her voice when she quickly answered, "Okay. I can do that. Promise."

So he told her.

He told her the condensed version of why he was different. Told her a couple stories from the past—the less dangerous type of stories—showing her how his talents had been used to help people, and some humorous tales of how he'd used them to help himself. She'd laughed at these, but he could see the gears turning behind her eyes, could see her brain scrambling frantically, trying to decipher what exactly it was she was hearing, probably wondering if this was all a dream.

He did not tell her that he occasionally saw ghosts, or spirits, or worse. That part was always the kicker, always the part where even the ones who'd begun to trust him finally held up their hands and said they'd heard enough. If the time came, and it was needed, then he'd tell her.

He also did not tell her two mysterious and powerful men (*Are they really men?*) were after him. Hunting him.

He finished talking, and Leah was quiet for a moment. She looked absently around the office, eyes darting from place to place as she thought. Finally, her eyes found his again and she said, "So ... you're like a psychic?"

"A little."

"Or maybe ... clairvoyant?"

"Sort of."

"You've got, like, a sixth sense?"

"Maybe more than six. I'm a lot of things, honestly. I don't fully understand it myself."

"How do you sleep at night?"

"In a bed, usually." He knew the joke was dumb, and sure enough, it fell flat. Leah looked at him for a moment, not realizing at first he was attempting to be funny, lighten the mood a bit after his speech. Finally, a small grin twitched her lips, and she reiterated, "No, seriously, how do you sleep with all that going on?"

He nodded. "It's not always easy ... but ... think of me like a radio, okay? I can sort of ... switch on and off, or not tune into certain channels unless I want to. Sometimes things tune in *for* me, but that's not an everyday thing."

Leah nodded, trying desperately to understand.

"But," Lance continued, "things can also tune into me. I guess ... I guess I sort of broadcast my own signal all the time, and other ... things can pick up on it. And that's not always good."

And a realization lit up Leah's face. "And that's what happened outside?"

Smart girl. Smart, smart girl.

"Yes. That's what happened outside." Lance told her about the strong sense of dread he'd been picking up since he arrived in town, then added the bit about feeling as though whatever evil was present had noticed him (picked up his signal) and was concerned. "It knows I'm here, and it knows I can feel it. It's worried I'll intervene with whatever it's got its teeth into around here." He told her about the flickering lights, and then the gust of wind that'd knocked him out.

"It can control the weather?" Leah had asked, eyes wide.

Lance thought about it. "Yeah, maybe."

Leah was quiet for another moment, deep in thought. When she came back to the present, she said, "So, you're kind of trapped in between, aren't you? You're here, with all the rest of us, but it's like you've also got one foot on the other side—wherever that is—right?"

Lance thought about the analogy. "I don't know if I have a whole foot on the other side, maybe just a toe or two, but yes. I'd say that's accurate."

Leah's expression had turned to one of pure excitement and fascination now. "Do you have any idea how you got to be this way?"

"My mother had a theory," he said. "But forget about that for now. I've done a lot of talking. Tell me what you think is wrong in this town."

So she did.

[6]

"You lost the newspaper I gave you?" Leah asked, mocking heartbreak.

Lance grinned, and a streak of pain bolted through the back of his head. "Sadly, yes. I would have gone after it, but, well ... I was unconscious."

"I suppose you think that's an excuse." Leah got up from the couch and walked back to the check-in counter.

"My mother never allowed excuses," Lance said. "So it's merely a fact. Conscious awareness or not, the paper is gone and I was the last to have it in my possession. Hold it against me if you want."

Leah crouched behind the counter, disappearing from view. Lance could hear her rummaging through whatever lay behind the wooden panels. "Daddy doesn't particularly care for excuses either," she said, "though I doubt he and your mom had similar parenting styles." She popped back up and triumphantly held a newspaper above her head, like she'd just won a trophy. She came back to the couch and tossed it into Lance's lap.

"It's not the same paper," he said, noticing different headlines and pictures.

"You're right," Leah said. "You are gifted."

Lance said nothing, just looked at her.

"It's from two weeks ago," she said.

Lance looked back down at the black-and-white pages. "So there was a story about what's wrong in this paper too?"

She smiled a little, and Lance knew she was playing some sort of game with him. "There's a story about it every week. At least for a few months out of the year."

Lance scanned the headlines again. Quickly skimmed an article about a farmer out on Route 19 having to rescue two of his cows after they got stuck in a ravine. Not exactly worthy of print, in Lance's mind.

Leah sighed. "I'm sorry. I was just ... I guess I wanted to see if you could, you know..."

"Read your mind?"

She grinned.

"I don't work that way," Lance said. "I don't ... I told you, I don't understand how I work. Things just happen sometimes, and sometimes they don't."

Leah shrugged. "Worth a shot. You're the first psychic I've ever met."

"I'm not a—"

Sports! There would be an article about sports teams every week!

Lance was a quiet for a moment, his mouth frozen midsentence as Leah's clues clicked together. Then he looked down and opened the paper, finding the sports section. When Leah saw where he'd ended up, she whispered, *"Not psychic, my ass."*

He shook his head and said. "No, really. It just suddenly made sense. The weekly article. Small town like this, it was a logical conclusion."

"Uh-huh, sure."

Lance looked down at the front page of sports and said, "Okay, I made it this far. Help me out."

Leah scooted across the couch, so close now he could smell her shampoo and a whiff of what remained of the perfume she'd probably administered early this morning before coming into work. Lance was suddenly very conscious of his lack of deodorant and toothpaste. He'd need to get to a store as soon as possible, especially if girls were going to be sidling up to him on couches.

Not what should be concerning you right now, Lance.

Whatever...

Leah leaned over further and tapped her index finger, the nail clean but unpainted, on the top story, the headline in large bold font.

MCGUIRE LEADS WESTHAVEN TO 3–0 START

Lance recalled the sports page from the newspaper he'd lost. "They're four and oh now. They beat a team from"—he paused to think—"Newberry, last week. They scored a touchdown and a field goal in the fourth to seal the win."

Leah nodded. "Nice memory."

"Like you said, I am gifted." Lance looked at the black-and-white snapshot chosen for the article's picture. A Westhaven High School player was walking off the field toward the sideline, helmet off and dangling from one hand while he used his other to high-five a man who Lance assumed must be the coach. The photo's caption read: WESTHAVEN QUARTERBACK ANTHONY MILLS AND HEAD COACH KENNY MCGUIRE CELEBRATE VICTORY OVER NON-DISTRICT FOE.

Coach McGuire was somewhat atypical for a football head coach. He was a small man, short and very thin, and he wore small rimless glasses that sat low on his nose, a look that seemed more fitting for somebody closer to sixty than the early forties

McGuire appeared to be. He wore a Westhaven High ball cap on his head, and a pair of large earphones with built-in microphone were draped around his neck. An iPad was clutched in his non-high-fiving hand. Lance smirked; the man almost seemed to be a biology teacher playing dress-up as a football coach.

Leah was quiet as Lance read the full article detailing a Westhaven blowout. He finished, considered his location, and then said, "Small town like this, I'm guessing high school football is a big deal, right?"

Leah threw back her head and laughed. "A big deal? Go ask for a tire rotation and oil change down at Clarence's Tire and Lube on the morning after a Westhaven loss and see for yourself. Service with a smile? Forget it."

Lance understood. His hometown had been enthusiastic about high school sports as well. The time junior year he'd missed a ten-foot jumper to win a close one midseason had haunted him for weeks. People had still smiled at him in the streets, but he had known deep down they blamed him for the loss. Fortunately, Lance knew better than most that sports didn't exactly rank high on life's important bullet points.

Leah leaned back against the couch cushion, kicked off her sneakers and pulled her feet under her. Her socks were so white they could blind you. Lance remembered the overwhelming smell of disinfectant from his entrance earlier and thought: *She keeps everything so clean, and I look and smell like a stowaway.*

"Would you like to guess how many AA state championships Westhaven has won in the last three years?"

Lance hedged his bet and guessed two.

"All three," Leah said. "Three years, three titles."

"Wow," Lance said. "That seems ... improbable."

"You think?"

"No competition? Weak district? Region?"

Leah shook her head and passed on the question. "You know how many games they won the season before their first title?"

Lance knew she was playing to some sort of buildup. Shrugged and said, "Six?"

"One. They beat one stinking team. I remember because it was my sophomore year, and my date to the homecoming dance, a safety who was terrible, just like the rest of the team, sprained his ankle on the second play of the game."

"So no dancing?"

"*That's* your question?"

"No, I have others. I just ... my mind's funny, remember?"

She smiled. "Try and focus here, okay?"

"Yes, ma'am. So the local high school team went from being the Bad News Bears to winning three titles in a row?"

"Correct."

"Doesn't seem like the sort of thing that happens overnight. Or in one off-season, in this case."

"Exactly."

"So what changed?"

Leah looked up to the ceiling, in contemplation of her answer. Lance looked up too, and another sharp crack of pain shot through his skull. He'd really hit that door hard, and was about to ask Leah if she had any ibuprofen when she said, "Everything changed. Everything except the players."

"I'm not a football expert, but I've played enough basketball in my life to know that it's going to take at least *one* new player for a team to improve from a nearly winless record to winning a state title."

"Well, there was *one*, but he was just a placekicker." Leah closed her eyes and thought. "Okay, yeah, sure there were a few seniors from the losing team that graduated, and then some JV kids moved up, but the core team was still there, and none of the rising players were what you might call game-changers."

"So ... the change?"

"The coach, for starters. Coach McGuire's first year at Westhaven was the first year they won state."

"Did he have a winning record where he coached before?"

Leah's face went blank for a moment, then she looked at him and said, "You know, I've never even thought about that. I've only focused on him since he's been at Westhaven. All I know is he and his wife came from Georgia. They were both schoolteachers. She worked at the library part-time the first year they were here, then she took over as vice principal at the high school a year later. That was my senior year."

"Big jump from putting books back on the shelf at the library to being vice principal of a high school. Small town or no small town."

"Mr. Barnes, the vice principal she replaced, retired and moved to Florida with his wife, who'd just been diagnosed with dementia. Apparently they had a son there."

Lance thought about this, somewhat surprised that no internal candidates, no longtime high school staff, might have gotten the job. But he moved on. "So the team got a new coach. What else?"

"The paper mill sold to new owners."

This seemingly unrelated bit of information made zero sense to Lance. So he nodded his head and said, "Elementary, my dear Watson."

"What?"

"Sherlock Holmes. Well ... it's a misquote. He never said that exactly, but people get the idea."

"Uh, okay."

Another fallen-flat joke. He was on a roll. "I don't understand why a paper mill selling to somebody new affects the foot-ball team."

"Ah, right." Leah readjusted her legs under her. "It wouldn't normally, I guess. But in this case, it did, in a big way. When the paper mill sold to the new owner, some big business out of Atlanta, they moved in a new general operations manager. Glenn Strang. Glenn's son, Bobby, was the placekicker I mentioned."

Lance's brain was trying to figure out how any of this had anything to do with the team's miraculous turnaround. "Unless Westhaven's offensive strategy was to kick fifteen field goals a game, I fail to see why this changes much. And you've already suggested that the new kicker wasn't a big deal."

Leah shrugged. "Well, he wasn't, in terms of being an on-the-field contribution. But ... his daddy quickly became the piggy bank for a school football program that'd been having the players wash their own uniforms at home. Before Strang, it would be generous to say the Westhaven athletic department was on a shoestring budget. It was more like a stray thread of a budget. But Glenn Strang is apparently a huge sports fan, played D-1 football somewhere out west and then had a somewhat lucrative stint as a pro. Now that he's got more money than he knows what to do with, he's living vicariously through Westhaven players by making sure they've got the shiniest, most sophisticated every-thing. Uniforms, training equipment, you name it. He contributes to the other sports programs as well, but I think it's just so he doesn't appear biased. Everybody knows football is his baby."

Lance thought about this. Could understand the situation fully. He knew some people could never let go of a game they loved, and he also knew from his one and only season of offici-ating peewee basketball that parents were just about always borderline insane and dangerous fans of their kids. He supposed dumping a ton of money into a program was a good enough way to support that habit.

"But, a new placekicker and fancy new equipment still doesn't take them from zeros to heroes. You can't buy a game."

Well...

"Wait, are we talking about bribery? Payoffs? Kickbacks?"

Leah closed her eyes and took a deep breath, shook her head. "No. Well, I don't know, maybe. There ... there's something else, too. Something worse. The thing that came to mind when you asked me earlier if I thought something bad was going on around here."

"Enlighten me."

A dull, thunderous sound was suddenly heard in the distance. Faint, but noticeable. Leah's eyes widened and her face went pale. She jumped up from the couch and quickly pulled on her sneakers, hopping from one foot to the other as she did so. Her eyes darted around the office, checking everything and nothing at the same time. "You've got to go!"

The booming noise was closer now, very close. "That's Daddy's truck! He'll kill you if he finds you with me!"

Lance jumped up from the couch, the threat of death always a motivation to move quickly if needed. "I thought you said he was working. Never takes a sick day. Employee of the year. Master of—"

"*He doesn't!*" Leah spun around on her heels, her eyes darting over every inch of the office. Lance headed for the door and she yelled, "No! He'll see you!"

The booming of what Lance now realized was a truck's exhaust muffler was nearly shaking the windows in their panes. He stopped halfway to the office door, almost turned back, and then continued. He heard Leah begin to protest again, but then he quickly flipped the NO VACANCY sign off and unlocked the office's door. He turned around and Leah was disappearing into the black mouth of the now-open door at the rear of the office. She was half-hidden in shadows as she waved frantically for him to follow her.

Lance ran across the freshly polished office floor, one continuing thought in his head.

It knows I'm here, and it definitely doesn't like it.

[7]

LEAH HAD PULLED LANCE INTO THE DOORWAY AND THEN
told him to hide. She'd given him one hard shove, pushing him
out of the way of the door she was closing behind her, and then
she was gone, leaving Lance alone in a dark, unknown space,
hiding from a man he'd never met, for a reason he didn't fully
understand. He chalked it up to an overprotective father,
remembered the supposed shotgun behind the check-in counter,
and quickly decided any man who'd give his young daughter a
shotgun to use at will on any human being who might pose a
threat was a man whom Lance would like to try and remain on
proper terms with. Lance also remembered the panic he'd seen
in Leah's eyes when she'd first recognized the sound of her
daddy's truck. It was a true panic, one which alluded to fierce
repercussions should she be caught.

Lance did as instructed and tried to find a place to hide.
Because apparently being behind a closed door in the near pitch
black wasn't good enough.

Lance turned around and closed his eyes for a moment, then
reopened them, trying to let them adjust. The thundering from
the truck muffler was now right on top of them, Leah's daddy

having clearly arrived in the parking lot. It rumbled on for another ten or fifteen seconds and then stopped completely. The newfound silence was almost as deafening as the noise had been. *Need to move fast now. He's here.*

As things came slowly into focus, Lance was surprised at what he had found. He'd seen the door at the rear of the office from the first moment he'd stepped inside Bob's Place earlier that day and had noticed it again as Leah had helped to nurse his injuries after the Great Ghost Gust and their subsequent conversation. But the entire time, he'd assumed it was some sort of utility closet, laundry room, or storage area. A place where you'd find the mop buckets and the bottles of bleach and boxes of mini-soaps. A room with a musty smell and a hard concrete floor with edges lined with mousetraps, a small grubby window perched high that was so covered in grime you couldn't see out. As the room's objects became clearer, what he found instead was a bedroom.

The space was small, but well furnished. To his immediate left, flush against two walls, was a twin-sized bed, made neatly and with a small stuffed animal of some sort propped between two pillows. A wooden nightstand sat next to the bed with a small lamp atop it and a paperback novel with a bookmark sticking out the top of the pages. On the opposite wall, a tiny square desk with an office chair hugged the corner. From atop the desk, the dull green glow of a power cord plugged into a laptop provided just about the room's only light. To the right of the desk was a wide dresser, a mirror mounted to the back that showed Lance a dull reflection of himself in front of the door. A small TV cart was in the corner opposite the desk, and the flat-screen resting there was no more than fifteen inches. A spark of light from his right caught Lance's eye, and he finished his scan of the room by noticing another door. It was open just a crack, and a small amber glow was beckoning him.

Outside the room, a door opened and heavy footsteps fell on the hardwood.

"*Daddy?*" Lance heard Leah say, her voice traveling from the direction of the check-in counter. "I thought you had to work tonight."

There was no answer, and Lance imagined Leah's daddy—who was surely a large lumberjack of a man who could grab Lance by the shoulders and rip him in half—standing in the center of the office, furrowed eyebrows above eyes trained directly onto the door Lance was still standing behind. Waiting —no, *hoping* to hear a tiny sound, any excuse to kick the door open and destroy whoever was behind it, whoever was dumb enough to try and spend the evening with his daughter.

This day is going a lot worse than I was expecting it to. And that's saying something.

"Boss told me to go home." A new voice, deep with bass and fitting Lance's imagery perfectly, sounded no more than two feet from the door Lance was still standing motionless behind. "Told me he'd made a scheduling error. Didn't need me tonight."

Leah, closer than she'd been before: "Why didn't he call you? Did you have your cell phone off again? I keep telling you—"

"I had it on." A quick, powerful retort. Leah stopped talking. "Boss said he'd forgotten until right when I showed up. He'd been in a meeting with Mr. Strang and some other folks, something about a fundraiser, he told me, and he forgot all about the scheduling error until he saw me at my post."

There was a moment of silence before Leah ventured, "But..."

"I don't ask questions, Leah! I do what I'm told."

Lance heard footsteps across the hardwood, heading his direction. He held his breath and the amber light caught his eye again. He turned toward the partially opened door and walked as softly as he could across the floor toward it. Grabbed the handle and pulled gently, begging for the hinges not to whine. They didn't, and Lance slid into the new room and closed the door softly behind him.

"So why'd you come back here, Daddy? Why aren't you home, or out with your buddies."

There was more silence again, and Lance didn't like it. Leah's daddy was thinking about something, contemplating some move he wanted to make. Lance could nearly sense it. Somehow, in some fashion, Leah's daddy knew Lance was here.

Maybe.

"On my way out to the parking lot, Strang himself found me and asked if you were minding the shop tonight. I said you were, and he'd mentioned that he'd heard on the police scanner earlier that there'd been reports of a suspicious-looking man heading down Route 19, toward the motel."

Though they were slightly muffled, Lance could still hear the words, and his heart stopped in his chest for a moment. *He knows. He knows I'm here and he's going to kill me. Okay, maybe he won't kill me, but I doubt he wants to sit down and talk about things.*

The paranormal and supernatural and whatever else you wanted to call the things Lance had dealt with his entire life didn't scare him half as badly as a pissed-off human being with easy access to a loaded weapon. Especially one with an attractive daughter to protect.

"Daddy, you worry too much. Been business as usual here. And besides, I've got Bonnie behind the counter if I need her."

Bonnie?

Lance hadn't met Bonnie.

A loud sigh, clear as day, was followed by, "If I'd known you were going to pick something so girly, I'd never have told you about people naming their guns."

Oh. Bonnie.

"It's not girly! It's because of Bonnie and Clyde! She was a badass!"

Silence again, and Lance looked around the room, waiting for the bedroom door to be flung open any second now and the search to commence.

He was in a bathroom. One larger than he'd expected, based on the size of the bedroom. There was a porcelain bathtub to his left with a showerhead sticking out of a crudely tiled wall like a weed. The shower curtain ran along a circular rod, half-open, swirling with a pattern of flowers and vines. A toilet to Lance's right, and between tub and pot was a wooden vanity with a single sink. A medicine cabinet with a mirror front was mounted above the sink, and Lance again looked straight into his own reflection. There was a neatly organized arrangement of products on the countertop, and a toothbrush holder held a single brush. *No boyfriend, then, I guess.* And Lance wondered why this information mattered to him.

The source of the amber light that had caught Lance's eyes was a plug-in nightlight glowing beneath a plastic cover next to the sink. Lance's other senses kicked in and he inhaled the sweet smells of shampoos and lotions and perfume, briefly imagined Leah standing in front of this mirror and—

"Seriously, Daddy, everything's fine here. I was just going to read a little bit until I was ready to go to bed, then I'd lock up and go watch some TV."

Another long, pregnant pause. Lance found himself just wishing the man out there *would* kick the door down, try and come find him. At least then he'd know what the heck was going on out there.

Expecting some sort of demand for an explanation, or at

least words of warning uttered in a threatening tone, Lance was surprised when all Leah's daddy said was, "Leah, you'd tell me if there was something I needed to know about, right? You know I only want what's best for you. Always have."

Leah laughed. "Yessss, Daddy, of course I would. But you got to believe me. Things are just as boring here as they've ever been. You're being paranoid."

"I'd rather be paranoid than regretful."

Lance had to agree with the man. And he noted how good of a liar Leah was turning out to be.

And then nobody spoke for what seemed like an eternity. Lance pressed his ear against the closed door and heard nothing. He contemplated opening the door a crack but feared the noise it might make. Finally, he heard Leah giggle and say, "Okaaaay, Daddy, now go get out of here and enjoy your night off."

The heavy footsteps started to retreat, the bell above the door gave its jingle, and soon after that, the booming muffler was once again rattling Lance's eardrums. It idled for a minute or two, and then the noise dissipated as Leah's daddy, thankfully, drove away.

Still, Lance did not move. He would stay right where he was until Leah came to get him.

He turned away from the door and moved to sit on the toilet and wait, but he froze midstep. Twirled back around and faced the door, his heartbeat drumming in his ears. He saw nothing but the closed wooden door. He looked back over his shoulder, into the mirror, and saw only his reflection.

A second ago, there'd been somebody else with him in the darkened bathroom. Somebody else's reflection looking straight at him. It'd all happened so fast that Lance hadn't had a chance to make out much, but he was certain of two things.

The young man looking back at Lance had skin as white as milk and blackish-gray eyes like a shark that seemed to pierce

Lance's skin. Dark lips that looked swollen. The person who'd stared back from the mirror was dead, Lance was certain of that.

The second thing Lance was certain of was that the boy had been wearing a t-shirt with some sort of graphic and writing on the front. Lance closed his eyes and forced himself to think, to rebuild in his mind what he'd only briefly seen—or hadn't seen.

He stood still in the bathroom, eyes closed tightly and his mind closed off to everything else. The graphic came to him first. It'd been a single letter, printed large in the middle of the shirt in a fancy script, words printed above and below.

The letter was a W.

And then, just like that, the words fell into their places.

WESTHAVEN FOOTBALL

[8]

THIRTY MINUTES HAD PASSED AND LANCE HAD TO PEE, which was an ironic task to be avoiding because he was sitting on a toilet. But he didn't dare use it. Not until he was absolutely sure he was in the clear from whatever potential there might still be of Leah's daddy giving him a face-to-face introduction to Bonnie.

So Lance sat alone in the darkened bathroom, amber glow from the nightlight letting him see just enough to notice whether any more dead football players were hanging out with him, waiting their turn to use the john.

Lance could only assume the young man he'd briefly seen in the mirror was a Westhaven player. There was the t-shirt, sure, but the boy had also seemed to be built like a person who'd spent more than a few afternoons in the school's weight room, throwing around dumbbells and downing protein shakes like water. He'd been big, broad shoulders filling out the neckline of the Westhaven Football t-shirt's fabric. But all those muscles couldn't stop whatever had ended the young man's life. And that was the part Lance was curious about.

Not just the cause of the boy's death, but also why his ghost had been present. Unlike the spirit of Annabelle Winters, which had been what Lance could assume was an accurate representation of Ms. Winters at the time of her death—old, but pleasant enough and without physical wounds or oddities—the football player's spirit had been more like a corpse. Something long dead and rotting and full of blackness. The image reminded Lance of a drowning victim, one whose body had been submerged for far too long.

The eyes... the eyes were the worst part.

Was the football player's ghost supposed to frighten Lance? Its presence supposed to cause him to flee back to the bus station and get the heck out of Dodge? Or was it possible this young man's ghost had been some sort of spy, doing the bidding of whatever dark and malevolent forces were obviously at play.

Neither option seemed appealing to Lance. But, neither much bothered him either, at least not in the sense his assumed-antagonist was surely hoping for. He would not flee, because where would he go? Plus, he'd done nothing of any significance worth spying on, other than sit on a closed toilet lid for half an hour after listening to his new friend's father come within what seemed like inches of making things much worse than they needed to be.

He was rolling all these thoughts around in his head like a handful of marbles when Leah nudged open the bathroom door, stuck her head in, and said, "You are extremely patient."

Lance looked up to her, startled. He'd been so deep in thought he'd not even heard the bedroom door open. He'd seen two ghosts in one day, which was something that had happened only one other time. Back when...

"It didn't seem like you wanted me to meet your father, and from what I gathered, he didn't seem too keen to meet me either. It was in the interest of both parties for me to stay put until called for. I figured he might be the type to stake the place out, peek through the windows and wait to see if you'd lied to him."

"Well, you're right. If he'd have seen you... well, I'm not sure what would have happened, but it wouldn't have been good." A pause. "For either of us. But he does trust me. He's been long gone."

Lance stood from his sitting position and stretched his lower back. "So why'd you keep me waiting?"

Leah shrugged. "Just being cautious, I guess. And maybe I was curious just how long you'd wait." She gave him a grin, and Lance returned the favor by telling her he needed to pee.

"But you've been in a bathroom all this time!"

He shrugged. "Just being cautious, I guess."

Leah left and closed the door, and Lance relieved himself with the level of self-consciousness reserved for every guy the first time or two he urinates with a new female companion within earshot. He was certain he sounded like a firehose open full-strength into a swimming pool. He flushed, washed his hands and dried them on his shorts. Then he opened the bathroom door and found Leah sitting on the edge of the bed. She'd turned the bedside lamp on and was staring at him intently.

"You're the first guy I've ever had in my room. You should feel very privileged."

Lance stood in the open doorway connecting the bathroom and bedroom. "It is an honor I will receive with respect and gratitude."

"Do you always talk so weird?"

"I didn't know I talked weird. So, yes. Probably."

"You're just different, that's all."

No kidding. "Different than what?"

"Most people I talk to."

"Well, if you spend most of your time here, I can certainly believe that."

The words were out of his mouth before he realized how rude they must have sounded. He blushed, his face warm with regret, and quickly stammered, "I mean ... it's just ... you said the folks who come through here usually aren't the... what I meant to say—"

She giggled, cutting him off. "Ah, so you are human. It's good to know you can get flustered. You struck me as kind of robotic earlier."

Lance recomposed himself, leaned against the door frame. "It doesn't happen often. So now *you* should feel privileged."

"Noted."

The silence sat in the air before them like the last slice of pizza, waiting for somebody to make a grab for it. Lance reached first, tackling what he figured to be the elephant in the room. "So, you live here, at the motel?" He gestured to the room, the bathroom.

Leah sighed. "Yes, and it's just as glamorous as it seems."

Lance recalled his home (*It's not your home anymore, Lance. You'll never go back there again. At least not for a very long time*), the small two-bedroom house he'd shared with his mother his whole life. The unkempt look of the place, the flea market furniture and garage sale knickknacks. Glamorous was a word Lance knew wasn't necessary to make someplace a good home.

He recalled the conversation he'd overheard earlier, when Leah had been fibbing to her daddy. "But your father doesn't live here?"

"You think we'd be sitting here if he did?" And that was all she had to say on the topic.

Lance shrugged. "Doesn't look so bad to me."

"Yeah. It'll do for now. One day I'll get a better place. One day I'll leave this whole town. At least, that's what I keep telling myself."

Lance wanted to tell her he'd just done exactly what she

was longing for, left his hometown behind in a cloud of bus fumes, but that wasn't something he was ready to talk about. It was something he might *never* be able to talk about. So, he moved on. "Before you sequestered me in your bedroom, you were about to tell me what else was bothering you about the football team. You said there was more to it?"

"See, that's what I'm talking about! Who says 'sequestered'?"

Lance thought for a second. "People who know its definition and can intelligently use it in a sentence, like they do with most words?"

Leah looked at him for a long moment, as if unsure if he was kidding or being mean. *Way to go, Lance. You're a real winner with these one-liners.*

"Are you hungry?" Leah asked.

The change of conversation was drastic, but by no means unwelcome. "Famished."

Leah jumped from the bed and headed back into the motel's office. "I'll order a pizza. I'll tell you what I know once it gets here."

Lance watched as Leah picked up the desk phone at the check-in counter and placed an order, not bothering to ask him what his preferred pizza toppings were. She ordered a single large with grilled chicken, green peppers, and mushrooms. Lance was impressed with the selection, though he might have added some pineapple. Leah hung up the phone and looked at him as he made his way back to the couch. "That okay with you?" she asked.

"Sounds great. I'm not too picky with my pizza."

Leah nodded. "I figured as much."

"What's that mean?"

"Guy as big as you, and as lean ... I didn't figure you'd find much to complain about with pizza toppings. Or any food, for that matter."

Lance remembered his breakfast. Remembered Margie's laugh after he'd ordered his slice of pie to wash down the rest of his meal. The thought of pie caused the image of his mother's face to jump to the front of his mind, half-hidden behind her mug of tea, steam curling around the edges of her brow as she listened intently to anything he'd ever had to say to her at the kitchen table.

"Hey, you okay?" Leah's voice snapped him back to the present.

He shook his head to clear it, the dull pain at the back of his head having throttled down to only a minor ache. His vision readjusted to the girl before him, this nice young woman who'd been able to sense in him some sort of genuineness—the way he'd been able to sense it in her—and allow this near-instant friendship to mature so rapidly. And, allowing himself one last glance back to the memory of his mother's face, Lance thought to himself, *Mom would like her.*

"Yeah, sorry. I just...."

"You spaced out on me. Am I boring you already?"

Lance smiled. "No. No, you're not."

They sat on the couch together while they waited for the pizza, Lance constantly glancing in the direction of the windows and straining his ears to pick up the noise of a rumbling muffler headed back their direction. Leah turned on the television and they watched a rerun of *The Big Bang Theory*, both of them happy to have the show's laugh track fill the silence of the room. Lance knew they were both growing more comfortable around each other, but the white noise definitely helped to make things a little less awkward.

The sound of a small, whining engine in the parking lot was quickly followed by three quick knocks on the office door.

Lance jumped in his seat at the noise, still on edge with the threat of Leah's father's wrath, but Leah calmly stood from her curled position on the couch and said, "It's just Brian with the pizza."

Lance stood anyway, ready to make a run for it, or at least be able to defend himself, if Leah was mistaken. But when she opened the door, Lance only saw the face of a young man dressed in baggy jeans and a pizza shop polo standing on the sidewalk. Leah greeted him and they exchanged common pleasantries, handed him some cash she'd pulled from her pocket, took the pizza, said goodnight, and then closed the door. "I went to school with him. He was a year older, but we had some of the same friends."

"Didn't seem too talkative," Lance said.

"You probably made him nervous."

Leah sat back down on the couch and set the pizza box on the cushion between them. She opened it and took a slice for herself and began watching TV again. Lance devoured four slices in the time she'd eaten two and declined any more when she asked. She closed the box and then went behind the check-in counter, bending down and reappearing with two bottles of water. "All I keep in the mini-fridge is water, so I hope you're not a soda addict."

Lance took the bottle she'd extended to him and quickly downed half of it. "I hate soda," he said after gulping. "Nothing but sugar and poison."

Leah nodded as she watched the television show's final scene. When it was over and the credits began to play, she used the remote to mute the volume and then turned to face him, her demeanor serious.

Lance picked up on her sudden mood shift, could practically feel the sudden burst of sorrow and fear that had flooded her system, as if she'd done well most of the evening in blocking out whatever troubling thoughts haunted her, but was now ready to let them break the dam.

"So what's the *real* problem?" Lance asked, as gently as he could.

Leah took a sip of water, glanced once at the TV and then back at Lance. "Westhaven football has won three straight state titles. Each year, one player from the team has gone missing. None of them have ever been found."

THREE YEARS.

Three football state titles.

And now, with a sinking feeling in his gut that threatened to dislodge his recently ingested pizza, Lance feared there were three dead high school students to round out the statistics. One of them for sure was dead, because Lance now had a good idea who the young man was he'd seen in Leah's bathroom mirror. He hoped he was wrong, suddenly wanted to be wrong about this more than anything in his life. But he recalled that feeling of dread he'd experienced since arriving in town, the attack in the parking lot, and even Leah's daddy's somewhat inexplicable night off from work, and could not shake the feeling that they were the result of nothing but true evil. And true evil didn't play games. True evil went for the kill.

An entire country, forty-eight contiguous states, and this is what I end up in the middle of on my first stop from home. Talk about luck.

"You already knew, didn't you?"

Lance looked up from the floor, where he'd been staring as he'd processed what Leah had told him. She was looking at him longingly, expectantly, as if she desperately wanted him to say yes, he did already know, and he had the answer to fix it all. Maybe he'd made a mistake in telling her about his abilities. Maybe he'd inadvertently made himself out to be something bigger in her eyes than he truly was. The girl looking back at him from the opposite side of the couch was a girl looking for the truth she figured only he could provide.

But Lance wasn't ready to tell her the whole truth. He would not tell her about what he could see. What he *had* seen. Not yet. It was still too early, and he was still afraid he'd come off as some sort of lunatic and she'd feel foolish and embarrassed and disappointed in herself for even considering trusting him. Leah was smart and headstrong, but she was still young and carried a lingering bit of innocence. Lance did not want to accidentally take that away from her.

But there was something else, a new feeling Lance could feel coming from her. Mixed with the look in her eyes—that *longing* look—that seemed to be more than just simply pleading for his help, but begging, Lance could feel her sorrow washing over him like a fine mist, cold and sticky and making his skin prickle. Again he got the impression that she'd been keeping something buried, something more important than she'd been letting on, and now she was tired of the masquerade and had removed the mask.

There was something very familiar about the pain coming from her. Lance quickly recognized it as a weaker version of what he himself was currently—

Oh. Oh no.

Lance ignored Leah's question and asked one of his own. One he was terrified he already knew the answer to. "One of those boys ... one of them was your brother, wasn't he?"

At the mention of her secret, of the truth Lance had somehow managed to excavate from her inner thoughts, Leah closed her eyes and a single tear spilled from each, slowly trailing down her cheeks until they fell to the couch with audible *plops*. Lance sat still, unsure of what he should do. Part of him wanted to reach out a comforting hand, be a reassuring shoulder to cry on. But another part, a part that carried the echoes of his mother's voice, told him that Leah was strong enough not to need those things right now; she'd been down this road before, often, and the best thing to do was to let his new friend move at her own pace. Lance was there to help, and a big part of that was going to be to listen.

So he remained where he was on the couch, slouched into the corner with one leg pulled under him, his other size fifteen sneaker flat on the floor. He never took his eyes off Leah, and when she was finally able to regain the composure she'd been so effortlessly displaying, she looked up at him with wet eyes and smiled. Lance smiled back.

Leah wiped her eyes with the back of her hand and sniffled. Lance wished he had a tissue to offer. "He was the first," Leah said. "The first casualty of Westhaven High School's historic football run." Leah smiled again and gave off a small laugh. "God, he wasn't very good, but he tried so hard. Loved the stupid game. I think he'd have been happy just being the water boy, just to be around it, you know?"

Lance nodded. He did know. He'd known plenty of guys like that in high school. Ones who would shoot baskets and run full-court with anybody all day, every day because they loved to play. But they didn't quite have the skillset to back up the passion. They'd gladly volunteer to be equipment managers, statisticians, videographers, anything to be at every game and have an inside connection to the team. To be a part of the basketball family.

"It's ironic, isn't it?" Leah asked.

"What?"

"The thing he loved is the thing that ended up killing him."

Lance bit his tongue, citing compassion as the reason he asked, "What makes you sure he's dead? You said none of the players had been found."

Leah looked at him, and instantly Lance had known his bluff had been called. "Don't patronize me, Lance. Don't act like everybody else and pretend that bad things haven't happened and that there's still hope and all that other bullshit people always say to a victim's face before going home and closing their doors and then shaking their heads and saying things like 'Oh, that poor thing. Bless her heart. Such a tragedy. Blah blah blah.' You know the truth, and I didn't have you pegged as the type of person who would shy away from it."

Lance sat, stunned. *This girl is ... wow. Just ... wow.*

His level of guilt at hiding the true nature of his abilities was growing stronger by the minute, but still he refrained. It wasn't the time. He needed more information about what he was up against. "Okay," he offered. "Your brother—oh, what was his name?"

Lance quickly regretted the use of past tense, but the damage was done.

"Samuel," Leah said.

"Okay, so Sam was the—"

"No. Never Sam. He always liked to be called Samuel." She smiled another sad smile. "He said it was more distinguished. No wonder he wasn't a superstar athlete, huh? Concerned about things like that."

Lance waited a beat before continuing, letting Leah finish off her memory. "So Samuel was the first of the three players to disappear, correct?"

"Yes."

"Okay, then that's where I need to start. Tell me exactly

what happened, as best you can. Maybe we can put some pieces together."

Leah looked at him for a long moment, and Lance wondered if she'd suddenly decided this was all a bad idea. Maybe she'd finally realized she was talking about something she normally kept locked away down deep to a man who was practically a stranger. But then, softly, she said, "You know, I've been over the details of Samuel's disappearance a million times—with the police, with Daddy, with friends—and another ten million times in my own head. It's never done a single bit of good. Nothing I saw and nothing I know has ever helped anybody come any closer to helping me get any sort of closure. My brother is dead, I know that." She paused. "And I can't explain it, honestly I can't, but you're the first person I've ever met who I think for some reason might be able to finally help me figure out why."

And then, in a move that both melted Lance's heart, and also made his skin come alive with electricity, Leah reached across the cushion that separated them and squeezed his hand.

With that simple touch, Lance's own demons and problems dissolved for an instant, and all that remained was a will to help this young girl find out what had happened to her brother.

Him and two other boys who had obviously suffered at the hand of whatever force was after Lance as well.

For the next fifteen minutes, Lance sat in his corner of the couch, eyes fixed on Leah as she did her best to summarize her story.

Leah and Samuel's mother had "gotten sick" a year and a half before Samuel had disappeared. Leah didn't say what exactly had been wrong with the woman, but sadly, she'd passed on just a few quick months after falling ill. From there,

Leah's family home had become a disaster zone. Her father, who'd been an overly aggressive social drinker to use the politest of terms, had let go of whatever small part of the wagon he'd been holding on to. He was rarely seen at home without a bottle in his hand and rarely seen in town unless it was on a barstool. "He always went to work, though," Leah said. "He never missed a single day at the mill. Even the days he could barely stand. Daddy's got flaws—bad ones—but he's loyal."

Lance chewed on this information for a moment before asking, "And how was his relationship with you and Samuel, after your mother passed?"

Leah's face fell, and Lance had a good idea what she was about to admit. "Not the best," she said. "He loves us, don't get me wrong, but he just ... after Momma, and the drinking ... he ... I don't think he ever meant to...."

"He hit you," Lance said. It happened every day in this country, but that didn't make the sting any duller as he looked at this sweet girl's face and imagined a burly fist connecting with one of her eye sockets.

Leah offered a sad, small grin and shrugged. "Only once with me. Nothing so bad. Just a hard slap across the face one day when I talked back. I knew he felt terrible about it as soon as it happened."

"And Samuel?"

Leah closed her eyes, and Lance didn't want to know what she was seeing behind her closed eyelids.

"Yes, it was worse for Samuel. I don't know why. He never did anything wrong. But he just always seemed to be in Daddy's way when the time came for an outburst. After all this time, part of me can't help but wonder if he was doing it on purpose. Trying to protect me."

"Sounds like a good brother."

Leah's face lit up. "He was the best." Then she continued on.

When football practice had started and the new coach—Coach McGuire—had the team doing two-a-days in what could only be an attempt to figure out why these young men had only won a single game the previous season, Leah had started spending more and more time helping out at the motel.

"Daddy's daddy owned this place until he died," Leah said. "Daddy inherited it, and since it was all paid for and, like I said, Daddy's loyal, we've always kept it. At that time, we had more hired help here, but I was sixteen and looking for a good reason to get out of the house and out of Daddy's way. So I asked Daddy—one day when he was surprisingly sober—if I could work part-time. I said I wanted my own spending cash so I could go out with friends. I think he knew the real reason I was asking, but he was too ashamed to admit it."

"And now you basically run the place?" Lance asked.

"Basically."

"Impressive."

"I don't have much else to do. It keeps me busy, and I like helping people."

"That's a nice way to look at it."

The two-a-days seemed to have helped, because Westhaven had won their first game of the season. And their second, and their third. The parents were happy, the fans were happy, the sports boosters were happy, but more importantly, the players were happy. The morale and camaraderie of Westhaven's football team were high, and the intense schedule of grueling practices that Coach McGuire had created suddenly seemed more than worth it. Leah said that Samuel looked forward to practices and pre-game meals and film sessions even more than he usually did, and from what she gathered, the rest of the team felt the same way.

After the fourth victory in a row, Coach McGuire invited the entire team over to his house for a barbecue. Parents were invited as well, and even though Leah and Samuel's daddy was unable to attend, Glenn Strang, father of Westhaven's new placekicker and largest new donor to Westhaven's athletic programs, was in attendance. He'd announced to everybody there that if Westhaven could win their fifth game in a row, they'd all be invited to a pool party at his home.

"He stood on top of Coach McGuire's lawn mower to make sure he could be seen and heard," Leah said. "Samuel said he looked like an expensively dressed meerkat, the way he suddenly popped up over the crowd."

Westhaven won the next game, and Strang kept his word. After the first pool party, the Strang home became somewhat of a regular hangout for Westhaven players. Glenn Strang told the team that his door was always open if any of the boys needed a place to study, clear their head, stay the night, or anything.

"It was pretty weird, if you ask me," Leah said. "It was like he was running some sort of shelter for the football team. I mean, his house is practically a mansion by this town's standards, and Mrs. Strang was always home to help the boys with schoolwork, or fix them a good meal, and everybody seemed to genuinely like Bobby—that's the Strangs' son. But some parents started grumbling that their sons were spending too much time away from home. More specifically, too much time at casa de Strang."

Lance had had similar team barbecues and parties hosted by parents of players or the coaches, and even the high school principal. But none of these people had essentially given him a key to their home and asked him to come by anytime for any reason. It wasn't exactly a red flag, but it certainly was an oddity.

"But the trouble really started when word got out that a lot of *female* students were making their way to the Strang house along with the players."

"Uh-oh," Lance said. "So the place went from shelter to brothel?"

"Brothel is a little harsh. Some of those girls are my friends, thank you very much. But basically it didn't take long for a group of horny high school boys to realize that if their parents wouldn't let them take a girl to their bedroom and close the door, maybe they could find someplace to be alone with a girl at their home away from home. A place as big as the Strangs' house, and with limited adult supervision, it was worth a shot. And it paid off for quite a few."

"Interesting."

Leah leaned forward, as if about to divulge some secret bit of evidence. "What's always bugged me about the whole situation is, I don't know if the Strangs knew about and were encouraging what was happening at their home, or they were simply naïve and ignorant. I mean, they obviously cared about the players and Bobby's friends, but I've always wondered how involved they actually were in everything. How hands-on. Does that make any sense?"

Lance nodded. "I think so. Basically you want to know if the Strangs were the problem. Point-blank."

Leah thought for a moment. "Yeah, basically. I just think their whole open-home policy was bizarre. And there's no denying the link between the timing of their showing up and entering the players' lives, and the team beginning to win, and ... and my brother's disappearance."

"Did Samuel spend a lot of time at the Strangs' house?"

Leah nodded. "Oh yeah. I used this place as my escape"—she gestured to the room around them—"and Samuel jumped all over the Strangs' freestanding invitation to use as his. He was constantly there. He and Bobby Strang got to be very close."

"What did your father think of that?"

Leah shrugged. "Daddy was still drinking a lot, and I think, just like with me and the motel, he knew Samuel was protecting himself. Daddy's not dumb, he was just ... broken for a while."

"He's better now?"

"He's getting there."

Lance left things at that. "So when did Samuel disappear?"

"Three days before the state championship game."

"And that's all? He was just here, playing football, spending a lot of time at his friend's house, and then one day he was gone?"

"Yes."

"And you didn't notice him acting different at all, like something was wrong? Who was the last person to see him?"

"No, he seemed completely normal. Funny enough, it was Bobby Strang who saw him last. They had been in town, getting some burgers for lunch, and Samuel told Bobby he had to go, that he was going to see his girlfriend."

"He had a girlfriend?" Lance asked.

Leah's face grew somber again, and she took a deep breath. "This is the other part that kills me, the part I can't understand. Samuel and I were always close, being only a year apart. It's just the way we grew up together. We had no secrets. He still came by the motel as often as he could to say hi, or bring me some takeout for dinner, and we always talked about what was going on in our lives."

"Okay."

"And not once in all those visits, all that time together, even two days before he vanished, did he ever mention a single word to me about having a girlfriend."

Lance had no brothers or sisters of his own and briefly let his mind wander to explore what it might be like to have somebody who shared his blood and was that close to him, somebody he could always trust and count on and speak freely to without fear of judgment. Somebody he could share his world with.

He quickly realized this person had been his mother, and his heart thumped a beat of anguish. God, how he missed her.

"So who was this girlfriend?" he asked.

Leah threw her hands up in frustration. "That's the worst part of the whole thing. Nobody I've spoken to, not the other players, not other students, and not even Bobby Strang, even knew Samuel *had* a girlfriend. She's a phantom. Nobody has the slightest clue who she was."

"But she could very well have been the last person to have seen your brother alive."

"Exactly."

"Well, then, we have to find her."

[10]

LANCE OPENED HIS EYES AND WONDERED WHEN HIS
bedroom ceiling had become so dirty. He didn't remember ever
seeing it so filthy, with blackish-gray smears of dust and cobwebs
dancing in the corners with unseen swirls of air. It was an odd
thing. His mother had always kept things very...

The memories flooded him, and he sat up, remembering
everything that had happened. His eyes focused on the dull
surroundings of his motel room, and he remembered where
he was.

He remembered last night.

After Leah's revelation about her brother's mysterious girlfriend, she'd quickly gone on to explain that Samuel had been
the first, and one Westhaven football player had followed in her
brother's disappearing footsteps in each of the past two years.
Two years in which Westhaven had won state titles.

Three years.

Three championships.

Three missing

(*Dead?*)

boys.

Lance had had more questions, and Leah had seemed to have more information, but at that point it had gotten to be a few minutes after midnight and Lance's headache was starting to kick up again. Plus, his afternoon nap was wearing off, his body once again beginning to feel weary, and he knew he needed sleep.

"Let's meet for breakfast in the morning, then we can get to work," Leah had said as he'd thanked her for the pizza and made his way to the office's door.

"Get to work?"

Leah had cocked her head to side. "Well, yeah. You know ... solving the case."

Lance had been tired and had hated to admit that Leah's enthusiasm to begin chasing down what he knew to be something neither of them were likely capable of dealing with was beginning to irritate him. A normal person might have been quick to vocalize such annoyances, but Lance had better sense. He knew Leah was hurting and had been for some time now. Whatever small flame of hope she'd been holding on to had been doused in gasoline and had exploded the moment Lance had told her what he was and shown an interest.

"I'm not a detective," he'd said.

"No," she'd said. "You're better than a detective. You actually care."

It was the truth. "You know Annabelle's Apron?"

She'd rolled her eyes. "Hello, I've lived here my whole life, and there aren't a lot of options. Daddy says Ms. Winters used to make the best pies in the state."

Lance had nodded. "She told—" He'd caught himself. "That's what I've heard. Meet there at eight?"

Leah had shaken her head. "Nine. That way the kids will be in school and the adults at work. You heard Daddy earlier. Folks have already reported you as *suspicious*. The fewer people who see us together, the better."

Lance agreed but knew that no matter how careful they were in their appearances, there was something worse than peeping human eyes keeping tabs on him. Something that would not be easily deterred. He had said goodnight and taken the few short steps to his motel room, his sneakers crunching the shattered plastic from the overhead light that had exploded earlier. He had shuffled a few of the broken shards around on the concrete and looked up at the now-blackened hole where the bulb and globe had been, looked across the parking lot to the road, the single streetlamp still casting its dull glow.

The air had been still and cool, but Lance knew better than to think it innocent.

After a quick check of his small room, which included looking into the mirror for surprise guests and pulling back the shower curtain to examine the empty tub, Lance had kicked off his shoes and fallen asleep almost instantly when his head had touched the pillow.

And now he was awake, a stranger in a town that held secrets that did not want to be revealed. *But how far will it go to stop me?*

The motel room's window was traced by an outline of gold as the early-morning sunlight squirted through the cracks. Lance stood and stretched, felt the lump on the back of his head and was pleased to find that it'd gotten much smaller than the night before. After rubbing his eyes, he found his vision to be fine and his headache to be gone. All that remained was the tender area of skin around the knot at the base of his skull. In time, that would heal.

He checked his flip phone and saw it was a quarter to seven. No missed calls or voicemails had been logged, which didn't surprise him in the slightest. He'd gotten few phone calls before, and he imagined, with his mother gone, he'd get even fewer now. He sighed, found his phone charger in his backpack and plugged it into the wall behind the nightstand. Once his phone was sucking down juice, Lance went into the bathroom and took a shower, extremely thankful for the motel-provided mini bar of soap, even if it did look as if he were scrubbing himself with an oversized Tic-Tac.

Finished with the shower and having dried himself, he looked at the pile of clothes he'd discarded on the floor and was slightly repulsed at the fact he would have to wear the whole outfit again. Socks, boxers, everything. He needed to go shopping, as soon as possible. He looked suspicious enough as it was, so wearing the same outfit every day to go along with eternal morning breath and his pits likely reeking of BO did not seem like the best option.

He shook out his clothing, a half-hearted attempt to de-wrinkle them, and then dressed. He unplugged his cell phone and slid it into his pocket, then repacked the charger. After a thorough check of the room to be sure he'd not left behind any personal items, he slid his backpack onto his shoulders, peeked through the blinds and scanned the parking lot for any movement. He went outside.

His hand went immediately to his face, shielding his eyes from the sun. He squinted and looked down to the asphalt, letting his eyes adjust. When they finally did, he looked to his right, toward the motel's office door, and found himself wanting to go in that direction. To pop his head inside and offer Leah a quick "good morning" and tell her he was looking forward to their breakfast

(*It's not a date*)

together. But then he was stepping off the sidewalk and making his way across the parking lot. *Stop being silly, Lance. That's not why you're here.*

The pickup truck was gone, but the Jeep with the stuffed Garfield suctioned to the window was still in the same place. Lance met the cat's plastic eyes as he walked past the car and wondered who it was that owned the vehicle, what kind of person he or she was, where they were headed.

His sneakers found Route 19, and before he turned to walk back toward town, he noticed the plume of smoke rising high above the trees in the distance. It had to be miles away, but still it was impossible to miss, a great gray pillar growing toward the sky. "That's got to be the paper mill," he said to the road, and he wondered if he'd make his way there, if whatever mystery he was attempting to solve would draw him toward that black smoke.

He walked along the sidewalk, back into town. A few cars passed him by, one going so far as to drive in the other lane as it passed, making sure to give Lance all the room he needed. *Well, at least I know not everybody's out for blood around here.*

Back in the heart of Westhaven's downtown, Lance turned off the main drag and walked two blocks down a side street. He found a small CVS on the corner and went inside, an elderly gentleman greeting him with a large smile and a loud "G'morning!" Lance returned the greeting with a smile and a nod and grabbed one of the plastic baskets from a stack near the door. Ten minutes later he'd made his purchases: toothbrush, toothpaste, deodorant, shampoo, soap, shaving cream, disposable razor, a small travel first-aid kit, a three-pack of white athletic socks, a three-pack of boxer shorts, and a pack of spearmint gum. "Is there someplace close where I could buy some clothes?" Lance had asked the man at the counter as he paid.

"Depends what sort of clothes you're looking for, son."

Lance looked down at his t-shirt and cargo shorts, his scuffed sneakers.

"I see," the man said. Then he pointed over his shoulder, as if this was a display of precision direction giving. "Sportsman's is a block over, but Harry doesn't open until nine."

Darn. Looks like I'm wearing the same thing for breakfast as dinner.

"Thank you very much," Lance said, and then asked, "Restroom?"

Lance followed another of the man's pointing fingers and carried his shopping bag to the back right corner of the store, where he found the men's room. Inside one of the stalls, he changed his boxers and put on a fresh pair of socks. Then he brushed his teeth and applied a thick layer of deodorant. He stuffed everything into his backpack and then headed toward the front of the store to leave. The elderly gentleman behind the counter was reading the day's newspaper, and as Lance was about to exit the store, he had an idea. "Excuse me, sir?"

The man peered at Lance from atop the paper. "Yes, son? Something else I can do for you?"

Lance hesitated for a moment, realizing this could be a bad idea, but he wanted to get a feel for things. He knew he had to ask. "I'm just passing through, on a way to visit a friend of mine a little further north. I told him I was coming through here, and he mentioned to me that he thought he heard that a bunch of high school boys have disappeared around here over the years. Is that true, or was he just pulling my leg? Trying to spook me, or something?"

It was like the air had suddenly been sucked out of the room. The man's smile faltered and the newspaper went all the way down to the counter. Then the man looked Lance dead in the eyes and said, "What are you, a reporter? Somebody looking for a scandal, to stir up trouble?"

"No, sir. It just sounded to me like you already had trouble. You know anything about it?"

The man stared at Lance for another hard second and then

picked up his newspaper. "Move along, son. Your friend is waiting for you."

Lance left the store and stood on the sidewalk outside the automatic doors. When he looked over his shoulder, he saw the man behind the counter looking at him through the window, his face partially hidden by a large advertisement promising Buy One, Get One Free for any bottled beverage. Lance waved and smiled. The man's face disappeared.

Lance sighed. *Well, that didn't go well.*

He checked his phone and saw it was nearly 8:30. Time for breakfast.

As he walked to Annabelle's Apron, he wondered if the man from CVS was already on the phone, letting everybody know that a *suspicious* man had stopped by this morning ... and he was asking questions.

[11]

HE WALKED THROUGH THE DINER'S DOOR AT TEN BEFORE nine and found Leah seated at the counter on one of the stools. She had one hand curled around a coffee mug, the other wrapped around her iPhone, her thumb aimlessly scrolling the screen. Her hair was down this morning. It looked clean and was shining in the sunlight pouring through the diner's windows. Gone was the black business suit, in its place a pair of green khaki shorts and a red t-shirt, a pair of white-and-red Converse sneakers on her feet.

Lance loved the girl's sense of style. He felt even more conscious about his lack of different clothes. He'd never been one to care much about his own appearance, but he didn't want to come off as a bum, and he hated feeling dirty.

As usual, because of his size, many of Annabelle's Apron's guests' eyes followed Lance as he made his way toward the counter. He smiled at a few that were close enough to notice, and they offered quick grins before turning their attention back toward their plates and newspapers. He had barely reached the counter when Margie came through the kitchen door and saw him, her stern face noticeably softening for a moment as she said, "Well, good morning! The man with the bottomless pit for a stomach returns. I told the afternoon staff all about you yesterday. They thought I was making it up. Said nobody could eat all of that and still walk out the door of their own accord." The woman laughed, and Lance noticed that her smile was very nice. He hoped that she got the chance to use it more often.

He waved back and sat himself on a stool, leaving a one-stool gap between himself and Leah. "Sounds like folks around here need to eat more," Lance said to Margie as she slid a coffee mug in front of him. "I used to put away twice that on game days back when I played ball."

Margie filled his mug. "Football?" she asked, her eyes lighting up.

Lance shook his head. "No. Too skinny for football. Basketball."

"Oh," Margie said, seemingly disappointed.

"Margie, sweetie, I'll take some of that coffee over here, and some of your sugar to go with it." Hank Peterson was in his same spot at the end of the counter, coffee mug held out like a street beggar.

Margie rolled her eyes. "Your wife's sugar not good enough, Hank?" Then she winked at Lance and went to fill Hank's coffee.

"Well," Leah said, speaking to him for the first time, "you've certainly made a reputation for yourself. Never known Margie to take to a stranger so quickly. She's usually, well, sort of a bitch. You know, in that Great American Diner sort of way."

"I think she just likes me because my bill is high. Plus, well, I'm downright charming."

Leah had no comment on Lance's level of charming. Instead, she stood from the counter, grabbed her coffee mug and said, "Come on, let's go get a booth so we can talk without everybody listening."

Lance stood, and when Margie saw him and gave him a questioning look, Lance raised his eyebrows and shrugged his shoulders, as if to say, *What am I going to do?*

He followed Leah through the smattering of tables, only a few of which had actual diners seated at them, and ended up sitting in the same rear corner booth where the family with the young child had been yesterday morning. Lance sat with his back to the side of the building, facing the front. Leah had her back to everything except him and the window behind him.

Remembering Margie's look, Lance said, "It's not going to be a secret very long that we're here together."

Leah shrugged. "I know. I thought it'd be better coming in later like this, but I wasn't even thinking about the people working here. Oh well. It's not like we're making out and causing a scene. For all anybody knows, you could be my cousin, or something."

Lance's brain had stopped listening at the words "making out" and he had to push away the images they conjured in order to bring his focus back to the present. "Okay," he said.

"Okay, what?"

A waitress brought them menus just in time to save him. Leah held up her hands and said, "I'll just have some wheat toast and jelly, Sarah."

Lance handed his menu back as well and ordered his same breakfast from yesterday.

"You know her?" he asked once the waitress was out of earshot.

Leah nodded and took a sip of her coffee. "Few years older than me. She used to be a cheerleader for Westhaven. Was supposed to go to college on a scholarship."

"What happened?"

"She got pregnant by the high school math teacher."

Lance swallowed a steaming-hot sip of coffee faster than he

wanted to. He coughed and said, "Whoa. That's pretty scandalous."

Leah raised her mug in a toast. "Welcome to Small Town, USA."

They were quiet for a bit, both sipping coffee and waiting for their food. "Who's watching the motel?" Lance asked.

"Renee. It's her normal shift, but I told her today I might need her to work some extra hours. I told her I had some things I needed to take care of. She doesn't mind. She needs the money."

"How many people do you have working for you?"

"Technically, they work for Daddy, but ..." She looked up, mentally tallying. "Five, if you count Martin. He's a handyman that Daddy pays a fee each month to be on standby. In case something needs fixing."

"A handyman on retainer," Lance said. "Not a bad gig."

Leah nodded. "And he's the sweetest guy in the world."

Their food came, and as Leah spread jelly on her toast and Lance poured syrup on his pancakes, Lance asked a question that had been nagging at him from the early moments of Leah telling him the town's troubled past. "So, what exactly do the police have to say about everything?"

Leah took a bite and wiped her mouth with a paper napkin. "Not much."

"Come on. Three kids gone missing. They've said *something*." Lance forked eggs into his mouth and washed it down with a bite of pancake.

Leah sighed. "You're right. Sort of. They honestly did seem to make a decent effort when Samuel disappeared. At first, anyway. But when the leads—which were essentially zero—led to dead ends, they started looking a little closer at the home life."

Lance swallowed another bite of food, knowing all at once where this was going. "They think he ran away." It wasn't a question. It was fact.

Leah nodded. "Again ... small town. Sheriff's office all knew about Momma passing and knew Daddy was drinking a lot." Then, embarrassed, "He's spent more than one night in the drunk tank after having a few too many and getting started on the wrong topic of conversation. Daddy's got a short fuse."

And the alcohol makes it shorter, Lance thought, feeling a twinge of anger at the memory of Leah's confession that her father had struck her and her brother.

She continued, "Everybody knew things weren't the best at our house. They knew I'd been working extra hours at the motel, and then ... well, when they found out Daddy'd hit us a few times, that was the final nail in the coffin. They immediately assumed Samuel had had enough."

Lance shook his head. "And just like that, case closed?"

"More or less. I mean, technically the case is still open—cold now—but nobody's following up with it. The last time any member of the sheriff's office came to see me was after the second boy disappeared. After the third, the state police got involved, or at least pretended to, but that fizzled out almost as quick as it started."

Because he was trying his best to give Leah his undivided attention, Lance was eating slower than normal, but still he was almost finished with his meal. Leah had only eaten half a piece of toast. "They can't possibly think they're *all* runaways. That's asinine."

Leah took another bite, her toast surely cold by now. "Do you read a lot?"

"What?"

"Asinine. That's what I was talking about last night. Who says that in daily conversation?"

Lance finished his coffee, thought about the shelves and shelves of books he'd left behind at his and his mother's home. The tattered paperbacks from yard sales, the hardbacks from library sales and used bookstores. He'd been making his way through all the titles, even going so far as to make a list in a notebook he kept in his nightstand. His mother *had* read them all. She was the most well read person he'd ever known. His stomach tightened at the thought that he'd never get to finish his list. "Does my vocabulary really bother you that much?"

She smiled. Shook her head. "No. I just think it's fun to give you a hard time about it. Honestly, I kinda love it."

The tightness in Lance's stomach was replaced by a warmth and fluttering.

"Anyway," Leah continued, "yes, the other two boys were also assumed to be runaways. Actually, that's the only thing that seems to make sense out of any of this."

"How so?"

"All the boys, Samuel included, had reasons enough to make the sheriff's office believe that their wanting to fly the coop was acceptable. On top of that, they were all eighteen. No longer juveniles."

Sarah stopped by the table to refill their cups, and Lance ordered a slice of pie. He asked her to make sure Margie knew he was ordering it, and to tell her that it was the best pie he'd had since his mother's. He figured a little damage control couldn't hurt. Maybe if he was polite enough and sucked up enough, Margie wouldn't label him suspicious as most other folks seemed eager to do.

"You know Samuel's story," Leah said. "Chuck Goodman's family had owned the hardware store for like a billion years, but the new Walmart fifteen miles up Route 19 finally put them out of business. Chuck's father took it pretty hard, and there were rumors they were going to move during Christmas break to be closer to Chuck's mother's family."

"And the police thought Chuck was unhappy with the arrangement and lashing out by running away?"

"Pretty much." Leah finished her last piece of toast. "Martin Brownlee's brother was in the Marines, got killed overseas somewhere. His father shot himself a month after they got the news. Martin's mother seemed to be handling things as well as she could, but when Martin vanished, nobody asked a lot of questions about him. Why would he want to stick around in that sort of situation, a lot of people asked."

"To take care of his mother?"

Leah shrugged. "I'm just telling you what people were saying."

Sarah brought Lance his pie, and he started to eat. Then he asked, "So what does the town think? What do they think happened to those boys?"

Leah's face was calm, but her words carried a tremor of anger that was only barely being suppressed. "You grew up in a small town?" she asked.

"Not as small as this, but yeah, pretty much."

"Well, around here, football is the only goddam thing that matters to these stupid people. It's like ... like ... like they've got nothing else to live for, like there isn't a whole vast world out there with other things to see and explore and people to meet. Football. And now that we've been winning, it's only gotten worse." She took a sip of coffee, as if trying to let herself settle down. "People around here accept the idea of those boys being runaways because that's the easy way out. It means that nothing's wrong except those boys' heads, and as long as Westhaven keeps winning games, people can keep on smiling and everything will be all right."

Lance was quiet, thinking about all Leah had told him. He finished his pie, and when he looked up, she was staring out the window. He thought he saw a tear in her eye, but it might have just been a glare. "And you think it's going to happen again?" he asked.

She turned her head and looked at him. "Don't you?"

Lance closed his eyes and took in a deep breath, letting his mind reach out through the town, sending out the sensors that he didn't understand how he could sometimes control. It was out there, that permeating sense of dread that seemed to hang throughout Westhaven like invisible fog. He'd felt it when he'd gotten off the bus, and he felt it now. And it could feel him. "Yes. I do."

Leah's face looked thankful. "So what do we do now?"

Lance pulled out his flip phone. "I don't want to sound too forward here, but may I please have your phone number?"

Leah looked at his phone as though it were something recovered from a time capsule. "As long as you promise not to wait three days before calling."

Lance opened his phone and went through the laborious process of typing out Leah's name to add a new contact. "Does your thumb get cramps working that thing?" she asked.

Lance smiled, keeping his eyes on the screen. "Number, please?"

Leah laughed and recited the digits, adding, "Man, I just got a wicked chill. Must be a draft somewhere."

Lance's thumb froze over the keypad, one last digit stored away in his memory that needed to be typed. He pressed the button slowly, the cold chill Leah had brought to his attention enveloping him, the booth, everything around him. He hit the SAVE button and then shut his phone.

"You going to give me yours now?" Leah asked.

Lance lifted his eyes from the scratched tabletop. Used all his willpower not to show how startled he was.

The young man standing directly next to their booth had been burned badly. He was muscular and well built, just as the boy in Leah's mirror had been. Only that boy's swollen face and blackened eyes were nothing compared to the charred and disfigured body Lance was looking at now.

The boy was naked, every inch of his skin marred and melted, a hideous orange and red and black swirl of blood and blisters and bone showing through splotches of missing skin. The boy's eye sockets were empty, traces of white and yellow and green fluids caked and dried to the remaining caverns where eyeballs should have been. Half the boy's left cheek was gone, slightly yellowed teeth winking out at Lance from a blackened and drooping gum line.

Lance felt his food shift in his stomach.

"Hey," Leah said. "You holding out on me?"

Lance's vision blurred for a moment. He shook his head and looked at Leah, the dark figure next to their booth still looming in his peripheral vision. "I'm sorry, what?" he asked, doing his best to sound cheerful.

"That antique phone you have—it does receive incoming calls, yes?"

There was a slow movement out of the corner of Lance's right eye.

"Oh, yeah, sorry. Let me know when you're ready."

The boy was reaching his right arm toward Leah, skeleton-like fingers, more bone than skin and tendons, outstretched in a menacing claw.

Leah held up her iPhone. "Been ready."

Lance recited the beginning of his number. *It can't hurt her. It can't hurt her. It can't—*

"Okay. Next."

He finished rattling off the remaining digits just as the tip of one of the blackened fingers touched a few wisps of Leah's golden hair. Lance wanted to jump up, wanted to grab her and pull her away and get the heck out of there. But that would mean he'd have to tell her the truth. All of it.

"Hey." She was looking at him, concerned. "You okay over there?" She laughed. "Did you eat too much?"

The door to the diner exploded open, slamming against the wall and rattling the windows. All eyes in Annabelle's Apron locked onto the source of the noise.

A short man, maybe five-five but built like a refrigerator, his width nearly filling the entire doorway, stormed into the diner and looked around, eyes wild. "Leah!" he called out.

Uh-oh.

"Daddy?"

Lance looked to his right. The burned boy was gone.

[12]

Annabelle's Apron was overcome with a hush. It was like a scene from an old-time Western, the eyes of spectators flicking back and forth between two opposing foes and waiting to see what would play out before them. Waiting to see who would make the first move.

Leah's daddy's eyes locked onto his daughter, and he quickly made his way down the walkway between the rows of booths and tables, his girth causing him to bump a few chairs along the way. Some of those chairs had people sitting in them, but nobody seemed to mind. Especially not Leah's daddy.

And then he was there, standing in the exact spot the burned boy had been just seconds ago.

Lance preferred the burned boy.

Up close, Leah's daddy was even wider. His forearms and biceps looked ready to rip phone books in half, and his chest and shoulders stretched the white undershirt the man was wearing to the point that it seemed ready to explode off his body. The legs of his blue jeans looked more likely to be covering tree trunks than human thighs. The heavy, steel-toed work boots seemed primed and ready to kick a man's teeth in or stomp a rib cage until the bones inside rattled around like castanets.

And the man was completely bald. Not a single hair on his egg-shaped head. Whether this was by choice or by genetics, Lance didn't have time to ponder, nor ask. The man's bloodshot eyes squinted, the blood vessels road mapping his nose squished together as his face grew into a snarl. "Who the hell are you?"

Lance wished he had been standing. At least then he'd have a significant height advantage. And could run away. But there was no running now. If he tried to make a move out of the booth, the walking cinder block of a man before him would surely snatch him up and slam him down. Lance liked his clavicle in one piece. So, he did the only thing he knew to do. He played dumb, and he hoped he was as charming as he thought he was.

Lance stuck out his hand. "I'm Lance, sir. Pleasure to meet you. Would you like to join us?"

Leah's daddy's snarl intensified. "Don't give a fuck what your name is. I asked who you were."

"*Daddy!*" Leah said. "What's gotten into you. We're just—"

"Shut your mouth. Now!"

Leah's face reddened, and Lance felt his anger begin to rise. But he had to keep it cool, otherwise this definitely wasn't going to end well.

"I'm sorry, sir," he said. "I don't know how else to answer you. You asked who I am, and my name is Lance. If you want to know more, I'm afraid you're going to have to be more specific. Otherwise, I fear we may be here awhile, and well... I've already eaten."

Leah couldn't stifle her laugh, a noise that seemed to catch everybody off guard. Her daddy shot her a look that could have knocked over bowling pins. Then he turned back to Lance, the muscles in his arms practically twitching, the veins pulsing.

"You want specifics? Here they are. Why in the fuck are you in this booth with my daughter?"

A number of answers filled Lance's mind, the truth being one that he thought would get the biggest reaction out of the man, but might also cause the most damage. Leah, fortunately, had the golden answer.

"*Daddy!* If you'd shut *your* mouth for a minute, you'd know that I'm interviewing him for a job."

Lance and Daddy both looked at her and said, "What?"

"Yes," she said. "Travis is going to start taking classes at the community college at night, and he's looking for another job to work in the daytime. So Lance here is interested in taking his spot at the motel. He stayed with us last night and asked if I knew of any place that was hiring, so I mentioned he could maybe work for us."

Lance marveled at Leah's quick thinking. "That's correct, sir. I've always had a bit of an interest in the hospitality industry, and your establishment seems like just the right type of environment to—"

Leah's daddy held up a scarred and calloused hand. Lance stopped talking. The man's features softened, his stance shifting to one less intimidating. He eyed Lance for a hard fifteen seconds, and Lance felt an absurd urge to smile big, as if for the school picture. Then the man's gaze switched to Leah. He took a breath and said, "That's really all this is? You're tellin' your daddy the truth?"

"*Yes*, Daddy. I know the rules."

The rest of the diner patrons slowly began to turn their attention back to their own tables, the sound of forks on plates and coffee mugs refilled by waitresses helped to bring the place back alive. The idle chitchat began to start up again.

Leah's daddy took one more glance at Lance before saying

to his daughter, "Come by the house sometime soon. I'll make dinner. It's been a while."

Leah smiled, but Lance already knew it to be artificial. "Yeah, sure. That sounds nice."

Her daddy nodded once, then turned and went to the counter, saying, "Margie, I'd love some coffee."

Lance watched as the woman gave the man a mug and filled it, then she leaned over and the two of them started talking quietly, Margie's eyes flicking in Lance's direction every so often.

"Don't take it personally," Leah said. "Gossip is gossip is gossip."

"I guess," Lance said. "But word sure did travel fast."

Leah turned and looked across the diner, scanned the few remaining customers. "And the worst part? It could have been any one of them."

Lance stared at the wide back of Leah's daddy, imagined all the hours spent at the paper mill, building those muscles to the shape they now were. "What's his name?" Lance asked.

"Who? Daddy?"

"Yes."

Leah glanced toward her father. "Samuel. My brother was a junior."

And in that moment, after feeling as though he'd narrowly averted a beatdown of the greatest magnitude, Lance felt pity for the man at the counter. He'd lost his wife, and then he'd lost his son. The only thing that mattered at all anymore was currently seated directly across from Lance. Lance's mother had told him that alcohol poisoned the mind and the body. But it sure as heck didn't dampen a father's urge to protect his only daughter.

"That was some quick thinking," Lance said.

Leah shrugged. "Thank God it worked. But now I have to

tell Travis he has to lie to Daddy if the topic ever comes up. Shouldn't be that big a deal, though. Daddy doesn't come around that often. He leaves most things up to me."

Lance nodded, took a sip of coffee that had begun to grow cold, bitter.

"So what do we do now?" Leah asked. "What's the first step?"

Lance had considered this during his walk from the motel to the CVS, and after listening to Leah tell him the stories of the rest of the boys who'd gone missing, he was certain of one question he wanted asked. "I want you to go do your best and see if any of the other two boys had girlfriends at the time they disappeared. Ask around, talk to people. You'll know much better than I would who to go see."

Leah nodded, but Lance could tell something was disappointing her. "And what are you going to do?"

Lance looked out the window to the mostly empty parking lot. "I'm not sure yet. But I'll figure it out. Times like this, I usually do."

"You know that makes, like, no sense at all."

Lance nodded. "Yeah, I know." He pulled some cash from his pocket and tossed it on the table. "I'm going to get out of here. That should cover yours too, so now we're even from the pizza." He stood from the booth. "Call me if you find out anything, and I'll do the same."

He made a show of waving to Margie as he left. "The pie was delicious!" he called to her. And then he wondered if Annabelle Winters had heard him, and was shaking her head.

If she was there, he wondered if she'd seen the burned boy.

LANCE WALKED BACK TO THE CVS AND THEN NAVIGATED A few more blocks until he found Sportsman's, a large storefront nestled between a dry cleaner and a martial arts studio that was advertising free first lessons to kids ages six to twelve. Lance looked through the glass front of the dry cleaner and saw a small woman with gray hair perched on a stool behind the counter, the eraser of her pencil bouncing against her bottom lip as she studied the crossword puzzle book she held. The rack behind her held only a few garments waiting to be picked up.

Lance pulled open the door to Sportsman's and was greeted by modern pop music playing through overhead speakers— something by one of those trendy new boy bands who liked to wear skinny jeans and slick their hair up and sing about love and sex at the ripe old age of seventeen. Lance didn't care for the music, but the décor was refreshing, like finally finding a person who speaks your native tongue after traveling abroad. The store was large and separated by category: hunting and fishing, camping, baseball and softball, basketball, football, golf, you name it. The entire back wall displayed athletic shoes of every make and model. Large cutouts and posters of the likes of Kevin Durant and Cam Newton and Rickie Fowler were bright and flashy and surely convinced folks they *needed* the same shoes these insanely gifted athletes wore.

The air smelled of leather and rubber and new shoes and competition.

There didn't appear to be any other shoppers in the store. Lance figured this was because it was still early. A store like this wasn't going to survive long in this town without some revenue. And if Leah's words were true, which Lance figured them to be, athletics really did appear to be more and more the lifeblood of Westhaven.

Lance's eyes gravitated to the basketball goal on display in the corner, an expensive model gleaming and beautiful, and he was hit with the urge to find a ball and go dunk it as hard as he could. Just to feel normal for a bit, to relax. But there was no time for that. He wasn't here to have fun.

A man wearing chinos and a Sportsman's embroidered collared shirt stepped out from behind one of the aisles. He held an old-fashioned clipboard in his hand and a pencil tucked behind his ear. "Hi there, welcome to Sportsman's. Can I help you find something?"

Yes, I'm looking for something that's been killing off your town's football players. Something from the supernatural line, probably. Not very flashy, but gets the job done.

Lance smiled and nodded toward the racks of clothes near the wall of shoes. "Need some new outfits. I think I see where I need to look."

"Be sure and let us know if you need any help." The man flashed a quick smile and then disappeared back into his aisle.

Lance found a clearance rack of t-shirts and managed to find three in his size. Then he did the same with basketball shorts. In the hunting and fishing section, he found a pair of brown-and-green camo shorts.

At the checkout counter, the man in the chinos rang up Lance's purchases and the total exceeded the amount of cash Lance was carrying. He slid his debit card from his wallet, wondering for the first time just how far his money would stretch. He'd saved up a decent amount from part-time work back home, odd jobs here and there. But he'd never held a full-time position anywhere, and sooner or later, he was going to run out of money. He'd have to find work. Or play the lotto.

His mother would scowl at him for that joke. The lotto was for the unambitious.

The transaction was approved, and Lance asked the man if he'd mind terribly if he used one of the fitting rooms to change. The man gave him a quick glance up and down, as if his question had suddenly provoked concern, but then smiled and nodded and said that was no problem at all. As Lance thanked him and began walking toward the fitting rooms the man called out, "Did you buy that backpack from us?"

Lance turned and smiled. "No, sir. It was a gift from a friend."

The man nodded. "I didn't think I'd seen you in here before. You new in town?"

"Just passing through," Lance said, then wondered just how true of a statement that was. His thoughts of the future were too overwhelming to dwell on. He had to focus on the task at hand.

Lance changed his clothes, pushing his two-day-old t-shirt and cargo shorts into the bottom of his backpack and pulling on one of the new shirts and pair of basketball shorts. He instantly felt better, almost reenergized, and as he was walking back down the center aisle of the store to make his exit, he caught himself whistling along with the tune playing overhead.

Then he saw the pictures and stopped.

To his left, the wall next to the exit door was a collage of photographs of local sports teams and athletes and newspaper clippings of exciting headlines, some framed, some not. The wall was meant to look causal, haphazard, abstract, but Lance knew that somebody in the store had taken great pains to make it only appear this way. This was somebody's baby, a side project that was fueled with passion.

Here was a shot of a basketball player shooting a three, a defender's outstretched arm desperately trying to prevent the shot.

There was a team photo of the Westhaven 2011 women's tennis team. A small group of young girls wearing white skirts and matching red sleeveless tops, their rackets all held sideways across their bodies like they were posing with a trophy.

Below this was a framed front page of the *Westhaven Journal*'s sports section, the headline screaming: WESTHAVEN WINS FIRST EVER STATE TITLE!

And next to this, large and framed and clearly meant to stand out, was a team photograph of the Westhaven football team. They were in celebration in the end zone of the field they'd just played on, organized but excited and jubilant in their victory. There were three rows, the rearmost row standing while the middle row knelt and the front row sat on the ground. Some boys held their helmets high in the air, cheers frozen on their faces. Others had tossed their helmets to the ground, dotting the green of the field with their discarded armor and making it look like a ravaged battlefield. There was a large—insanely large—trophy on the ground between the middle boys in the front row. It towered up and gleamed in the sunlight, a lens flare popping from one side. The boys' faces were sweaty and dirty and tired, but they were clearly living in one of the best moments of their lives.

The frame was a dark polished wood without a speck of dust, and there was a large gold placard in the center of the bottom panel. The engraving read:

WESTHAVEN HIGH SCHOOL FOOTBALL TEAM
2012 VIRGINIA STATE AA CHAMPIONS
FINAL SCORE: 28–7

Below the header in a much smaller script were the names of the players and coaches. Lance scanned the names, recognized Coach McGuire and Chuck Goodman and Martin Brownlee. He didn't see Leah's brother Samuel's name. This would have been Samuel's team, the year he'd disappeared. The lack of even an honorable mention or in memoriam side note was more unsettling than Lance cared to admit.

He looked at the photo, with no way of knowing which boy was which, as the names on the placard were simply alphabetical. Then he moved on to the two smaller framed shots to the right of this large one, each one inching folks closer to the door. They were the team pictures for each of the following two state titles Westhaven had won. Chuck Goodman was not listed on the second picture. And on the third and final photograph, showing last year's team once again celebrating with another large trophy and more large smiles, Martin Brownlee's name was nowhere to be found.

Something else caught Lance's attention, and he went back down the row of photographs to take a second look. The rear row of boys in each picture was bookended by coaches and staff, clearly recognizable by the headsets and ball caps and khaki pants and shirts and playbooks and Gatorade-soaked shirts. Kenny McGuire, Lance knew because of the picture he had seen in the newspaper Leah had shown him, but the other men's faces were anonymous to him.

But it wasn't the coaches who caught Lance's eye. In each picture, starting with Westhaven's first state title, there was another man with the group. He was tall and broad-shouldered and clearly built like a player past his prime. His hair was peppered with gray, but his face appeared younger than the rest of him. In the first picture he was standing by the coaches, a small gap between himself and coach McGuire. He wore a dark blue sweater and crisply pressed jeans with loafers. The second and third picture, he was kneeling on the grass with the middle row, beaming just as big and bright as the players. And in the last picture, the man was again adorned in a sweater and loafers, only he'd decided to casual it up some with a Westhaven ball cap. This time, he was seated on the grass next to the front row, his arm draped around the player to his left.

There was a clear resemblance between the man and the boy, and before Lance's mind fully made the connection, a voice next to him said, "Never seen anything like it in all my years."

Lance, startled, turned and found the man with the chinos and clipboard next to him. "What haven't you seen?" Lance asked.

"That team." The man pointed to the picture of the first title team. "They were about the sorriest group of ball players I've ever had the misfortune to witness. And then"—he snapped his fingers—"state title the very next year, and every year since." He shook his head. "If I was a betting man, I'd have lost big-time. Hell, the whole town would have lost. Don't get me wrong, we'd support those boys and cheer and holler 'til our throats went raw, but we knew they stunk up the place."

Lance nodded and asked the same question he had asked Leah last night. "What changed?"

The man shrugged. "Got to be the coach. McGuire doesn't look like much, but he's whipped those kids into shape. Can't deny it, right?"

Lance didn't answer. He wasn't so sure. Instead, he pointed to the man in the picture, the outlier. "Who's that? He doesn't look like a coach."

Chino man leaned forward for a better look, then his eyes brightened and he smiled like he'd just found twenty bucks in his pocket. "Oh, that's another blessing our poor team received. Glenn Strang has given those kids every advantage he possibly can. Don't know what we'd do without him"—then, in a whisper —"or his money." Chino man laughed, and Lance went along with it. The connection his brain had started before was finalized. The boy Glenn Strang had his arm around in the last picture was his son, Bobby.

"Yeah," Chino man said, "McGuire and Strang—those guys really turned it all around. Thank God they showed up when they did."

Lance thanked the man and left the store, wondering just what else had shown up in town the day Kenny McGuire or Glenn Strang had ridden in.

[14]

LANCE WALKED AWAY FROM DOWNTOWN, INTENT ON dropping his purchases off at his motel room—now that he was clearly staying another day, at the least—and then deciding where he should go. If Leah had done as he'd asked, then hopefully she'd be well on her way to trying to dig up any info she could about whether either of the other two missing boys had had girlfriends at the time they'd disappeared.

Ordinarily, a high school boy having a girlfriend wouldn't be enough to set off the alarm bells in Lance's head. But it was the fact that Samuel had hidden his relationship from Leah that made Lance suspicious. He knew she wasn't the type of person who would exaggerate the closeness she shared with her brother. If she said they were thick as thieves, Lance believed her. Plus, in a town this small, Lance had a hard time understanding just how a member of the football team, an active member of the town social circle, could even manage to keep something as significant as a girlfriend a secret. It seemed fairly impossible for Samuel and his girl to go out to dinner, a movie, a walk in the park, *anything*, without eyeballs noticing and word of mouth traveling.

There was, of course, the possibility that Bobby Strang was not being honest. Leah hadn't mentioned whether Bobby's statement about Samuel needing to go see his girlfriend had been given to her straight from the horse's mouth, or passed on via the police during the investigation. Either way, if Bobby Strang had made the girlfriend thing up, that meant he was either covering for Samuel, or for somebody else. Maybe even himself?

By the time Lance made it back to the motel, he'd all but decided he'd like to have a chat with Bobby Strang, and he hoped he didn't have Leah out chasing a red herring. But there was nothing wrong with leaving no stone unturned. Her brother had been missing for years now. His case wasn't going to be solved instantly, no matter if Lance was helping or not. His gifts helped with things like this, sure. But life wasn't an episode of *Murder, She Wrote*. Jessica Fletcher, he was not.

The Jeep with Garfield as a passenger was gone from the lot, as were all other cars except a dirty early-model Honda Civic with an Obama bumper sticker from his first campaign. There was a long scratch along the passenger-side door, and as he walked past, Lance saw a tattered copy of *The God Delusion* by Richard Dawkins lying on the floorboard and thought the car seemed entirely too Democratic for a town like Westhaven. The car was parked directly outside the door to the office, and Lance figured it must belong to Renee, the woman Leah had watching over things. He contemplated poking his head inside to say hello but thought better of it. Enough folks around Westhaven had already pegged him as a suspicious weirdo. No sense adding to the list. He'd keep his attempts at making friends to a rule of necessity.

He approached his door and saw that somebody—Leah, more than likely—had swept up the broken bits of plastic and glass. He looked up and found that she'd replaced the lightbulb as well.

Who needs Martin the handyman?

Lance slid his key into the lock and opened the door.

He stopped.

His bed had been made, and fresh tracks on the carpet showed that it'd been vacuumed since he'd left. *Leah?* he wondered. *Or was it Renee, or somebody else—a housekeeper? Does a place like this even have housekeepers?*

Even though he'd had zero personal belongings in the room at the time it'd been straightened up, his stomach still did an uneasy twirl at the thought of Leah poking around in here while he was gone. Not that he didn't trust the girl, and not that he possessed anything physical that would unravel his secrets, but it was the age-old tale of guy-meets-girl self-consciousness that even Lance himself was not immune to.

He liked Leah. Even at this disastrous, tragic, and earth-shattering moment of sadness and confusion in his life, human nature and biology and a human's desire to find love and companionship refused to take a backseat.

He pushed the thoughts away. He couldn't ignore what he was feeling, but nothing said he had to accept it.

He wasn't ready. It was too soon.

He didn't even have all the details of exactly what had happened after he had left town, after the night when—

His cell phone buzzed in his pocket, a hard vibration that caused his heart to lurch and snapped him back from his thoughts. He dropped his backpack onto the bed and fumbled with his phone, flipping it open. He'd received a text from Leah: *Working on more, but Chuck Goodman's sister is meeting me for lunch. 1 @ Frank's Pizza. Can you come?*

Lance studied the message, first impressed with how quickly Leah had managed to drum up a potential lead for information, but also concerned that his presence would make Chuck Goodman's sister uncomfortable, especially when dealing with what was already sure to be an uncomfortable subject. But again, he was going to trust his new friend. He convinced himself that Leah would not have invited him if she felt Chuck's sister would not be okay with it.

He began thumbing his worn and faded keys and texted back: *See you there.*

He had no idea where Frank's Pizza was located, but he usually had a way of finding things.

He went to the restroom and relieved himself and washed his hands. There was a freshly wrapped bar of soap at the sink, and clean towels hung from the rack next to the shower. He glanced back at the toilet bowl to make sure he hadn't dribbled or dripped any on the visible surface. He'd probably die if he ever knew Leah had wiped up his dried urine.

Back by the bed, he unzipped his backpack and separated his dirty clothes from his new purchases. He stuffed all the dirty items into one of the Sportsman's bags and then placed his new items in the other bag. He left his toiletries in the CVS bag and walked to set it and the bag of dirties in the bathroom. Back in the bedroom, he checked his phone once more for new messages, found none, and then left.

Outside, the sun was at its peak, and Lance was glad it was fall and not summer. Otherwise he'd bake to a crisp having to walk everywhere. He kicked himself for not buying a cheap pair of sunglasses at CVS. He didn't particularly care for sunglasses, or the way he looked in them, but they sure would help right about now. He squinted his eyes against the brightness and headed across the parking lot, a soft breeze helping to push him along and making the air feel crisper than it looked.

He had about forty-five minutes before he had to find Frank's Pizza and meet Leah and Chuck Goodman's sister, so he figured he had enough time to see Westhaven High School.

He couldn't say exactly why, and he didn't know exactly

what it was he planned on learning during the middle of a school day. With times the way they were, you couldn't hang around near a school for long without somebody calling the police. Whether you were wielding a candy cane or an AK-47, somebody would notice, and the repercussions would be just as swift either way.

Still, he walked.

He headed back toward town, but at an intersection he usually continued straight through, he stopped, closed his eyes for a moment, and then turned left, heading down another rural route that seemed nearly as desolate as the previous. The sidewalk vanished, and he was forced to walk on a grassy shoulder, the blades growing high enough in some spots to reach above his sneakers and tease his shins. Far off to his left he could still see the black plume of smoke rising above an expanding tree line, only now he could begin to make out the top of the smoke stack that spewed it. There was no doubt it was the paper mill.

The Strang family was another oddity in Lance's mind. On the surface, they seemed harmless, maybe even the good guys. Glenn Strang was an ex-player who still loved the game, loved his son, and used his fortunate financial means to help provide for an underfunded athletic program at a small-town high school. Admirable. Bobby Strang, from what Lance had heard from Leah, was probably the placekicker because he didn't have the skill or talent to play other positions. This could have been a point of discontent for Glenn Strang, but the man seemed to be taking it all in stride, being just as enthusiastic about his son and the team's accomplishments as he would if Bobby had been the quarterback. Aside from this, all Lance knew was that Bobby and Samuel had become close friends. And if Samuel was anything like Leah, that meant that Bobby couldn't be too bad a character. Lance still wanted to talk to him.

It was Mrs. Strang that Lance knew nothing about. Leah

had told him that she stayed at home and cooked meals for the boys and probably played team mom more than other actual mothers liked, but she hadn't factored into the story much at this point.

Before Lance could think about her any further, Westhaven High School began to grow out of the weeds ahead on the right like a desert mirage.

The school had a larger campus than Lance had expected, with three one-story buildings separated by covered sidewalks, giving the appearance of an eagle spreading its wings. The architecture was dated—fifties or sixties most likely—with weathered brick walls and peeling white paint on the overhangs covering the sidewalks. In front of the center building, which Lance assumed to be the office, a wide traffic lane looped across the buildings and connected on each end to the main road. There was a single bus parked here, along with several cars that probably belonged to office staff. A larger parking lot flooded out from the side of the right-most building, and it looked like a used-car lot where the dealings were in cash only and *warranty* was a foreign word. There were more pickup trucks and mud-splattered SUVs than Lance could count.

The door to the office building swung open, and a blond-haired woman wearing a simple skirt and light sweater stepped out and held the door wide. A single student walked out of the office with a yellow slip of paper in his hand and headed toward the left building. He was staring down at the sidewalk as he went, downtrodden and slow-moving. *That's a boy who just got in trouble,* Lance thought, then realized that if a bell rang then, the students would come flowing out of the buildings like a school of fish and he didn't want to be standing out here all alone, sticking out and being noticed. Lance's eyes followed the boy until he disappeared inside the other building. He looked back to the office just in time to see the door swing shut.

But he needed to see more. He was looking for something else.

Lance walked a little further, taking a few steps up the cracked asphalt leading toward the school's lot. There was a flagpole in a small section of grass outside the bus loop, the Stars and Stripes flying proudly alongside the deep blue of the Virginia state flag and the black and white of the DARE program's own banner. Lance's own high school's flagpole had looked exactly like this, and he again felt that twinge of longing for home.

Keeping in the grass, he continued up the entrance just enough to try and get a look behind the buildings. Halfway to the parking lot, he was able to see a fourth building behind the middle one, a large domed roof rising up over what was clearly the school's gymnasium. He thought back to his four years on the basketball team and tried to remember if he'd ever played against the Westhaven team. It would have had to have been in the state tournament, which he had only been privileged to go to his junior and senior year—no titles, unfortunately. He didn't think they'd ever played each other.

He wanted to see the football field. It was probably behind the gym, Westhaven's pride and joy stuck in the middle of what otherwise looked like a cornfield. But Lance didn't dare venture further. He was probably trespassing as it were, and he didn't want to push his luck.

He looked back toward the flagpole and studied the small brick marquee beside it. Beneath the WESTHAVEN HIGH SCHOOL insignia, a white message board with black plastic letters advertised upcoming school events. Lance read through the list, stopped, pulled out his phone to verify the date, and then smiled. He'd picked a good day to show up in Westhaven.

The football team had their next game that night. It was a home game, and he wished he'd thought to ask Leah about when the next game was sooner. It would have saved him a trip out here.

Thinking of Leah, he remembered lunch, and as he turned to head back to the road and start back into town, he heard the crunching of loose bits of asphalt and gravel under tires as a car slowly pulled into the drive behind him.

Without even looking, Lance immediately knew he would see a police cruiser when he turned around. Cops, for some reason, were easy to sense. The good ones ... and the bad ones. The problem was it was difficult to tell at first.

You took too long, Lance. He scolded himself. *This was a bad idea.*

Or ... or something knew you were here.

The sound from the tires stopped, and Lance heard the gentle hum of a car window being lowered. "Help you?" a voice dripping with Southern accent asked.

Lance, slowly, turned around and offered his best smile to the man behind the wheel of the sheriff's department car. "Afternoon, Officer." He waved. "No, sir. Just on my way into town to have lunch with a friend."

And then the thing Lance had hoped would not happen, did happen. The man behind the wheel rolled up the window, unfastened his seat belt, opened the door, and stepped out.

15

LANCE HAD SEEN ENOUGH NATIONAL NEWS TELEVISION footage ("*Such a sad place our world is,*" his mother often said as they watched. "*So much hate. So little love*") and he knew that being a stranger in town was recipe enough for a potential disaster, so he stayed perfectly still and didn't say a word as the sheriff's deputy stepped out of the car and stood with his hands on his hips, one palm resting on the butt of his holstered pistol.

It had been unwise for Lance to come here, but it was too late for regrets. He knew from Samuel Senior that he'd already been on the police radar since yesterday, and now he was only fueling the fire of the town's suspicions of him. He'd been caught loitering around a freaking school, of all places.

Lance stood. Waited. The deputy took another step closer and his eyes met Lance's, and all at once Lance let himself relax a little. The man had kind eyes, not the eyes of a power-abusing ruffian dressed as an officer of the law. He took another step forward and—Lance could hardly believe this—stuck out his hand. "Deputy Miller," the man said, and boy was that accent heavy. "What brings you to Westhaven, young man?"

Deputy Miller was almost as tall as Lance, but even thinner, an Ichabod Crane physique with spaghetti limbs and an Adam's apple that looked as if the man had swallowed an arrowhead. His uniform was loose-fitting, and he'd adjusted his hat twice since stepping out of the car. Lance shook the man's hand and

(*Single-story house in the nice section of town, green lawn, likes to garden, wife named Jen with red hair, pregnant with baby number two, first son's name is Ben, they joke because it rhymes with Jen, there go Ben and Jen, Jen says he works too much, but he says they need the money and Jen says they aren't that bad off, church every Sunday, third pew, plays on the softball team and always brings his famous triple-chocolate brownies to the potlucks*)

had to stifle his surprise as Deputy Miller's life flooded through his veins and into Lance's mind. He pulled his grip away fast, unintentionally rude. Deputy Miller's eyes scrunched in confusion.

I hate it when that happens. So weird.

Invasive was the word he used when he really thought about these occurrences, which took place at random in his life. He'd tried to make sense of whose touch prompted such visions, but the demographics were so varied and inconsistent it was hopeless to try.

Lance offered another big smile, hoping they could move on from the awkward handshake. "Nice to meet you, Deputy."

"Likewise, son." Deputy Miller looked right, down the road and toward town. "Meeting a friend for lunch, huh?" The question wasn't exactly accusatory, but Lance knew the man was trying to make sense of Lance's tale, trying to assess any potential threats to himself or his town he'd sworn to protect.

"Yes, sir," Lance said, speaking as casually and confidently as he could. "I'm on my way a little further north to visit some family, but I got off the bus here yesterday to say hi to a friend of mine I haven't seen in a couple years. Catch up a little before I

headed on." Then Lance relied on good ol' small-town camaraderie. "You probably know her, actually. Leah, over at Bob's
Place?"

Deputy Miller's face lit up, and Lance knew he was off the
hook. "Sam's little girl? Sure, I know her. Heck, I've known her
since she was this big!" He held his hand out, just below waist-
high. "Good girl, she is. Good girl."

Lance knew he had to try, for Leah, and for the town. He'd
take any info he could get. "Yeah," he agreed. "She is. Her
brother was a good guy, too. Always makes me sad, what
happened to him."

Deputy Miller's smile didn't falter, but his energy took a hit.
He stood still for a moment, as if Lance's most recent words
were taking longer to process than the rest. He looked directly at
Lance, but it was like he momentarily lost focus, thinking back
to something long ago.

But then he was back, snapping his fingers and saying, "Is
that who you're going to meet for lunch? Little Leah?"

Lance nodded. "Yes, sir." He was becoming increasingly
amazed at how folks in Westhaven said absolutely zero about
the missing boys. Not even the vaguest of acknowledgments.

Deputy Miller turned and motioned for Lance to follow,
and he opened one of the back doors to the cruiser. "Hop on in,
I'll give you a lift. I'm headed into town myself."

Lance didn't move at first, looking into the rear of the open
cruiser and calculating his options.

"I know, it's a little weird," Deputy Miller said with an
almost-embarrassed smile. "But I can't let you ride up front." He
shrugged. "Against the rules."

Lance took another glance toward Westhaven High School,
read the marquee again to verify there was a football game
tonight, and then sighed. What choice did he have? He could
refuse the officer's ride, but that might make him seem more

suspicious. It might cause more questions to be asked. He replayed the flashes of Deputy Miller's life in his mind, like the memory of a movie he'd seen long ago and could only remember the good parts. *He's a decent guy. He believes me. And Leah's smart. She'll quickly catch on and verify everything I've said if asked.*

Lance smiled and started toward the cruiser. "Hey, yeah, that would be great! Thanks so much. I really appreciate it. That's the problem with taking the bus into town. It's hard to get around afterward."

Lance folded himself into the rear seat of the cruiser, sliding his backpack off his shoulders and setting it in the seat next to him. "Yeah," Deputy Miller said, "we had a couple folks try to be Uber drivers for a while, but Uber's a little too sophisticated for a town like us."

Lance looked down to his shorts pocket, where his flip phone lived. "Yeah," he agreed. "I could see that."

Then Deputy Miller said, "Everything in?" Lance said it was, and the back door to the cruiser was closed and Lance was locked in.

The bell rang, an old-fashioned physical bell from the sound of it, not the new digital tones that got played over speakers at more modern and up-to-date schools, and like racehorses out the gate, a sea of students began to pour from every exterior door of Westhaven High School and scatter in every direction. Lance watched them through the window of the cruiser. Even at this distance he could see them smiling and laughing and joking. He could see the popular girls and the jocks and the FFA leaders and the chess club members. He saw them all and, as he'd done so many times in his life, he wondered what it must feel like to be normal. To be able to be a student and an athlete and only those things, instead of living with his gift, living with one foot firmly planted in a dimension of the world that nobody else could see.

The front door of the cruiser opened and the noise from the kids intensified as Deputy Miller folded his own long and lanky frame into the driver's seat and closed the door. He took off his hat and tossed it onto the passenger seat, and through the partition, Lance could see the man was losing his hair on top, a beanie of baldness starting at the center of his skull and working its way outward.

"Let me guess," Deputy Miller said, "You're going to... hmm ... Frank's Pizza?"

Lance smiles. "You got it. How'd you know?"

Deputy Miller shrugged. "Not a lot of choices around here, and Frank's is always popular with the younger crowd. Figured it was there or the diner."

Lance nodded. "I've been there. I liked it. Margie seems nice. Seems like she runs a tight ship." And then Lance wondered why he felt compelled to offer up this information to Deputy Miller, why he was telling more of his story than necessary. Not that there was anything wrong with him visiting Annabelle's Apron, but when you were sitting in the back of a cop car, you couldn't help but feel like you were under interrogation, no matter how casual the conversation.

Deputy Miller sat still in the driver's seat and watched as the last of the students disappeared back inside the school's buildings. Two boys wearing black t-shirts and baggy jeans were left alone outside the building closest to the parking lot, huddled around a large orange trash can. One boy produced something small and white and rectangular from his pocket, shook it, and as the other boy reached out, Lance realized it was a pack of cigarettes. Deputy Miller reached forward and flipped a switch on and off, creating a quick *bleep-bloop!* from the car, and the boys' eyes darted up, saw the cruiser. And then they dashed off around the rear of the building.

Deputy Miller shook his head and sighed. "There's always those kind."

Lance knew what he meant. Those kind were everywhere. Always.

Deputy Miller put the car into drive and made a three-point turn, then drove along the front of the school, following the same path the buses would drive in a few hours' time. At the stop sign, he waited for a pickup truck to pass by, and then a Jeep, and then a small sedan.

Then there was no more traffic, nothing coming or going in either of the two lanes. The car's engine idled and that was the only sound Lance could hear. They do not move. The gearshift was still in drive and Deputy Miller's hands were still on the wheel and the road was clear and they did not move an inch. Lance let a full minute pass, his pulse beginning to drum in his ears, and he was about to ask Deputy Miller if everything was all right when the deputy's arm reached up and flicked the turn signal up, signaling a right turn.

Lance felt his stomach tighten, and the drumming in his head grew louder.

The town, and Frank's Pizza, and Leah, these things were to the left, back the way Lance had walked.

The car began to move, slowly at first, and then with a sudden burst of speed, as if Deputy Miller had accidentally stomped on the gas instead of the brake. The car fishtailed out of the school's driveway and the tires squealed on the rough black-top. Lance's backpack slid across the rear of the cruiser and Lance followed it, both bag and boy slamming into the door of the car. Deputy Miller's hands seemed clumsy on the wheel as Lance watched the man overcorrect, whipping the wheel back in an unpracticed motion and rocking the car back and forth as it tried to straighten out. Lance reached up and braced his palms against the roof of the car to gain some balance, and as he sat up and the cruiser finally straightened out, he looked into the rearview mirror and instantly knew he had made a mistake.

Deputy Miller's eyes were nothing but solid whites, rolled up into his head like a man convulsing. His mouth hung open, slack, his tongue poking out and a bit of drool dripping down to the breast of his uniform. Lance sat up straighter and saw the speedometer needle pass seventy, and it felt like a hundred from the backseat. The car was straddling the center line, and all it was going to take was one car coming the other direction, cresting a hill or turning from a side road into their path, and they'd be dead. There was no question about it.

And Lance took another look at Deputy Miller's face that wasn't his face and knew that this had been the plan all along. He'd been found, and he'd been tricked. It was no accident that when he'd shaken the deputy's hand, he'd gotten a glimpse into the man's life. It had shown the life of a simple and good family man in order to disarm him, to have his guard lowered. Whatever force was here in Westhaven knew more about Lance than he'd imagined. It knew the specifics of his gifts, it seemed, and now it was exploiting them. He'd been baited and lured into the back of the cruiser, into a rolling cage from which he could not escape and in which he would now likely die.

He'd failed.

He'd failed the town, and he'd failed those boys and—worst of all—he'd failed Leah. She'd put so much faith in him, and he'd seen the hope he'd inadvertently inspired in her.

And now he was going to die and nobody would ever see him again. Just like Samuel.

His anger and his frustration and his fear overcame him. He pounded on the partition and began to shout. "Hey! You're never going to win, you know that, right? It won't go on forever!

If I don't stop you, there will be somebody else! I'm not the only one!" And then as he fell back into the seat, he thought, *I can't be the only one. Just can't be.*

Deputy Miller's head snapped to the right, so hard and so fast Lance heard something crack. The whites of his eyes were still all that was visible, and his throat muscles shifted and his tongue slid back and forth and his lips twitched as a series of deep gurgles and grunts spilled from his mouth. They were audible, but indecipherable, like the sounds of an animal or an invalid.

Lance was not afraid, only angered even more that this *thing* inside Deputy Miller thought Lance could understand it. Lance slapped his hand against the partition, and Deputy Miller snarled and bared his teeth and barked in response, spittle flying against the Plexiglas. Lance jumped back, and that was when he saw the semi in the distance.

The road was flat, and the truck was still a good distance off —a half mile maybe—but at the speed they were traveling, that would be eaten up in no time. Lance heard the air horn screaming through the air, imagined the driver wondering what in the world this policeman was doing. The driver would be braking, doing his best to avoid an accident, but unfortunately for Lance, the truck could be completely stopped and it would likely make no difference. If they hit it going this fast, the cruiser would crumple like a soda can and Lance would quickly be a lot thinner.

He smacked the partition again, Deputy Miller's white eyes still staring vacantly at him. Lance's mind raced, spun and spun and—*This is really it. I'm going to die. Less than forty-eight hours after my mother and I'm going—*

BEN AND JEN. BEN AND JEN.

The thought smacked him so hard he could barely register its meaning. Then he saw the face of the innocent man caught in a terrible darkness he deserved no part of, and Lance screamed, "Ben and Jen, Ben and Jen, Ben and Jen! You love them so much and they love you and you have a new baby on the way and you are so happy and so lucky and blessed and you don't want to leave them! If you can hear me, Miller, fight! Fight! Ben and Jen, Ben and Jen!"

The truck ahead was stopped, but the cruiser was not.

Lance pounded the partition, his hands stinging with each blow. "Ben and Jen, Ben and Jen, Ben and Jen!"

The eyeballs flickered, a small sign of life. Then the hands on the wheel shifted—marginally, but they shifted!

Lance's heart was about to burst from his chest, the truck getting impossibly closer with each millisecond. He sucked in a deep breath and yelled, "*BenAndJenBenAndJenBenAndJenBen-AndJenBen!*"

Deputy Miller's body shook, like he'd gotten the most violent of chills. His eyes rolled forward, bloodshot now and watering. He saw the road, saw the truck. He screamed. Lance screamed. The brakes were slammed, the wheel was jerked. The police cruiser missed the truck...

But it flipped over and rolled off the road and rolled through a field and came to rest upside down fifty yards away. Lance heard crashing metal and cracking glass and the sound of Deputy Miller's screams. And then he heard nothing.

16

LANCE SLOWLY OPENED HIS EYES, SAW A CEILING FAN *wobbling back and forth as it spun lazily above his head. The ceiling was cracked in a few places, but clean. He tilted his head and saw the rest of the room: warped wooden floor, antique dresser and full-length mirror, a nightstand with a glass of water and a Monday-through-Friday pill container beside a pair of thick reading glasses. Warm light spilling from a small lamp. He lay on his back atop a small bed, a hand-sewn blanket covering him up to his waist. The room smelled of apples and cinnamon, warm cider ... or maybe pie.*

"You need to be more careful."

His head darted left and found Annabelle Winters gently rocking back and forth in a rocker in the corner. There was an open book on her lap and Lance saw it was the Bible.

"You have the gifts, and you have the strength, but that's nothing if you're careless."

"Where am I?" he tried to ask, but his voice didn't work. His vocal cords pinched.

"You were lucky this time. Miller was always one of the good

ones. *If it'd chosen someone else—well..."* She trailed off, and Lance knew exactly what she meant.

He tried to sit up further and

There was an explosion of light and pain. His head throbbed and there was something warm trickling down the right side of his face. His right arm tingled, and when he squeezed his hand into a fist, he cried out. Something in his arm was on fire, burning beneath the skin with every twitch of his fingers.

He opened his eyes and the small room was gone, replaced by the sideways view of the rear interior of Deputy Miller's cruiser.

Lance lay on his side, his head pressed against what felt like a bed of needles. He sat up, slowly, and when the cruiser began to spin in his mind he vomited onto the floor. He closed his eyes and took deep breaths, willing his racing heart to steady a bit. He looked down to where his head had been and saw the bits of broken glass, touched the side of his face and felt a few loose shards stuck to his cheek. He pulled one out with a sting and dropped it, watching it fall into his pile of puke. He took another deep breath, closed his eyes again and mentally examined his body. Aside from the head injury and whatever was wrong with his arm, he appeared to be okay. If Deputy Miller hadn't—

Deputy Miller.

Lance looked through the partition and saw the lifeless body. Miller's torso had been nearly impaled by the steering column, his body slumped and askew and his neck hanging at an angle that told Lance all he needed to know.

Ben and Jen, he thought, and he was filled with a great sorrow in knowing the happy family would never be the same. They had suffered a tragic loss, and they didn't even know it yet.

And it's my fault. It's all my fault.

(You need to be more careful.)

He should have never gone to the school alone, a stranger walking down the road, looking like trouble. He knew better. He could have waited, asked Leah to drive him and show him what he needed to see. But he'd been careless. And now a man was dead.

He heard a voice, close but faint. He looked up and turned around, and through the rear glass he saw a man wearing faded jeans and a solid red t-shirt talking animatedly into his cell phone. In the distance, the semi was still parked in the middle of the road, its door hanging wide open.

The truck driver. He's calling for help. I've got to go.

He wasn't sure why the last part of that thought occurred, but it did. The man who'd been driving the truck was surely on the phone with 911 or whichever emergency services line he'd called, and the people who arrived would definitely be able to treat his wounds and make sure he was okay and handle the situation with professional training and skill sets.

But eventually, the questions would start. Questions Lance would likely not be able to answer truthfully.

And to make matters worse, if whatever plagued this town could possess one cop (*one of the good ones*), it could surely possess somebody else. Lance didn't have time to take chances right now. He'd gambled once today, thinking he'd made the right choice, and it had nearly killed him.

He glanced at the shattered glass next to him, then followed the trail of shards to the window. The pane of glass was half-missing, a diagonal section with jagged edges all that remained. Lance raised one his large sneakers up, his head pounding with the motion as he leaned back and his right wrist screaming, and then carefully kicked at the remaining glass. It was splintered and full of spiderweb cracks already, and it only took three soft kicks from Lance's size fifteen foot to finish the job. The rest of the window shattered outward and fell to the ground.

Lance took another glance toward the truck driver, heard the words, "I think they're both dead, you've got to come quick!"

He had to move quickly. He winced as he sat back up and pulled himself forward. He gripped the edges of door where the window had been, a few splintery remains digging into his fingers, and then he used his legs to push off and threw himself over the edge and forward, falling to the grass. He felt the urge to vomit again but closed his eyes and counted to ten and willed himself to keep it down. When he opened his eyes, the truck driver was staring directly at him, phone pressed to his ear, mouth hanging open like a man who'd just seen a magic trick.

Lance stood, slowly, and reached inside the busted window. He pulled his backpack from the wreckage, slung it over his shoulder. Just as the man came out of his startled state and started to say, "Hey! One of them is alive!" Lance turned and ran as fast as he could toward the trees, which were only a hundred yards away but in his current state felt more like a mile.

There was shouting behind him, screams to stop and wait and that help was on the way. When Lance didn't stop, the yelling became angrier, profanity interlaced with accusations of Lance being crazy and stupid and obviously up to no good.

Lance did not stop to turn and look. His head felt ready to burst and his arm hurt with every movement, but Lance was still in decent shape and his lungs didn't complain much. He reached the tree line and entered the woods and did not stop for another fifty yards. Only then did he bring himself to slow down and turn to see if the truck driver was following him.

He saw nobody.

He held his breath to listen and heard nothing but the rustling of the branches and leaves around him. The truck driver was not coming.

He had to move. He had to get away.

But he had no idea where he was.

Leah.

He slapped at his shorts pocket with his right hand and groaned at the pain. His cell phone was still there. He reached in and pulled it out and scrolled through his contacts. Found Leah's name and pressed SEND.

She answered almost immediately, and to her credit, she didn't interrupt or ask too many questions as he quickly explained he'd been in an accident and needed help. He told her he'd been at the high school, told her what direction they'd been heading, and told her he was currently a woodland creature.

She told him to keep walking, that he'd come out on the other side right along Route 19. She'd be waiting.

Lance ended the call, double-checked to make sure the truck driver wasn't following, and then started to walk.

17

LANCE HIKED HIS WAY THROUGH THE WOODS, AND eventually he heard the distant sounds of sirens, emergency crews coming to handle the wreck he'd just escaped. He wondered if they'd search the woods for him and quickened his pace. He covered what he guessed to be roughly half a mile before the tree line reappeared and he stepped out into the sunlight. Just as Leah had said, maybe twenty-five yards ahead, the faded blacktop of Route 19 stretched to his left and right, seemingly heading nowhere in both directions. He looked around at the empty fields and tried to get his bearings. He figured the motel was to his left, though he couldn't be sure how far. To his right, if he kept walking twenty miles, he guessed he'd hit the town with the Holiday Inn and other bigger-town amenities Leah had alluded to.

He was ashamed that for the briefest of moments, just a fleeting flash of an idea that popped into view and then vanished before it could be fully absorbed and comprehended, he wanted to walk right. Wanted to trudge the twenty miles on foot and maybe hope for a kind person to stop and offer him a ride and leave Westhaven and all its evil behind.

He'd left his home—been forced to leave was more accurate —to move on from his painful past and avoid the unpleasant drama that was sure to follow. It had taken every ounce of will he'd had to step onto that bus and leave behind the only world he had known. He'd picked the destination seemingly at random, the first ride out of town, never imagining that where he ended up would be just as problematic as where he'd left. In the brief time he'd spent in Westhaven, he'd been looped into a terrible secret, a secret he understood better than anyone else in town, and had now been attacked twice. This last time, it had nearly been fatal. How many more chances would he get? Despite his insatiable longing to see his mother's face again, he was fully aware that he was not ready to join her in whatever form of afterlife perhaps existed.

Lance wanted to live.

Between the choice of uncertainty and death, he chose uncertainty.

And was it really a coincidence he'd ended up in Westhaven? Was it really just happenstance he'd decided to stay at Bob's Place and had met Leah and learned of this town's horrible history? He almost rolled his eyes at his mother's words.

The universe is too smart, too calculated for us to accept the concept of a coincidence, Lance. Do you, a person with your gifts, honestly believe things could be so random?

They'd had a similar conversation on more than one occasion, especially as Lance had gotten older, but this particular speech had stuck with him for years, like a favorite scene from a movie. She'd said it after they'd watched an episode of *The X-Files* on Netflix one night. Something from the show's plot had provoked it, and Lance remembered that the only answer he'd offered was a half-hearted *I don't know*. He hadn't been in the mood for philosophical discussions that evening. He'd loved his mother more than anything on earth, but at times she could be exhausting.

And now, another of her tidbits of wisdom floated down to him, and he knew there was no way he was going to head right and find that Holiday Inn.

I know you didn't ask for this, Lance, but you have it. And whatever higher power decided you were meant for this, you are indebted. You have an obligation. Don't you see, Lance? You are a bright spot in a dark world. You are meant to help people. And that's not something you can turn your back on.

The sound of a car engine caused Lance to stiffen, and he briefly considered turning and diving back into the trees. But it was too late for that. The car was only fifty yards away and had definitely spotted him. He stayed in place and tried to look innocent—as innocent as one could look with a blood-streaked face—and watched as a black Toyota 4Runner slowed down and pulled off the road, parking directly in front of him.

The passenger window rolled down and Leah's face brightened his mood. "You look like crap," she said. "Get in the back."

Lance didn't comment or question. He got in.

The 4Runner was a newer model and its owner had kept it clean. As Lance squeezed into the rear seat, having to twist his feet sideways to fit behind the front passenger seat, he noticed the floorboards looked freshly vacuumed and the air smelled of pine and Armor All. The seats were black leather and the trim was tan. This was a nice car. He looked at the driver and saw a tall, heavyset woman wearing black yoga pants and a long-sleeved Westhaven High School t-shirt. Her black hair was short and spiked with gel, her mascara was heavy and her eyeliner was thick. She looked as if she could be about to step onstage with a punk rock group and smash a few guitars.

As Lance took in the woman's features in the rearview mirror, he suddenly realized she'd been staring right back at him. This silent staring contest had lasted nearly thirty seconds before Lance realized nobody had spoken since he'd gotten into the car. Embarrassed for being caught gawking, he said the first thing that came to mind.

"I'm sorry if I get blood on your seats."

The woman looked at him for another second or two, then turned to Leah, eyebrows raised.

Leah giggled. "I told you. He's not like anyone you've ever met." Then, quickly turning to Lance, "But ... you know ... in a good way!"

Lance's head felt woozy and he was still breathing hard from the run through the woods. His heart was beginning to settle, though, and it felt more reassuring than he'd expected to be back with a friend.

"Don't worry about the seats, honey," Miss Mascara said. "But I am worried about the blood. Let's get you somewhere we can take a closer look." Her voice was throaty and sultry. Based on her appearance, Lance would have guessed her to be close to Leah's age, probably a little older. But based on her voice? She could be forty-five and a chain smoker.

None of this mattered now. Lance felt the urge to vomit coming back, and he groaned a bit and started to lay down across the seats. "Need to go," he said, barely a whisper. "They might try ... and find me."

"Who?" Leah asked.

But Lance's eyes were closing as he felt the car begin to move.

Who? That was the question of the hour.

"The motel," Leah said. "Let's get him there and you can do your thing. Then we can talk."

Lance felt the car accelerate and then the woman craned her neck back to him and said, "Try and stay awake, honey. You might have a concussion."

Thankfully, the ride was short and Lance managed to let the girls help him out of the car and into his motel room. He sat on the bed and Leah ran to get him a bottle of water from the lobby, and the woman in yoga pants came in a minute later holding a large red first-aid kit.

"Lance, this is Chuck Goodman's sister, Susan," Leah said. "She's a paramedic. Lucky for us, right?"

(*Do you, a person with your gifts, honestly believe things could be so random?*)

Lance, despite the headache and the dull fire in his arm, could only offer a small laugh at this revelation.

Miss Mascara—Susan—gave Leah another questioning look. "I think he might be delirious."

Lance laughed again, harder this time, and then held up his hands. "No, no, it's just ..." *I miss my mother.* "You reminded me of a joke somebody told me one time. I'm fine. Mentally, anyway."

Susan set the first-aid kit on the bed next to him—it was huge, the real deal, not some tiny thing you'd buy at Walmart for your family fishing trip—and unzipped it, flipping it open and donning a pair of surgical gloves.

"Okay," she said. "Let's take a look."

Soon after Susan started her work, the sound of a police siren came fast and then faded as it traveled past on Route 19.

18

Susan Goodman asked Lance to lie back on the bed and he did so, his eyes focused on her makeup-heavy face as she asked him questions and probed at his head and body. She popped a few pills into his mouth and he swallowed them down with a gulp from the bottle of water, not concerned about what he was ingesting. He trusted this woman. He could feel her warmth the same way he could feel Leah's.

A short time later, and after nearly falling asleep twice in the process, Lance listened as Susan told him he had a small laceration on his scalp, but nothing a little glue and a small bandage couldn't fix. His wrist, however, was definitely sprained, and maybe had a small fracture.

"I'm leaning toward it being sprained," Susan said as she slowly helped him sit up, "because I think the pain would be a lot worse if it was broken." She poked and prodded at his wrist a little more, and only when she attempted to bend it down did Lance grimace in pain. "See?" she said. "I can wrap it now to stabilize it, but a proper brace would probably do you well."

Leah had brought a wet washcloth, and Susan cleaned Lance's face of the dried blood. Then she wrapped his wrist thick with gauze and clipped it tight. She stood back. "How do you feel?"

Lance stood, slowly, and was happy that the room didn't spin or wobble in the process. He took stock of himself, searching his nervous system for anything in disarray. Aside from a dull ache from his head wound and the pressure in his wrist, he felt fine.

"I think I'm okay," he said. Then, without thinking, he took a step forward and hugged Susan, the top of her head coming in just below his chin. "Thank you. This was very kind of you."

Susan laughed and stepped out of the embrace. "That might just be the drugs I gave you talking."

Leah laughed.

Lance shrugged. Drugs or no drugs, he was grateful for Susan's help. Her appearance was definitely out of the ordinary for a young Southern woman, but there was no denying her kindness and her skill.

"So," Susan said, "Leah here tells me you think you can tell us what happened to our brothers. I asked her what you could do that the police couldn't, but she wouldn't really tell me."

Lance looked at Leah. She gave him a *What was I supposed to say?* look.

"But," Susan continued, "frankly, I don't care what you know or do, or … whatever. All I care about now is answers."

The room stayed silent.

"So is it true?" Susan asked, leaning against the wall and crossing her arms beneath her broad chest.

"What?" Lance asked.

"Can you help us?"

Lance chose the honest answer. "I can try."

Susan, whose face had been hard and unreadable most of the time Lance had known her, offered a grin and nodded her head. "At this point, that's all I want. Somebody to keep trying."

Lance got the feeling that suddenly the woman's hard exterior was softening, and the resurfacing of her brother's disappearance was weighing heavily on her.

"It's been so long," Susan said, and now Lance was certain her eyes were forming tears. "But I've never given up hope."

Lance had been down similar roads before and hoped his face did not betray his knowledge that he was almost certain all these boys were dead—Chuck Goodman included. His mission was to find out why, and to save future victims. The answers would give families closure, but it would not bring their brothers and sons back. God, how Lance wished he could change the past.

Susan took a deep breath and composed herself, wiping under her eyes with her index fingers and offering a small chuckle. "Sorry," she said. "I'm not usually one to blubber all over the place."

Lance asked Leah, "Should we talk here, or go somewhere else?"

"Wait," she said. "You haven't told us what happened to you yet. How'd you end up in a police car, and how did it wreck?"

Lance shook his head. "No time right now, but trust me when I tell you it's bad news, and people—the police, for starters —are probably looking for me. So is it safe to stay here, or not?"

Leah considered this. "Let's go to my room behind the office. That way if somebody does show up looking for you, I can show them your room and they can see you're not here. Maybe they'll think you ran off, skipped town, whatever."

Lance nodded. "Fine." He grabbed his backpack and followed the two girls out the door, hoping there wouldn't be a Westhaven police cruiser sitting in the parking lot, waiting like a snake ready to strike.

The sky had grown cloudy, and the air had cooled. A strong breeze rattled through the motel's overhang, and Lance shivered at the memory of the wind that had knocked him back last night. But the parking lot was empty except for Susan's 4Runner and the Honda Civic he had assumed was Renee's. As they walked the short distance to the office, Lance glanced to his left and saw the paper mill's smoke curling up to meet the incoming gray clouds.

Inside the office, a middle-aged woman with long black hair graying at the roots was behind the counter. She looked up from a paperback she'd been reading and, upon seeing Leah, straightened up. "Hey, Leah, I didn't think you'd be back till later." The woman's face reddened softly, as if she'd been caught breaking the rules. She added, "I finished all the items on your list. Didn't take long." She laughed nervously. "Been a slow morning."

The woman's eyes were tired, and Lance wondered when the last time she'd gotten a full night's sleep had been. The dark circles said it had been a while. Her fingernails were painted red, but it was a sloppy job, and the black zip-up hoodie she was wearing had a few obvious stains on the arms and chest. She looked like a woman hanging on for dear life.

Leah smiled, and instantly the woman's face relaxed. Lance, special as he was, knew it didn't take his gifts to be affected by the warmth Leah exuded. "Thanks, Renee. I appreciate it. But, hey, why don't you go ahead and go home for the day? I can handle it from here. I've got some things to work on."

Renee's face fell, and it looked as though she was searching for something to say. Leah beat her to the punch. "Don't worry. I'll pay you for the whole shift. My treat—for all the hard work you do around here."

Renee smiled, and though her teeth were coffee-stained and an upper molar was missing, there was no denying the appreciation it carried.

"Go on, get out of here. Go spend some time with your kids. Get some rest." Leah nodded toward the door, and Renee thanked her again and again and then was gone without so much as a simple introduction to Lance and Susan.

When the office door closed behind Renee and the Civic's engine rustled to life, Leah said, "Daddy would kill me if he knew I'd just let her do that."

"It was nice of you," Lance said.

Leah nodded. "I feel so bad for her. Sweet woman, but she's made some bad choices. Great worker, though. Can always count on her. Amazing, when you consider she's got three jobs. I wish I could pay her more."

And that was the end of that. Leah took a look around the office, tidied some things up behind the check-in counter, and then headed to her bedroom. Lance and Susan followed.

The small television was on, but the screen held nothing but static. The volume was turned down completely. "Ugh, I hate it when this happens," Leah said, walking over to the set. "Thing turns on by itself sometimes and always just hits an empty channel like this." She reached to hit the power button.

"Wait," Lance said, his voice dry, his pulse quickening.

Leah froze, her hand an inch from the power button.

Lance stared into the black-and-white static of the television screen and watched as the gray outline of a figure revealed itself, popping in and out of focus in a strobe-like fashion. Just a gray mass at first, and then edges shifted and aligned and became more defined, falling into their correct place.

It was the dead boy from the bathroom mirror, staring back at Lance with those intense black eyes. Only now ... now, Lance would swear the face looked... sad. Pleading, almost. Lance wanted to reach out and touch the screen, wanted to talk to this ghost in the machine. But just as the thought hit him, the figure vanished, replaced by more blurred static.

"Okay," Lance said. "You can turn it off now."

Leah turned the television off and stared at Lance. Susan shifted her weight from one foot to the other, unsure what to do.

Lance thought about the boy's face, about the new sense of sorrow he seemed to pick up on. Then it hit him. He looked to Leah. "Do you have a picture of Samuel?"

[19]

LANCE HAD ASKED LEAH IF SHE HAD A PICTURE OF HER brother before he'd fully realized what he'd done. He was now desperate to see what Samuel looked like, but he knew that seeing the picture and then possibly being forced to explain his request in front of Susan Goodman was not something he should do right now. With Leah, in private, maybe. But not with Susan. Nice as she was, and regardless of how trustworthy Lance assessed her to be, there was no way he was going to share his biggest secret with two people in one day. It was too risky. Plus, he and Leah had bonded, formed more than just a hey-can-you-do-me-a-favor relationship. Lance was certain of this, and he figured Leah could feel it as well.

"Yeah, of course I do," Leah said, taking two steps toward her dresser.

Lance spoke quickly, trying not to sound panicked. "Okay, cool. Show me later, okay? I want to talk to Susan."

Leah stopped and met his eyes and—boom—just like that, she got it. "Yeah, you're right. Susan's already done more than she thought she'd do today. Right?" Leah gave the woman a playful swat on the arm and sat down on her bed, motioning for Susan to join her.

Susan's eyes shifted between Lance and Leah, clearly understanding that there was something more going on than she realized, but either she didn't want to understand or she just respected whatever the two of them were up to. *God bless her,* Lance thought.

Susan laughed, though it sounded forced. She sat on the bed, her weight sinking down into the old mattress. "No biggie. I have to work the game tonight anyway."

There was silence then. Outside the wind picked up again, and the building shook and rattled with a particularly strong gust. Lance's mind again floated to his attack the night before, and that jump-started his train of thought.

Lance's size had always intimidated people. Whether on the basketball court, or just in everyday life, when you were six-six, people noticed, and with this size came an unwarranted air of power and authority. Lance didn't really understand it, but he accepted it. He'd be lying if he said he hadn't used this to his advantage on an occasion or five. But this wasn't one of those times when he wanted to intimidate. Susan Goodman was a good woman who, like Leah, had suffered a great loss, and she might have some information that could help Lance keep others from having to experience the same thing. He needed Susan relaxed. He needed her to open up to him.

Lance closed the door to the bathroom and then sat down on the floor and leaned against the door, his long legs stretched out in front of him like he was just hanging out with some buds, about to shoot the breeze for a while.

Susan Goodman stared at his basketball shoes.

"Size fifteen," Lance said, grinning. "And, yes, they're real."

Susan looked up, looked back to Lance's shoes, and then up again. Then she busted out with a laugh so loud and infectious the three of them were in near-tears in a matter of seconds. When the laughter died down, Susan wiped the tears from her face and all at once grew very solemn. She took a deep breath and said, "Chuckie wore a size fourteen. I always joked he could be a clown if football didn't work out."

Lance gave her a minute to relish her own memory of her brother, then he softly asked, "Tell me about him. What was your brother like?"

Susan became a burst pipe, spewing anything and everything about the late (presumed) Chuck Goodman.

Chuck and Susan didn't seem to have had the same relationship that Leah and Samuel had enjoyed. Susan admitted to using her power as the older sister to torment Chuck—Chuckie—when he was a young child, and she'd continued the job well into their adolescence. As Chuck had gotten older, he'd started to tease and torment back. But at the end of the day, the harassment between siblings had been mostly of the playful nature, and the two had genuinely loved and respected each other.

"He punched a guy once," Susan said, looking past Lance and seeming to stare at the wall as she spoke. "For me, I mean. We were in the high school parking lot, and some guy said my ass was—how did he put it? 'Too big for my britches.'" She laughed. "Chuckie walked right up to the guy—some sophomore who thought he was hot shit because he dipped on school grounds and drove a pickup truck that clearly compensated for a tiny dick—"

Boy, she remembers this very clearly, Lance thought.

"And then Chuckie said, 'That's my sister,' and socked the guy in the gut. Poor kid hit the ground and gasped for air for what felt like five minutes."

"Did he get in trouble? Your brother?"

Susan and Leah both laughed then. "You kidding me?" Susan said. "Football players at Westhaven are like the celebrities out in LA that get arrested for DUIs and picking up hookers. It brushes right off."

Lance nodded. He understood. He'd been granted such privileges as a basketball player in high school. Not that he'd used it to get away with being a troublemaker, but there were definite perks to being a well-respected high school athlete. Just ask one.

Lance asked, "Was Chuck good at football? Like, could he play in college, even if just Division 3?"

Susan thought about this for a moment, looking up to the ceiling and closing her eyes.

When she finally looked down and opened her eyes, Lance watched as the tears began to stream down her face and his heart melted. "We always called him superstar, my family did," Susan said. "We built him up, acted like if he kept working hard and stayed passionate, he could make something of himself with football. We all encouraged him because he just loved it so damn much." She paused. "But honestly, no, he wasn't great. He was just ... big. I mean, look at me. My parents are big, and they made two big children. Not fat, mind you—though I could afford to lose a few pounds—but just ... wide. Stocky. Large frames. Chuck lifted weights to put on muscle, but he was big without it. But he wasn't quick. His footwork was always sloppy, and his reflexes were nothing to write home about. His size is what served him well on the team. If he got in your way, he was hard to move. But I don't think that would have cut it at the next level."

Lance said nothing, just nodded.

"But he always tried hard," Susan sniffled. "Every day he did his best."

Lance hated to continue the questioning. It made him feel like a detective. But, in a sense, that was what he was. "No other trouble at school, or at home? Leah told me about your family's store, about it having to close."

Susan nodded. "Yeah, that was a tough time. I had already graduated and was taking classes at the community college, so I wasn't too concerned about Daddy saying the family was going to move. I had means to survive around here on my own. But yeah, Chuck was pissed. He didn't want to leave his friends, and he certainly didn't want to leave the football team. I think even then he knew that whichever new high school he ended up at, he might not make the team. Chuck wasn't stupid. He knew his own limitations, even if we tried to give him a big head."

Lance waited to see if there was more, but when Susan didn't say anything else, he asked, "But was he upset enough to run away?"

Susan looked at Lance like he was stupid. "Didn't you hear what I just said? The last thing on earth Chuckie wanted to do was leave his friends and team behind. My brother did *not* run away. I don't give a shit what the fucking police said. These small-town Podunk bastards don't even know which end of the gun to point out."

Again, Lance nodded. Then he went for the million-dollar question. "What about a girlfriend?"

"Yeah, sure, he had a couple."

Lance and Leah both perked up at this, and Susan sensed their sudden interest, offering a concerned, "*Why?*"

Leah turned sideways on the bed and pulled one of her legs underneath her. Facing Susan, she asked, "Was he dating anybody when he went missing?"

Susan looked at Lance, then at Leah, and then she shook her head. "No … no, he wasn't. He'd broken up with that Yates girl during the summer, right before football started up. He told me it was just a fling, anyway, and that he needed his head straight for Coach." She laughed, a sad, weary laugh. "See what I mean? He loved that damn sport."

Lance felt let down, and he could clearly see Leah did as well. They'd wanted the answer to be yes. They'd wanted a name, a person to lay blame on and interrogate further. And then, as if their disappointment had sparked a rush of memory, Susan sat up straighter and said, "Although ..."

She looked down at the floor, her brow furrowed in thought. Lance stayed quiet, letting her work out whatever it was she was unraveling. When she finally looked up at him, she said, "He never said he was dating anybody, but there was the perfume."

"Perfume?" Leah asked, getting excited.

Lance stayed calm. It was nothing, until it was something. "What do you mean?" he asked.

"I used to stay up late, doing my homework at our kitchen table. Chuckie didn't have a curfew—town this small, good kid like he is—it just wasn't needed. Mom and Dad trusted him. In the last month or so before Chuckie disappeared, I can distinctly remember him coming home late—I'm talking one or two in the morning—looking half-stoned, and when he came through the front door and walked by me in the kitchen—I remember, God I remember like it was yesterday—I smelled a woman's perfume on him."

Leah's eyes darted to Lance, and he could see the fire in them, the flash of excitement that they might be on to something. Lance stayed realistic. "You ask him about it?"

Susan shook her head and sighed. "No. I never did. I mean, I didn't like to pry into Chuckie's life. Tease him, sure, but I respected his privacy. He did the same for me."

"So it's possible the perfume belonged to a friend, some girl who hung out in his social circle?"

Susan made a face. "I ... I guess so."

"But?"

She looked at Lance. "How much do you know about perfume?"

"Let's say zero, less."

"Right, okay." Susan thought for a moment. "I guess the best way to explain is that the scent I smelled on Chuckie didn't seem like something a high school girl would wear. It wasn't all sweet and sugary and fun like a lot of the Bath & Body Works lotions and sprays. It was, I guess, more mature. It smelled more like something a *woman* would wear. Not a girl. Stronger, more floral." When Lance said nothing, Susan said, "It smelled like something my mom would wear. That's the last thing I can think to say."

On the one hand, Lance was deflated. They hadn't really gained any new insight into what might be happening to the Westhaven boys. On the other hand, there was this one small connection: Samuel's last words had been about going to see a girlfriend nobody knew about, and Chuck Goodman had come home smelling of perfume when his closest family had believed he wasn't involved with anyone, having just gone through a breakup. Statistically, assuming Bobby Strang was truthful about Samuel's parting words, two-thirds of the boys who'd vanished had a mysterious female presence linked to their disappearances.

Lance, Leah, and Susan chatted a bit longer, and then Susan said she had to go. Lance gave her another hug and thanked her again for helping him with his injuries, and also for talking to them about her brother. At the door to the office, Susan stopped and said, "I don't see how it's possible, after all this time, but you'll let me know if you find out anything, won't you?"

"Of course," Leah said. "You'll be the first to know."

Susan gave Leah a pained smile and then cast one final appraising glance at Lance before leaving. When her 4Runner was out of the motel's parking lot, Leah turned to Lance. "What do you think?"

Lance studied the clouds through the closed office door for a moment. "I think I'm ready to see that picture of your brother."

She nodded and took his hand and led him back to her bedroom.

20

THE LAST TIME A GIRL HAD TAKEN LANCE BY THE HAND and led him to her bedroom, they'd done a lot more than just look at pictures.

But Lance was always careful. His mother's words, which had followed him when she was alive and now haunted him in her death, always echoed in his head during those certain "moments of indiscretion." There'd been no talk of birds and bees; thankfully his mother had allowed him to grasp those concepts on his own, along with the help of the public education system's health classes. But there had been a warning, one spoken with grave seriousness.

A child will only make you vulnerable, Lance. You carry enough of a burden as it is. Don't add to that load, not until you're good and ready and fully understand what you are.

Lance was unsure he'd ever fully understand what he was, so children seemed like a far-off dream he might one day catch up with. But ... he was a human male, after all. He had urges just like everyone else. He could never be too careful.

Leah left the bedroom door open and pointed to her bed. Lance sat, holding back a joke about not even getting dinner first. Leah pulled one of the dresser's bottom drawers open and took out a small stack of books—all of them were Westhaven High School yearbooks. She spread them out on the floor, checking the years on the front covers, and then selected one and joined Lance on the bed. He got another whiff of her shampoo and tried not to be obvious that he was inhaling deeply, enjoying the scent. Leah flipped through the yearbook's pages, the faces and smiles and scattered collages of hundreds of students flashing by, and then stopped, smoothing the pages open and holding it out for Lance to see more clearly.

"Here," she said, pointing at one of the small squares on the page. "That's Samuel." She laughed softly. "What a dork."

Lance watched Leah's face as the smile grew large and held, her eyes locked onto the eyes of her brother's picture. He wondered what memories she was visiting in her head, which of the best moments of her and Samuel's childhood was replaying and causing that grin on her face.

Lance looked down at the picture. Leaned in closer just to be sure.

Samuel was well built, broad shoulders and chest. His grin was forced, like somebody who didn't like to smile on cue. On his head was a mop of sandy-blond hair. The resemblance between the boy and his father was there, as well a small resemblance to Leah.

But one thing was for sure. Samuel was the dead boy Lance had seen in Leah's bathroom mirror, and again in the fuzzy television screen.

Lance tried not to let it show that he'd discovered this disturbing fact, so he quickly blurted, "Chuck Goodman in this yearbook, too?"

Leah thought for a moment. "Um, yeah, should be." She flipped through some pages, going to a different class. Her finger traced the list of names and then followed a row of pictures. "Yep, here he is. God, I'd forgotten how big he was."

Lance looked down at the picture. Leah was right. Chuck Goodman was a large boy, nearly filling in the entire square allotted for his picture, and Lance understood what Susan had meant about her brother being "hard to move." But the real reason Lance had asked to see Chuck Goodman's picture was to see if he'd been the burnt boy who'd appeared at the diner earlier that morning. He wasn't. It didn't mean Chuck wasn't dead—Lance now assumed all the boys were deceased. It just meant he'd yet to show himself.

Lance had just started to consider the differences between Samuel's appearance in the mirror and television screen, and the burnt boy in the diner, when Leah asked, "Why'd you want to see their pictures?"

Lance tried to be quick. Shrugged. "Just wanted faces for the names." He left it at that.

Leah wasn't buying it. "Bullshit."

Lance stayed quiet. Kept his eyes on Chuck Goodman's faded yearbook picture.

"You know something," Leah said. Then her eyes drifted toward to the corner where the TV sat on its cart. "When we first came in here and the TV was on, you made me wait before turning it off. You were just staring at it ... like you were ..." She trailed off. "Lance ... what did you see?"

He couldn't tell her. Couldn't bring himself to expose his secret just yet, couldn't break this girl's heart with the finality of her brother's death. Whether she'd already accepted the idea or not, Lance didn't yet want to deliver the final blow.

"Nothing," he said, and he couldn't meet her eyes.

"You're lying. Aren't you?"

Lance said nothing. Hated himself on the inside.

Leah nodded. "I'll take that as a yes." She stood up and

tossed the book into Lance's lap. He caught it, and as she stormed out of the bedroom, he called after her and she ignored him. He threw the yearbook onto the bed and followed her into the office. Leah was already behind the check-in counter, absentmindedly sorting papers and checking things on a laptop. She didn't so much as raise an eyebrow in Lance's direction.

Lance leaned against the counter and waited to see if she'd acknowledge him. After a couple minutes of cold-shoulder action, he finally said, "Look, I'm sorry."

"Great," she said.

"No, really."

"Really. Great."

Lance sighed. "Would you just—"

"Do you have any idea how much I'm risking for you?" Her words shot like darts from her mouth.

Lance stepped back. "For *me*?"

"Yes, you!" Leah pushed a strand of hair out of her eye. "Since you've walked into my life, I've lied to Daddy, twice. If he takes this job away from me, I don't know what my next step is, Lance. I've been here my whole life. This is all I know. I've got a high school diploma from the middle of nowhere and I've managed a roach motel. And now—now!—I'm harboring somebody the police are probably out looking for right now. I could be arrested, Lance. I'm not positive about that, but even the possibility scares me." She was on the verge of tears now. "Look … I don't have a lot, and I don't mean much to hardly anybody, and even though you say we're doing all this to try and find out what happened to my brother—and, yes, I know I sort of pushed your hand to help—I think we all know Samuel and the rest of the boys are already dead and nothing we do is going to change that and … and…"

The tears came now, spilling down her cheeks, and Lance did the only thing in the entire world he could think to do—the only thing in the entire world he wanted to do. He leaned his tall frame over the counter, grabbed the front of Leah's shirt and pulled her forward, kissing her hard on the mouth.

His heart pounded.

There was the smallest moment of resistance.

And then she kissed him back.

He tasted her tears, salty and wonderful, and drowned in her scent. The kiss flooded him with a warmth, melted the tension he'd built up, and he felt the same process occurring in Leah, watched her body relax and loosen.

When they finally pulled apart, staring at each other with faces more full of surprise than any sort of regret, Lance spoke first. "I'll tell you everything," he said. "But you just have to follow blindly a little longer. Just until I get a better understanding of what I think I know."

She stared at him, breathing hard after the kiss. Her tears had stopped, dried streaks on her cheeks.

"Neither of us can solve this alone," Lance said. "I need you. And I need you to trust me."

Leah was quiet for a long time, and Lance started to think she wasn't going to go along with it. Whatever damage had been done, the kiss, the new naked truth between them, couldn't repair it.

Finally, she said, "What do we do next?"

Lance felt the relief wash over him. "There's a football game tonight. Will you be my date?"

21

WHATEVER DRUGS SUSAN GOODMAN HAD GIVEN LANCE, they were starting to wear off. For nearly an hour after the kiss, he'd sat on the couch in the office while Leah did some work behind the counter. She would occasionally run outside to this room or that and return a short time later, always first glancing at him on the couch, as if she were concerned he might have run off.

His head was starting to throb behind his cut, and the pain in his wrist, while not unbearable, was irritating. He stood up, stretched, and told Leah he was going to go lie down to try and take a nap. And really, what else was there for him to do? He wasn't going to go risk walking into town again by his lonesome. He'd learned enough to know he wasn't going to learn much else today. The town's citizens answered his questions vaguely at best, and usually acted like he was off his rocker for even bringing the topic of the missing boys up at all.

But he was looking forward to the football game. Not because of the competition, but because of who all might be in attendance.

Leah told him she'd wake him if he wasn't back by the time

they had to leave. "As long as you don't mind me slipping into your room," she said with a grin. "But in all fairness, you've spent a lot of time in mine already."

Lance thought about covering the short distance between the couch and check-in counter and kissing her, but he restrained himself. *Keep it organic*, he thought. Then, *And by the way, you know this is a bad idea. What's your plan with her?*

He told his subconscious to shut up and headed outside. But as he stepped through the door, he took one last look back at her, suddenly wondering if it was a good idea to leave Leah alone. How guilty was she, now that she was tied in with him? Could the evil that had come after Lance sense the feelings between him and Leah? With the one kiss, had Lance instantly transformed Leah into a vulnerability? The phrase "collateral damage" lit up in his mind like a Vegas strip marquee. He could almost hear his mother's disapproving sigh, see the subtle shake of her head.

Lance stepped out through the door. Again, what could he really do?

The clouds were still dark, but any rain was still holding off. The smoke plume continued to rise up to the sky, and Lance stood on the cracked concrete walkway and stared at it, wondering if the blackness of the smoke symbolized a hidden threat somehow tied to the paper mill, tied to Glenn Strang.

He started to pull at this thread for just a minute before the burning pain of his cut forced him to turn away and enter his room and lie down on the bed.

He shifted restlessly atop the covers, careful not to put any weight on his injured wrist. When he closed his eyes, he saw Deputy Miller's kind eyes, heard the Southern hospitality in his voice. And then he saw the slack and broken body twisted in the front of the cruiser. He saw a mother and child

(*Ben and Jen!*)

standing over a closed casket being lowered into the earth, saw them returning to a home that would forever feel emptier than it should. An empty spot at the kitchen table, an empty half of a bed, an unfinished bedtime story bookmarked at a page that would never be read.

It's my fault.

He tossed, rolled over onto his side. Took a deep breath and tried to clear his mind.

It's my fault...

He forced himself to think of Leah, relive the kiss, that only-the-first-time heat of excitement that had accompanied it. And as he finally started to drift off—sure he'd be met by nothing by nightmares—he could almost taste her tears again, almost smell her shampoo.

But it wasn't Leah who he last saw in his mind before he fell asleep. Instead, he saw Susan Goodman, the way she'd gently and thoughtfully tended to his injuries, the way she'd laughed thinking about Chuckie, the tears that had come despite her best efforts to fight them off as she spoke.

Too many good people were getting hurt in Westhaven. He had to put a stop to it.

[22]

LANCE WOKE ON HIS OWN FROM A SLEEP THAT WAS DEEP, dreamless. He stretched, pulled his flip phone from his pocket and checked the time. He had time to shower, he assumed. He sauntered to the bathroom, his head feeling heavy, but mostly pain-free. He undressed himself and carefully unwrapped his wrist, trying to remember how to redo it after he had showered. As the water ran hot, he stood in front of the sink and checked himself in the mirror. He looked weary, but considering he'd been in a full-on auto accident that had resulted in a fatality earlier, he figured he could look a heck of a lot worse.

The water scalded his body, stung the cut on his head, but the pain and heat rejuvenated him. Cleared his mind. Helped him find his second wind for the day—both physically and mentally. He stepped out and dried off. Brushed his teeth. He dressed in more of his new clothes and, again, stuffed all his belongings into his backpack. He couldn't bring himself not to prepare for a rapid departure. For whatever reason. If he was forced to leave quickly, as he'd been from his home just two short days ago, he didn't want to be completely helpless and empty-handed.

With his backpack on his shoulders and his mind and body ready, Lance checked the time on his phone one more time before he would head over to the office and see what Leah was up to and when they were going to be leaving.

But there was something on his phone. A missed call. A voicemail.

He recognized the number, had had it memorized for years, though it wasn't stored in his phone's memory.

Marcus Johnston had just started out with Lance's hometown sheriff's department the first time Lance had met him. Marcus and Lance's mother had attended high school together, and Lance's mother had been able to urge Marcus to help her and Lance out during a particularly sticky situation they'd gotten into. The first of many.

Over time, as Lance had gotten older and his gifts had increased, he had been able to put them to better use—willingly, or not—and Marcus had continued to play a role in Lance's life. Eventually, Lance's secrets had been spilled to the man, sometimes one drop at a time, other times in great gushes of new information. Why Lance's mother had ever trusted Marcus Johnston enough to tell him what Lance really was, Lance would never know. Maybe she too had possessed a small bit of what empowered Lance, just enough to be able to see the truly great ones, the ones who she knew wouldn't let them down.

As Lance had grown and developed, so had Marcus Johnston's career, though the two ascensions were unrelated as far as Lance could tell. Marcus had climbed the sheriff's office ladder until, when Lance was a freshman in high school, he had become the actual sheriff. He'd held the position through Lance's senior year, and then a few more years just for good measure. And then, one year before Lance was forced to flee, Marcus Johnston had become mayor.

(Do you, a person with your gifts, honestly believe things could be so random?)

Lance had been lifelong friends with a man who'd eventually become the highest-ranking person in the city. A man who'd helped Lance and his mother in more ways than Lance could ever count. A man who'd helped protect Lance.

A man who was there that night.

A man who knew the truth.

Guiltily, Lance shoved the phone back into his pocket. He couldn't bring himself to listen to the message right now. Good news, bad news, it didn't matter. Whichever, it would only prove a distraction. Right now, he had more important things at hand.

Lance walked out of his room and went one door down to the office. The Honda Civic was back, and when Lance opened the office door he was immediately greeted by the sounds of laughing children. There were two small boys, no more than five or six, either of them, sitting on the couch, staring intently at the television screen. A brightly colored cartoon was displayed on the screen, and the volume was turned up too loud. Lance looked left and saw Renee and Leah standing behind the counter. Leah smiled at him. Renee looked apprehensive, but not all together displeased.

Leah gave the woman a small hug. "Thanks again, Renee. I owe you big-time."

Renee waved her off and said it was better than sitting at home and that the kids would have a great time. That it was almost like going to the movies.

Leah said goodbye to the boys, who didn't even twitch their eyes toward the sound of her voice, and then looped her arm around Lance's and pulled him out the door.

"I feel terrible, having to ask her to come back in like that," Leah said as the door closed behind them. "But she's right. The kids look like they're having a good time. I've only ever seen the outside of Renee's trailer, but that alone is enough to make me think the kids feel like they're in a castle right now."

Lance asked, "What did you tell her the reason you needed her back was?"

"I didn't really. Just said I had some things I had to take care of that couldn't wait, and she'd be doing me a huge favor and I would owe her one."

"The kids?"

Leah sighed. "Different fathers, both long gone. Like I said, I feel bad for the woman." Then Leah pulled a single key from her pocket and said, "Oh, and she's letting us borrow her car."

Lance crammed himself into the passenger seat, trying not to step on the debris on the floorboard—the book from earlier, as well as a children's picture book, an empty McDonald's bag, a tennis ball, a phone charger, unplugged and loosely coiled. This was a family car. A family that was constantly on the go. It smelled of apple juice and coffee and sweat. There was something sticky on the center console, and Lance made a note not to rest any part of himself there.

Leah started the engine—which began as a sputter before coughing to life with a whine—and backed the car out of the parking spot. Through the cracks in the cloudy sky, the sun had faded to orange and had dipped nearly below the tree line. "Calling for rain?" Lance asked.

Leah shook her head. "I don't think so."

She turned right out of the motel's parking lot and headed first toward town before shooting off down a side road Lance had yet to travel. "We're going to get dinner first," she said. "I hope that's okay."

Lance realized he hadn't eaten since breakfast, which felt like two days ago, and the hunger complaints from his stomach broke loose and were on him furiously. He knew things were serious when he forgot to eat. "Sounds great," he said.

Half a mile down the road, Leah turned into the lot of a Sonic Drive-In that looked startlingly out of place. While everything else Lance had seen in Westhaven was old, aged, and weathered, the Sonic appeared shiny and new. Bright signage and a freshly painted building and a recently paved parking lot. And they were busy. Leah nearly circled the entire lot before finding an open slot to pull into. The last one available.

"Place just opened about a month ago. So, yeah, Westhaven is sort of a big deal now, as you can see."

Lance grinned, looked all around him at the folks eating in their cars. Even through the windshields and windows he could see a mass scattering of Westhaven-emblazoned shirts and hats. Everybody was having their pre-game meal.

Football was important around here.

Lance ordered three cheeseburgers, fries, and a chocolate milkshake. Leah ordered a grilled chicken sandwich and looked at Lance like he was from Mars. "Where does it go?"

He shrugged. "Feet. I guess."

She laughed and he leaned over the sticky center console and kissed her. She smiled at him and said, "You better be careful. Lots of wandering eyes around here."

And he almost said it wouldn't matter, because he wouldn't be around for long. And this truth stifled his mood for only a moment before he pushed it away. It sounded meaner than it really was, that thought. He wasn't abandoning anybody, but he was fairly certain Westhaven was not where he was supposed to spend the rest of this life. He'd move on. Searching—even if he didn't know what for.

Instead, Lance said, "What if your father shows up? Comes for a coney and ends up shoving it down my throat when he finds us together. I know statistically it happens a lot in the United States, but I really don't want a hot dog to kill me."

Leah stared out the windshield. Didn't laugh at the joke. She sighed. "Daddy's protective of me. I guess I understand why, but..." She snapped out of it and said, "I'll just tell him it's part of the job interview." She smiled, and the food came and for a while they sat together blissfully eating. When Lance had finished his second burger, he took a long pull from his shake and said, "Tomorrow I want to try and talk to Bobby Strang. If he was the last person to see your brother alive, *and* they were such good friends, he really might know more about what happened than he thinks he does."

Leah nodded, sipped her drink. "Maybe you can talk to him tonight."

"How's that?"

Leah smacked her forehead. "Geez, I forgot to tell you! Bobby's the assistant football coach for Westhaven."

Lance turned in his seat to fully see her. "You're kidding."

She shook her head.

"Why would he stick around? He graduated, right?"

"Yeah, of course he did. He just ... I don't know. When he finished high school, he went to work for his dad at the mill. Nothing manual, mind you, some VP of such and such I think. But by the time the next football season started up, he'd found a place on the coaching staff."

"Nobody thought that was odd? That he didn't head off to college or anything?"

Leah laughed. "Around here, that's a lot more common than you'd think. No, I think if anything, people were surprised at him ending up coaching, considering he really wasn't much of a player." She shrugged. "But, with all Glenn Strang's done for the team—and still does, by the way—I guess folks figured it was all part of the process, part of the deal. He seems to do a good enough job, anyway."

Lance finished his last burger and again marveled at how much the Strang family had to do with the Westhaven football team.

His conversation with Bobby couldn't come soon enough.

Somewhere, somebody was hiding something.

WHEN THE FOOD WAS FINISHED AND THE TRASH DISPOSED of, Leah asked Lance if he was ready.

"I've got nowhere else to be," he said.

She started the car and headed back the way they'd come, crossing over Route 19 and heading toward Westhaven High School, the same route Lance had taken on foot earlier that day. Before he'd met Deputy Miller. Before somebody else had died.

The sun was gone now, and the headlights of Renee's Civic did the job well enough to light the way. Above, there were no stars, only the thick blanket of clouds. But ahead, looming in the distance less than a mile away, was another cloud, a bright explosion of white that hung in the air and lit up the sky and created a dome of light that only grew in size the closer Lance and Leah got.

"Those are some serious lights," Lance said, leaning down to peer up and get a better view through the windshield.

Leah stopped fifty yards from the turn-in for the high school, coming to a stop behind a line of brake lights as others waited their turn to enter the parking lot. "Glenn Strang had some connections, worked a few fundraisers. Those lights were installed the year after they won the first state title."

An elderly woman in a bright orange vest and wielding a light-up orange plastic signal cone motioned the cars in, one by one. She wore a Westhaven baseball cap and smiled brightly at Leah as she waved the Civic into the lot.

"Know her?" Lance asked.

"Mrs. Bellamy. She taught civics for about a hundred years before I had her, and she's still here."

"She liked you. Could tell by her smile," Lance said, feeling a pang of guilt as Leah drove by the exact spot where Lance had stood earlier when Deputy Miller had pulled his cruiser in behind him.

Leah shrugged, found a parking spot near the rear of the lot, and pulled in. Killed the lights and the engine. The engine ticked, something popped, and then all was quiet except for the murmur of the crowd noise and the booming godlike voice of the PA announcer from the field.

"Plan?" Leah asked, checking herself in the rearview mirror, adjusting her hair.

"You keep asking me if I have a plan. Did it ever occur to you I'm just winging this?"

"Are you?"

"Mostly."

Leah sat back in her seat. "And so far you've been blown over by a phantom wind and gotten in a car accident that could have killed you. It's not working out so well."

"I'm not dead yet," Lance said, opening the door and stepping out into the cool evening air.

"Not the most reassuring of statements." Leah got out and motioned for him to follow her. "This way."

Lance followed her, and they wove their way between an ocean of parked cars and finally fell in line with a mass of people who were being funneled from the parking lot and through a large gate that then funneled further toward a ticket booth window just outside the field's main entrance. The marching band's bass drum thumped along with the snapping of the snares. Trumpets and tubas tooted and honked. The crowd cheered randomly at whatever was happening on the field, though from what Lance could tell, the game hadn't started yet. They'd stood in line for five minutes before things began to get quiet and the PA announcer asked that everybody stand and turn their attention to the flag for the playing of the national anthem. There was a great shuffling and scuffling from the massive bleachers, and everybody rose up and angled them-selves toward a flag Lance couldn't see. A great many folks in the line, however, all turned and faced west, many putting their hands over their hearts. Lance followed suit, and Leah looked up at him and smiled.

There were a solid five seconds of what seemed like absolute silence before the band played the tune, finishing in a powerful barrage of sound that caused a great eruption of cheers from the stands and some muted clapping from the ticket line. The PA announcer did the usual pregame rigmarole, using the customary increased enthusiasm when announcing the home team, and then the game started.

Two minutes later, Lance bought two tickets and refrained from holding Leah's hand as they walked through the gate.

Leah and Lance passed on all the offers to buy 50/50 raffle tickets and Westhaven t-shirts and Girl Scout cookies being offered by a line of enthusiastic peddlers set up at tables just left of the main entrance. The tickets and t-shirt were an easy "no" for Lance, but the cookies didn't seem like such a bad idea. But he needed to focus. Thin Mints would have to wait.

Leah led the way, navigating the mosh pit of people who filled the large square of gravel and grass bordered by the entrance, peddler's row, restroom and concession stand, and the field itself. Lance smelled grilled hot dogs and nacho cheese. Leah was headed toward the fence that separated the viewing area from the field. Lance, a head above most people, scanned the crowd as he followed Leah, looking for any familiar faces, and, well ... seeing if he picked up anything, any vibe or premonition or whatever the words were. He got nothing except a few curious stares and one baby who seemed to start crying as soon as it made eye contact with Lance. He'd never been great with kids.

The game had started, and by the time Lance rested his elbows atop the chain-link fence along the field, Westhaven had the ball on the opponents' thirty-yard line and the running back took it straight up the gut through a hole big enough to park a bus, then dove into the end zone with outstretched arms as a defender wrapped up his legs. The referees blew their whistles and threw their arms in the air. Touchdown. An explosion of noise came from the bleachers, shouts and screams and air horns and cowbells and the band blasting a fight song. Lance ignored it all and stared at the Westhaven sideline.

Coach Kenny McGuire was smiling, but he wasn't jumping and celebrating with the rest of the team and coaching staff. Instead, he turned away from the action and consulted his iPad, surely flipping through plays and notes and preparing for what came next. He acted like a man who'd done this all a million times. Which, with three state titles, he had. What was one more touchdown?

In person, he looked even smaller than he had in the photograph Lance had seen in the newspaper. Short and thin and almost feeble-looking, as if a strong wind might carry him away like a kite swept away from an unsuspecting child. The rimless glasses made him appear distinguished, but not altogether handsome. The air of dorkiness clung to Kenny McGuire, despite his coaching accolades. He looked like a guy who should be spending his Friday nights playing Dungeons & Dragons instead of even attending a sporting event, never mind coaching one.

"That's Bobby Strang." Leah pointed, and Lance followed her finger down the sideline until he saw the guy.

Bobby Strang was down on one knee, also immersed in an iPad and shouting instructions to a semicircle of players around him. The guy was average height and had a buzz cut, a small belly already forming along the line of his Westhaven t-shirt where it was tucked into his khaki pants—which seemed to be standard attire for the Westhaven coaching staff. His face was red, and sweat dripped from his brow. Coaching must be tough work. Lance stared at Bobby, tried to will his mind to focus on the guy, to pick up something, anything. But he got nothing. Maybe he was too far away, out of Lance's reception area. Like Lance had told Leah earlier, he really didn't understand any of what he could and couldn't do.

"Think we can talk to him?" Lance asked.

Leah was about to answer, then got distracted by a play on the field. A fumble, which Westhaven recovered. More cheers. More celebrating. More cowbell. She looked at Lance. "It would have to be after the game, obviously. But, yeah, I think so. I think..." She looked away sheepishly and said something that got drowned in the crowd noise.

"What?" Lance said, leaning in closer.

"I think he always feels guilted into talking to me when we see each other."

"Because of Samuel?"

She nodded.

Lance wondered if the guilt was a general sort of thing, sympathy for a victim, or if there was more to it. If Bobby Strang felt guilty because he knew more than he was letting on.

Lance watched the game. The Westhaven quarterback—Anthony Mills, Lance remembered from the paper—heaved a long pass high in the air to a streaking receiver, and the entire crowd seemed to hold their breath as the ball flew. There was a collective "uggghhh" of disappointment when the ball ended up being overthrown by a good five yards. *Kid's got a good arm,* Lance thought, and then he asked Leah, "Where's Glenn Strang? I assume he still comes to all the games."

Leah snapped her fingers. "Right. Yeah, he does. I think so, anyway. It's been a while since I've been here."

This time she did take Lance's hand in hers and led him away from the fence, two other people quickly sliding into their places to get a better view. They walked down the fence line, gravel crunching beneath their sneakers, and Lance saw a pair of sheriff's deputies leaning against the bleachers, half-watching the game, half-watching everything else around them. Despite what were probably their best efforts, both men couldn't quite contain a downcast look of sorrow, and Lance knew the news of their fallen comrade was hitting them hard.

My fault, Lance thought as he walked past them. *I'm so sorry, guys. I was stupid and one of yours paid the price.* And then a second thought struck him. He wondered if there was an active effort to find him—the other passenger in the wrecked cruiser who'd fled the scene. Lance's description was pretty telltale, especially his height. But the two officers paid him no attention as Lance and Leah walked by. They were distracted.

The space between the fence and the bleachers was wide but still felt like a packed cattle chute with all the people walking either back to their seats or toward the restrooms and concessions. Lance purposely walked with a slight stoop, trying to make himself not appear so tall and stand out in the sea of people. Leah gripped his hand tightly, and he had to wonder how many folks were watching them from the bleachers and whispering to the person next to them, *"Isn't that Leah from the motel? Who's that guy she's with? New boyfriend? I wonder what her daddy thinks about that."*

Leah stopped right at the fifty-yard line and turned to face the field. Lance followed suit.

"He usually sits right here, about four or five rows up. I didn't want to just stop and stare. Lean sideways against the fence and casually look around, up toward the bleachers. Like you're just taking in the sights."

"Those are very specific directions. Spy on people often, do you?"

"Maybe you're not the only one with special talents."

Lance didn't know what to say to that, so he did as she asked. He turned sideways and propped himself up with his right elbow against the fence. He watched another play take place, a short run attempt by the opponent, which got them a gain of three or four yards. He checked the big, beautiful scoreboard behind the opposite end zone. It was now third down, four yards to go for a first down. Then he looked up to the sky, verified the clouds were still blacking out all the stars, and then—

"Okay, you're making it obvious. Just look already," Leah said, elbowing him.

Lance rubbed his rib where she'd hit him and looked toward the bleachers, counted four rows up, scanned the crowd. Went up to the fifth row and immediately found Glenn Strang.

The man looked exactly like he had in the photos Lance had seen at Sportsman's earlier that day. He was tall, his head looming above the others in his row, and his graying hair was cut close, but still long enough to comb. His face was smooth, and again Lance thought the man's face didn't seem to add up to his age, but this could be attributed to a strict regimen of moisturizers and creams, he supposed. He still appeared to be in decent shape, his shoulders still broad, and his biceps snuggled nicely beneath the sleeves of the Westhaven polo shirt he was wearing beneath a black sweater-vest. Glenn Strang's eyes were locked intently on the football game, darting from place to place along the field, his mouth constantly moving in bursts of cheers and unheard instructions he was mumbling to the players.

Here was a man who absolutely loved the game of football and would never let go.

Which wasn't a crime, Lance conceded.

But ... Glenn Strang was not what held Lance's attention.

"Is that his wife?" Lance asked.

"What?" Leah said, turning from the game.

"The woman next to Strang—is that his wife?"

"Oh." Leah looked over her shoulder, then turned back. "Yeah, that's her. Tasty, right?"

"Did you just say 'tasty'?"

"Come on, you know she's hot. Even I know she's hot. Though it's probably all tummy tucks and face-lifts and hair dye."

Women and jealousy. Lance was thankful he was a guy.

Leah sighed. "Her name's Allison and she's always been super nice, as far as I can tell. She brought me and Daddy dinner every day for a week when Samuel disappeared. And she brings me cookies sometimes at the motel." And then, almost regrettably, "And they're delicious."

"You sound like that's a bad thing."

Leah shrugged, a motion Lance was becoming quite familiar with. "She just seems so perfect, is all. It's sort of disgusting."

Lance took another look at Allison Strang. Blond hair to her shoulders and high cheekbones and smooth skin. A pretty face. She was wearing blue jeans and a light sweater, and Lance felt embarrassed to find himself staring at her breasts, which seemed a little too firm and upright for a woman who had to be midforties at the youngest, bringing back Leah's comments about enhancement surgeries. He hated the term MILF but couldn't deny where its definition applied.

And then he realized that at some point between Lance looking from the woman's face to her chest, Allison Strang had begun staring directly at him.

Their eyes met, briefly, and Allison gave him a small embarrassed smile, as if she was the one who'd been caught. Lance offered a quick, sheepish grin and then turned his gaze back to the field. "She just caught me staring."

Leah laughed. "I think she's used to young men gawking. Old men, too."

Lance waited a beat and then risked another look back. Saw Allison Strang talking excitedly to a woman next to her, a woman Lance had failed to even notice before, drowned in the shadow of Allison Strang's beauty. She was shorter and not quite as thin but still looked pretty good for a woman who might have been forty. Her face showed her age more than either of the Strangs' did, and she sat somewhat hunched over, her blond hair done up in a tight bun, dark eyes looking out toward the field and then constantly glancing to the sideline. Homely wasn't the word Lance would use, but maybe average. The woman listened and nodded as Allison Strang continued talking, but Lance got the impression she wasn't really interested. Something tugged at the back of Lance's brain, and it took him a minute, but he was finally able to firmly grasp it and pull it to the front. The woman next to Allison Strang was the woman Lance had seen escorting the boy out of the school's office earlier that day. The boy with the yellow slip of paper and the downtrodden demeanor.

"Who's that next to Mrs. Strang?"

Leah didn't even have to turn around. "That's Melissa McGuire. That's the coach's wife."

"The vice principal."

"Right."

Lance nodded. It made sense. Surely the Strangs and the McGuires were close. The women were probably great friends, at least on the surface.

It started to rain. Nothing hard or serious like the heavy clouds seemed to have been advertising all evening, but a light, spotty drizzle that was more irritating than problematic. Lance saw a few umbrellas go up in the bleachers, a few ponchos pulled on and a few hoods pulled up, zippers zipped. The rain was cold, but he didn't mind. Leah didn't seem to mind either.

"Let's move," he said. "I feel like they're watching us now."

"Who?"

"Mrs. Strang and Mrs. McGuire."

"Why would they be watching us."

"Just a feeling," he said, though that was a lie. He wasn't feeling anything right then, but the odds were great that the Strangs had something to do with the Westhaven boys' disappearances, and Lance didn't want to risk popping up on their radar quite yet. He nodded across the field, to the other set of bleachers. These were smaller, and less populated. "Let's go sit on the other side."

Leah turned and looked at him, confused. "The *visitors'* side?"

"What? Will that hurt your image?"

She elbowed him again. "No, I suppose not."

She didn't take his hand this time but left the fence and walked, heading away from the concessions and the entrance, meaning to walk around the other end zone and loop around to the opposite-side bleachers. Along the way, a couple of people said hi to her, and she chatted with one younger girl who was probably an ex-classmate. Lance stood silently a few feet away each time, trying not to stand out, trying not to make it too obvious he was with her. Despite what Leah thought or cared about, he didn't want to put her at any more risk, whether socially or otherwise, than absolutely necessary.

The rain stayed constant, but the wind picked up a great deal by the time they reached the end of the bleachers. Somewhere in the distance, a clap of thunder caused all the spectators' heads to swivel. Lance shivered and wished he had a jacket. Not so much for himself, but to offer Leah. He noticed the goose bumps prickling along her arms.

They rounded the edge of the fence and were halfway across the rear of the end zone area when a huge gust of wind rattled the goalpost, the uprights swaying and creaking. And it was then that Lance was slammed in the gut with an overwhelming feeling to stop, turn, and look back toward the bleachers and find the area the Strangs were sitting. Something was screaming at him, something was locked onto him, something was ... taunting him.

And then, without any warning, a single bolt of lightning blistered from the sky. It struck the large scoreboard and traveled down its metal pole of a base, slamming into the earth and shaking the ground. Sparks exploded and the scoreboard sizzled and metal burned, and then another powerful gust blew in from the west, and Lance's heart froze as he saw what was happening.

He had stopped walking before the lightning, hit with his intuition to turn and seek out the Strangs. In just those few seconds—*how long had it really been?*—Leah had kept walking. She was ten, maybe fifteen yards ahead now.

Directly behind the scoreboard.

The blast had knocked her to the ground, and she sat up dazed, disoriented.

The scoreboard started to fall backward, the base of its pole melted metal that gave way under the weight it had been supporting. Lance traced the trajectory and knew it was headed right for Leah. It was going to crush her.

"Leah!" he shouted at her with all his gusto. "Leah, you've got to get out of the way!"

He ran, but fast as he was, he knew he was too late. "*Move!*"

He screamed a scream that hurt his throat, and Leah must have heard him, because her eyes cleared momentarily and she looked up and she rolled to her left just as the massive scoreboard crashed down to the ground with a noise that sounded like the thunder.

And then Lance heard a sound that pierced his heart. He heard Leah cry out in absolute agony.

[24]

SILENCE.

The players on the field, the patrons in the stands, even the emergency crew that were standing by near the ambulance parked at the rear exit gate of the field—nobody moved or spoke. Even the wind had died down and the rain reduced itself to less than a drizzle, as if its job were finished. Faces were stupefied, eyes locked on either the place where the scoreboard had once stood or where it had crashed to the ground.

Lance felt as if he'd been sucked into a black hole. In the terrifying silence that had encased the field, the only thing he heard was his heart pounding in his ears, and his own conscience berating him with more obscenities than he even thought he knew. *You were too late. You should have never gotten close to her.*

All my fault.

And then Leah let out another cry of pain, a scream for help, and as if somebody had hit the play button on life's remote, all at once everything snapped back into action. The football players ran off the field, huddling on their respective sidelines, unsure what to do next. Folks in the bleachers jumped to their feet, a few scampering off to the parking lot, a great many more shifting to get a better view of what had happened. The PA announcer, in an effort to instill some sort of crowd control, advised people to remain where they were, to remain calm and stay clear of the "accident."

The lights on the standby ambulance danced and the siren whoop-whooped, and ten seconds later it had crossed through the grassy expanse behind the field and was parked right next to the collapsed sign, paramedics jumping out and going to work.

Lance was frozen. He wanted to run, that he knew for sure. But he didn't know which way. More than anything, he wanted to run to Leah, do whatever he could to help her. Take her hand and hold it as the emergency crew did their job. He wanted to make sure she was going to be okay, and most importantly, he wanted to tell her he was sorry. Sorry for ever showing up in her town.

But the other part of him wanted to run in the other direction. Wanted to run straight to the bus station and ride off and flee this place, just as he'd done his own home. He was tired of people getting hurt, and hurt seemed to be following him. His powers made him a threat to unseen things, and therefore endangered everyone around him.

"Lance!"

Leah...

She was calling for him.

"Lance, where are you?"

He snapped out of his paralysis, sprinted toward the sound of Leah's voice. Could hear the increasing murmur of the crowd behind him as he ran. *Well, if I wasn't on the radar to start with, I sure am now.*

He covered the ground quickly, three seconds, if that, but it felt too long, as if the ground under his feet was moving like the belt of a treadmill, keeping him in place as his legs worked hard to reach his destination.

He stumbled as he got near, and one of the paramedics stepped into his path and raised a hand to stop him. The man was middle-aged, out of shape, but heavy with fat and wearing a grim determination on his face. "Close enough, sir."

Lance tried to sidestep the man, hearing Leah once again call his name, her voice slicing through the raised voices of the crowd, the murmur steadily rising in volume. The man grabbed Lance's wrist, hard enough to get Lance's attention, and in that moment a hot bolt of anger shot through Lance's body, and he found himself about to give in to his temper. He was a split second from raising a fist to smash the guy's nose into pieces when another voice called out. A voice Lance recognized.

"Let him through, Harry! He's a friend, and she's going to be all right."

Susan Goodman stood from a crouched position, where she'd been helping to examine Leah. The dark eye makeup was still heavy, and her face still looked generally unfriendly, but right then and right there, she was beautiful in Lance's eyes.

Harry held on to Lance's wrist for another second, glancing from Lance to Susan. She nodded, and Harry sighed and let Lance go, his nose remaining in a single piece in the middle of his face. Lance jogged the small remaining distance and came to a stop just shy of Susan, who was now holding up a hand of her own to slow him.

"It's her ankle, maybe her leg. Could have been a lot worse, though. She rolled out of the way just in time."

Lance took a tentative step forward, and when Susan didn't stop him, he kept walking until he reached the scoreboard, which lay flat on the ground, its face split nearly in two, chunks of circuit boards and loose wires dangling from the crack running down its middle. The pole jutted out from the bottom and pointed straight out toward the end zone where it had once stood.

"Lance?"

Leah was sprawled out on her stomach, perpendicular to the pole, the bottom corner of the scoreboard pinning her left ankle against the ground. Lance stepped carefully over the pole and knelt down beside her. He had to get down low to see her face, nearly falling forward. "I'm here," he said.

She looked up at him, and even though her cheeks were wet with tears, she smiled at him. "I take it this wasn't part of the plan. At least I certainly hope not. If so, you could have at least warned me." She laughed, then grimaced in pain.

Lance laughed, relief so abundant in him he felt weightless. "I told you, I'm just winging it."

He winked at her, and she laughed again and rolled her eyes, and then Lance and the paramedics and a few spectators who'd been brave enough to wander close enough to get pulled in to help worked together to lift the sign off Leah's ankle enough to allow her to be pulled out. Free.

Susan convinced everyone to let Lance ride in the back of the ambulance on the way to the hospital. He watched impatiently as they carefully put her on a stretcher and loaded her into the back. Lance waited for the signal and then climbed in. He looked back out to the bleachers, scanning the crowd, watching thousands of faces watch him climb aboard, all probably curious as to who he was.

Then he remembered the feeling he'd gotten just before the lightning strike, that nagging feeling that something was screaming toward him, taunting and cocky and nasty. He looked to the field and found the fifty-yard line. Followed it up to the fence, then the bleachers. Counted the rows.

Glenn and Allison Strang were gone. He squinted and tried to focus his vision. Melissa McGuire was gone, too.

The ambulance doors closed and they headed off, a bumpy ride through the grass and then up onto the smooth asphalt of the road. He held Leah's hand as Susan and Harry carefully removed her shoe and sock and examined her on the way. Leah lay perfectly still, her eyes closed, the occasional grimace or whimper of pain at a bump in the road or a prod or poke from Susan and Harry. Lance used the short ride to the hospital to calm himself, center his feelings. He'd almost snapped, back there with Harry. He'd almost punched the man. He needed to get himself under control. The important thing was Leah was okay, in the grand scheme of things. A broken ankle, maybe, but nothing life-threatening.

Lance was feeling better when the ambulance slowed, and once Leah was settled in he'd be ready to figure out what his next move was. The ambulance came to a stop and the doors opened and Lance was told to get out first.

He did so, stepping carefully to the ground, looking up to see the two-story Westhaven Hospital in all its glory. He'd barely registered the bright neon EMERGENCY above his head when a pair of strong hands grabbed him by the shoulders, twisted, and slammed him to the ground.

[25]

LANCE'S FACE HIT THE ASPHALT PARKING LOT HARD enough to rattle his teeth and create a starburst in his vision. Instinctively, he rolled away from the direction the attack had come, scrambling to try and stand again before another blow fell on him. He heard a rushing noise coming at him, something large and moving fast. He was pushing himself off the ground, halfway up before an uppercut caught him in the gut, slammed the air out of him and sent him back to the pavement. He gagged and gasped for air, raising his hands to shield off a further assault. Then the stars in his head finally began to clear and he looked up to stare into the face of his attacker.

He wasn't surprised.

Samuel Senior stood over Lance, fuming, hands balled into fists, his bald head so red it looked hot to the touch. The veins in his arms pulsed. His eyes were narrowed to slits, trained on Lance. Standing over Lance in the darkened parking circle with the bright neon EMERGENCY sign lit up behind him, Leah's daddy looked like a prize fighter basking in the glory of his latest knockout, waiting for the ref to turn the other cheek so he could really finish the job.

But he wasn't moving. He'd stopped his attack. Lance kept his hands raised, both in surrender and defense, and slowly stood, finally regaining control of his breath. Samuel Senior's eyes flicked to something behind Lance, and he said, "It's fine, Roger, we're done here. Just a bit of a misunderstanding." Then the man took a step backward.

Lance twisted his neck around to look over his shoulder and saw a Westhaven sheriff's deputy standing with his hands on his hips in the open doorway leading into the emergency room's entrance.

"Had anything to drink tonight, Sam?" the deputy named Roger asked, as if he were exhausted.

Samuel shook his head. "Not a drop. Honest."

"Is he telling me straight, son?" Roger asked, looking at Lance. "Just a little misunderstanding, and now you two are going to go your separate ways?"

Lance swallowed down his anger, looked from the deputy, to Leah's daddy, and then to the ambulance doors, where Susan and Harry were standing, shielding Leah from viewing what was happening. But she must have recognized the sound of her father's voice just then, because from inside the ambulance, she called out, "Daddy? Is that you? What's going on?"

At the sound of his daughter's voice, Samuel's expression softened, and he took a step toward the ambulance. But then he stopped, turned back to Lance with a refreshed hatred in his eyes and said, "Get the fuck out of here. If I ever see you near my daughter again, I'll kill you. I promise. I knew you was trouble the moment I saw you." Then he turned away and stood by the ambulance as Susan and Harry disappeared back into the rear and came out a minute later, carefully extracting Leah's gurney, then the four of them were swallowed by the large electric doors leading inside, Leah turning her head to see Lance one last time before she was wheeled out of view, her eyes apologetic.

Lance stood, staring at the now-closed hospital doors and then watched as the ambulance drove away, off to wherever magical place they go to hide before the next call. A breeze blew by, and a few drops of rain splashed on top of his head. He looked up, saw the starless sky, the gray clouds just visible against the black backdrop. He sighed, at a loss, a loss of everything.

He turned and started to walk away, nodding to the deputy, who was now leaning against the hospital's brick wall, one leg cocked back, the sole of the shoe pressed against the brick.

"You okay, son?" he asked as Lance passed.

"Yes, sir. Thank you, sir," Lance said.

Lance had made it another ten yards when he heard the electronic *whoosh* of the doors opening. He didn't turn back, didn't look. But then he heard Susan Goodman's voice calling his name. He turned and saw her jogging toward him across the parking lot, her large body bouncing with each stride. She stopped a few feet short of him and waited a second to catch her breath, then tucked a few loose strands of hair back behind her ears. She was sweating, some of the dark makeup around her eyes smeared ever so slightly. Lance could smell her deodorant.

He asked the only question that mattered to him right then. "She okay?"

Susan shrugged. "Probably. Doctors are looking at her now, but I'm positive it's broken. Question is how bad. X-rays will tell. But look, that's not why I came out here."

Lance raised his eyebrows. "Okay."

Susan tossed him something and he caught it, reflexively. It was a set of car keys.

"Leah said go get the car and take it back to Renee," Susan

said. "And she said to wait at the motel for her to call you. Which she'll do as soon as she can."

Lance stared at the keys for a long few seconds, then looked back up to Susan. "I don't ... maybe I should just go."

Susan looked at him. Cocked her head to the side and studied him. Then she looked up to the sky for a moment and back down to Lance. "Look," she said matter-of-factly, "I don't really know who you are, or why you're here. I know Leah thinks you can figure out what happened to our brothers, and yeah, that'd be great and all, but honestly, we all know the odds are slim." She paused. "What I also know is that, despite all the mystery-solving bullshit, Leah likes you. A lot. Like ... really likes you. We're not the best of friends or anything. Hell, I maybe see her once or twice a month, just around town and whatnot. But I haven't seen her smile this much in a long time. You should have seen her, the way she was talking about you when we were headed to pick you up from the side of the road earlier. She lit up like a Christmas tree."

Then she stopped talking. She just shrugged, looked back over her shoulder toward the hospital and said, "I've got to get back to work. Take care."

She jogged away, leaving Lance standing in the hospital parking lot with no better idea of what he should do than he had before.

He turned and started to walk.

LANCE HAD MADE IT ROUGHLY A QUARTER MILE FROM THE hospital before his mind focused enough on the present to realize he had no solid idea where he was. He'd been unable to see from the back of the ambulance as it'd rushed from the football field to the hospital, and the hospital was something he hadn't come across during his brief exploration of Westhaven. But he knew the ride had been short, and he knew the bright, expensive lights from the field were surely still illuminating the sky. He needed to locate the lights and use it as his North Star, let it guide him back to the car.

He followed the sidewalk from the hospital parking lot, stopping every so often to listen to what was around him. A half mile from the hospital, he stopped and swore he heard a faint echo from the PA announcer. Nothing he could make out, but a familiar sound. Through the darkness, the downtown buildings came into view, slowly growing shape the way a monster from a closet might in the middle of the night. He was approaching them from the south side, from the rear. A side he'd yet to see. He followed the sidewalk into town and then stopped, looked left and right, and then turned, headed down a now-familiar path.

The shops and stores were all closed, shut down and locked up and dark. The few small cafes and restaurants were the only signs of life, keeping things from looking quite like a ghost town, and probably hoping for some postgame customers to stop by and help the day's profit.

Lance walked, ignoring everything but his thoughts. He reached the Route 19 intersection he'd found earlier that day and turned right, the lights from the field visible, but not needed now. He'd been this way before. Right before he'd caused a man to die.

And as he made the walk, the last leg of the trip before reaching the high school parking lot, he replayed the past thirty-six hours' worth of events. He watched himself get off the bus, walk to Annabelle's Apron. He recalled his conversation with the diner's deceased owner. Her subtle plea for help. From there he watched himself stumble upon Bob's Place, and then he remembered the first time he'd seen Leah. The thought filled him with a sudden warmth he'd not been expecting, despite his current affection for her.

You're too close, Lance.

He had seen the face that he now knew to belong to Leah's brother, Samuel, staring back at him from both the mirror and later the television. The face that he now felt wasn't malicious or hostile in any way, merely that of a loving brother, trapped in some terrible in-between place—not living, not in whatever afterlife might exist—forced to stay near a sister he could no longer protect, no longer talk to. So close, but so, so far. Keeping a watchful eye, despite the limitation. Curious about Lance.

You're too close, Lance.

He saw Susan Goodman's large but gentle hands working to treat his wounds from the car accident.

BEN AND JEN!

Saw her tears fall as she fondly remembered the kid brother she used to pick on but had loved so deeply. Susan and Leah were just two of the people who'd had their lives destroyed by something selfish and uncaring and ... something that needed to be stopped.

Lance had tasted Leah's lips, her tears. Smelled the shampoo.

Seen the pictures of the state championship teams, their missing teammates not even mentioned.

Seen Glenn and Allison Strang, the town's power couple, sitting side by side on the bleachers.

Seen Melissa McGuire, petite and unremarkable and almost out of place, beside the Strangs, half-watching her husband command his team.

Lance had heard the thunder roar and the lightning crack, had seen the scoreboard begin to fall.

Heard Leah scream.

The anger rose, and the bile in his throat was hot and bitter.

You're too close, Lance.

He felt a chill at the memory of that odd sense of taunting he'd felt just before the scoreboard had fallen. It had been there, and it knew it was winning.

Lance pushed away the thoughts and turned into the high school's parking lot. The announcer's voice came back into focus over the PA, and Lance heard a whooping from the stands, followed by the announcement of a Westhaven touchdown. A collapsed scoreboard and an injured fan were not enough to stop a football game in this town.

Lance pulled the car keys from his pocket, unlocked the door and got in the driver's side, sliding the seat as far back as it would go. Then he sat, waited, thought.

You're too close, Lance.

He looked up at the bright lights and heard another cheer from the crowd and made his decision.

He had nobody. He *was* nobody. And he had nowhere to go.

But here, in Westhaven? There was a girl, and she'd shown him that

I don't care if I'm too close. It doesn't change anything.

a town needed him.

Lance sat back against the seat, his mind made up.

He would get to the bottom of this, even if he had to die in the process.

Lance waited for the game to end. He was going to talk to Bobby Strang, whether Bobby was willing or not.

[27]

LANCE CRACKED THE CAR'S WINDOW, LETTING BOTH AIR and the PA announcer's voice blow through the vehicle's interior. The gentle breezes kept him cool and the announcer's voice kept him updated. Westhaven was winning twenty-eight to seven. Not a blowout, but by Lance's best guess the game had to be nearly over, so Westhaven would add another tally to the victory column.

Sure enough, five minutes later there was a barrage of horns and cheers, and the announcer shouted the final score with gusto and then thanked everybody for coming out and asked them to please drive safely.

And then the people came. They spilled from the too-small gate like a flood breaking through a dam, a densely packed group that seemed never to end, fanning out and widening and scattering loose once past the gate's confines and into the parking lot in search of their vehicles. It was a chaotic scene, the type of thing where children get separated from parents, or an elderly woman falls down and gets trampled, like those disgusting videos they play every Black Friday on the news where somebody nearly dies to get a discounted television. Humanity at its absolute finest.

But while the parking lot was busy and fast-paced, the people were smiling, laughing, high-fiving and celebrating their team's victory. And when the cars switched on their headlights and began the slow process of vacating the lot, they did so in courteous and cautious maneuvers, waving cars in, letting pedestrians through the seams. Lance didn't hear a single horn blow or see a single fist shake from an opened window.

He turned around in his seat and watched cars fall into single-file and follow a path in front of the main office building. In the distance, he saw a police cruiser, lights spinning, parked near the exit and directing traffic in a well-organized manner. Apparently getting cars out of the school's lot was too much a task for Mrs. Bellamy, the legendary civics teacher.

The lot was half-empty, but Lance wasn't concerned about missing Bobby Strang. The team might just be finishing up their postgame coach's speech, and then they'd be stripping off their uniforms and equipment. Some would shower, others would stuff their sweaty bodies into their normal clothes and head out. Eventually, the players would all be gone, but the coaches would stay behind, discussing the game with each other, putting away equipment, tidying things up. Aside from any janitorial staff, the football coaches would be some of the last folks to leave the high school tonight, and Lance had all the time to wait.

Most all the patrons had left the lot, and what remained was three densely packed rows of cars at the very front of the parking area—those who'd arrived first. Players ... and coaches. Sure enough, a few large high school boys began to trickle from the rear of the school, all carrying duffle bags or having tossed light jackets over their shoulders. They wore the faces of winners, the taste of another victory still sweet on their tongues. They climbed into pickup trucks and battered SUVs and lowriders, even one minivan. Engines started and music blared from windows—a hodgepodge of country and rock and rap that mixed into an unruly mess of sound—and then the boys drove away one by one, leaving just Lance in Renee's borrowed Honda, and five other cars parked side by side in the far right corner of the lot.

Twenty minutes later, as Lance was fighting his urge to doze off in the now quiet and still parking lot, Bobby Strang emerged from the school's shadows.

Bobby had untucked his t-shirt, a creased line of sweat visible in the dimly lit parking lot, and he'd put on a Westhaven ball cap. He had a gym bag slung over one shoulder and was fumbling with his car keys as he crossed the lot, heading toward one of the remaining few cars parked in the front.

Lance sat up quickly, ready to make a decision. Ready to make a move.

But then Bobby Strang stopped midstride, maybe ten feet from the closest car, as if something had caught him off guard. He started to turn around, and for a brief moment Lance felt his stomach tighten, figuring somehow Bobby had caught him, knew he was watching. But Bobby's turn continued past Lance's direction, and then he stopped, looking back toward the school.

And then Lance heard a woman's voice, faintly entering the Honda's cab through the cracked windows. Lance couldn't make out the words, but apparently Bobby could, because he suddenly shouted, "Tell him that play might have worked twenty years ago! Tell the old man to let the past go!" He said the words with a smile, and Lance heard laughter coming from the school. And then from the shadows came two figures.

Lance slouched down in the seat, his eyes just above the steering wheel, his knees nearly jammed to his chest. He watched as the figures came into focus, stepping into the cones of light cast by the parking lot's lamps.

Allison Strang—Bobby's mother—said, "You know your father is only trying to help." Her voice was smooth as silk, carried on the night's breeze. Behind her, the second woman came into view. Melissa McGuire entered the light and then put a hand on Bobby's shoulder, gently. "Don't feel bad. He gives Kenny play advice all the time."

"Which I'm sure Kenny promptly and politely ignores," Allison said, and again the group fell into a fit of laughter.

Lance sat up a bit, leaning closer and trying to hear as the laughter fell away and the group continued a conversation at what became a whisper. Too far away to make out well.

What are they talking about? Lance wondered, but then he thought, *Nothing that's going to help me, that's for sure. Why would it?*

There was a buzzing in his pocket and Lance started so fast he hit his head on the car's ceiling. *"Crap!"* he mumbled, swallowing his heart back down. He clawed his cell phone from his pocket and checked the number on the display.

Leah.

His felt a jolt of happiness. Smiled.

He wanted so badly to answer but knew now was not the time.

He ignored the call and looked up.

Allison Strang was looking straight at him.

Lance froze. In the poor light it was tough to tell if she was actually looking directly at him—right at Lance's body—or if she was simply looking in the direction of the car. Could she even see him through the windshield? Lance basically played dead, holding his breath, not blinking, not moving a single muscle or tendon. Not even sure why he was so concerned. So what if she saw him? He was nobody. Just a random guy who'd shown up to watch the state's best team. Here to see what all the hype was about.

But still, he felt fear. He just didn't know why.

Allison Strang looked away, and Lance allowed himself to breathe.

A minute later, Kenny McGuire and Glenn Strang joined the group in the lot, and a few more jokes were made and a few more laughs were had. They all just seemed like decent people having a good time after a great win.

Then they all got into their respective vehicles: the Strangs a BMW SUV, Kenny and Melissa McGuire a newer-model Ford Explorer. Lastly, Bobby got into a Toyota Tundra pickup that looked new and shiny and too flashy for the small town of Westhaven. Maybe a gift from Dad—apparently a bottomless wallet —or a company car, perk of being a VP.

Reverse lights came on and the cars drove out of the lot.

With no real choice, his task not yet completed, Lance started Renee's Honda and followed the caravan.

Yep, he thought, *I'm definitely winging it.*

LANCE CREPT UP TO THE STOP SIGN AT THE EXIT TO THE school. The police car and officer who'd been directing traffic were gone, and Lance idled the Honda for a moment, letting the line of vehicles he planned to follow get a little bit of a distance ahead. They'd turned right. The same direction Deputy Miller had turned earlier. But Lance couldn't think about that right now. He pushed the thoughts of his accident, of Miller's ... *possession* was the only word for it ... away and focused on the present. He flipped open his cell phone and saw Leah had left a voicemail earlier when he'd been forced to ignore her call. He hit the button and listened to it.

"If you're still here ... call me, please."

If I'm still here?

Leah's voice had been soft, apprehensive. Almost timid, as though she was trying hard not to let her real emotions translate through the call.

Lance remembered his conversation with Susan Goodman in the hospital parking lot, right after they'd wheeled Leah inside. He'd been in a bad place then mentally and had fully expected to walk out of the parking lot and then out of town.

Yet here he was.

He scrolled to Leah's number, pressed SEND, and then drove past the stop sign and followed the sets of taillights in the distance. Nothing but darkness on either side of his car.

Leah answered the phone on the first ring. "Are you on a bus?"

"No."

"Are you waiting for a bus?"

"No."

Silence. Then, "So, what are you doing?"

"I'm following Kenny and Melissa McGuire, and the entire Strang family. But really just Bobby."

Silence again. Then, "So you're still doing this?"

"Why wouldn't I be?" He tried to sound convincing.

Leah sighed. "Lance, don't feed me bullshit, please."

Lance kept his eyes locked on the taillights. He'd driven about a mile from the school. A battered speed limit sign said things should move forty-five miles per hour, but the caravan ahead seemed to be moving much faster. "Sorry," he said. "You're right. I thought about leaving. Things are getting dangerous, and it's because of me." The truth was the only option right now. "Whatever's happening in this town, it's not ... I know it's not completely human. It's something ... worse. And it knows I'm here, and it knows I care about you, and therefore you and I and anybody we associate with from this point forward could be considered targets."

There was more silence now. Longer than before. Finally, Leah spoke, slowly. "You ... you think this—this *thing* is what caused the sign to fall on me?"

"I do," Lance said. He had no doubt about it.

He was amazed at how accepting Leah was. She didn't question him about what he'd just told her and didn't sound dubious when she spoke, as if she wasn't quite sure she could swallow that particular pill. She just went with it.

She trusted him. Completely.

"Well," she said, "it missed."

Despite himself, Lance chuckled. "Not completely. How bad is it, really?"

"Not terrible. No surgery needed, but it's in a cast. Hurt like hell."

"I'm so sorry," Lance said, because he was. He truly was.

"Don't worry about me right now. Why are you following Bobby?"

"I'm going to ask him what he knows."

If Leah thought this was a bad idea, she didn't say so. "I guess I'll need to call Renee and tell her she can let the kids sleep in one of the motel rooms until you get back, since I'm sure it'll be past their bedtime. You've got her car, don't forget."

Lance nodded. "And it's coming very much in handy at the moment."

Ahead, the McGuires and Bobby Strang both turned on their left turn signals and slowed. Glenn and Allison Strang kept driving, surely headed to their luxurious abode in a more secluded area.

Lance slowed as well, letting Bobby and the McGuires keep their distance. "How pissed was your dad?" he asked.

"Oh," Leah said, as if she'd forgotten. "Very. I'm pretty sure you're a dead man if he ever sees you again."

"Yeah, I gathered that."

"I tried to tell him you had nothing to do with what happened to me, but ... well, it doesn't matter. You're a boy, I'm his girl. Enough said."

Lance nodded again. "Well, I'll try to keep my distance."

"From him or from me?"

Lance smiled. "Him, ideally."

Silence again. Then, "Good."

Lance made the left turn and found himself in a cluttered suburban neighborhood. Modest, but nice. Middle-class and tidy. A neighborhood watch sign reflected in his headlights. The McGuires' Explorer made a right turn a quarter mile up the road, heading deeper into the guts of the rows of houses, but Bobby Strang's Tundra kept straight. Alone.

"I need to go," Lance said. "Just me and Bobby now."

"Okay. Be careful. And remember, Bobby's a nice guy. Let me know what you find out. And I'll text you when I get out of here."

"Where are you going?"

"The motel, hopefully. But I think Daddy is hoping I'll go home with him for the night."

Lance said his goodbye and hung up the phone, following Bobby's Tundra and wondering just how nice of a guy Bobby truly was.

Bobby Strang turned left down a side street, and then three houses later, the brake lights came on and the large truck slowed and flicked on a turn signal. Lance slowed, watched as Bobby drove into his driveway and an automatic garage door began to open, its chain and motor whirring in the still night. Lance drove past, taking note of the house, trying not to look too much like he was spying.

Bobby Strang lived in a two-story brick home with an attached two-car garage. Nothing special architecturally, a big brick box with the standard window placement and roof slants, but way more house than a single man in his early twenties needed. Lance again wondered at just how deep Glenn Strang's wallet was. The front porch lights were on, and Lance could see a sparse but well-kept flowerbed lining a stone walkway leading from the driveway to the front door. The yard was empty otherwise. No trees or bushes or gazebos or anything decorative. No basketball hoop out front. Of course not. The Strangs were a football family.

Lance drove down the street and found it to be a dead end. A cul de sac that had a house to its left and right sides, but nothing straight ahead at the end. Lance killed the headlights and carefully pulled the car into the soft, grassy shoulder, the passenger-side mirror maybe two feet away from a tree line, dense and dark. He could have just pulled into the driveway—he was only there to talk, after all. But, as Lance had learned throughout his life, as well as during his brief time spent in Westhaven, things had a way of not always going as well, or as regularly, as you often planned. If things got out of hand and he had to make a quick exit, he didn't want potential witnesses to remember seeing the car parked in Bobby Strang's driveway. In a town like Westhaven, eventually the information would point back to Renee, which might lead to the motel, which might lead to Leah. It was a risk Lance wanted to avoid.

He waited five minutes after parking. He wanted to let Bobby Strang take care of whatever small things most people did as soon as they got home—kick off the shoes, toss the keys in the bowl by the door, check the day's mail, grab a drink. After waiting, Lance got out and walked back up the street. The night air had grown warmer and had mixed with the moisture, causing Lance's shirt to feel as though it were sticking to him. The front porch lights were still on outside Bobby's front door, and as Lance walked up the driveway, glancing over his shoulder at the houses across the street to see if any prying eyes might be peering out behind pulled-back curtains (the neighborhood watch sign flashed across his memory), he realized that what he was about to do seemed pretty crazy. Oh well, he'd never been one for normalcy.

He followed the stone walkway and stepped up onto the stoop, debated between knocking and ringing the bell, and then decided and pressed his finger to the button, hearing a soft melody of chimes from inside the home.

The door opened almost immediately, Bobby Strang appearing and standing with the door fully open. Sure enough, there was an open beer bottle in his hand, and behind him Lance could see the flickering blue reflection of a television screen.

"Who are you?" Bobby asked. Not so much with malice or mistrust, but genuine confusion, as if maybe he'd been expecting somebody else.

Somebody who has no idea what he's doing, that's who I am, Lance thought.

"My name's Lance. I'm a friend of Leah's."

Bobby's brow crinkled, further confusion sweeping across his face. "Leah?"

"From the motel," Lance said. "She, uh, she asked me to stop by and see you." Lance figured maybe playing the friend angle would help him out, if only to offer an opening to really get to his point without a confrontation.

"Leah?"

I did say that, didn't I? Or is my head injury acting up?

"From the motel," Lance said again.

"The motel," Bobby said slowly, as if the puzzle pieces were slowly sliding together, but not quite interlocking.

"Samuel's sister," Lance said, hoping the new name would jump-start Bobby's brain.

It did more than that. At the mention of Samuel, the color literally drained from Bobby's face. He recovered quickly, taking a swig from his bottle to help hide his brief change in emotion, but Lance saw it all the same. "Right, Leah," Bobby said. "She's a great girl, love her to pieces, that one." Then, slowly, more cautiously: "Why did she send you to see me? Oh, and hey! Wasn't it her who got hurt tonight at the game, when the scoreboard fell? Man, that was *insane!* Oh man, is she okay? Is that why you're here? Oh God, does she want to sue the school or something, because look, I don't really have any—"

Lance held up his hand. Bobby looked at it, stopped talking.

Lance was getting tired, and his head was beginning to hurt again, and honestly, for some reason he found himself not liking Bobby Strang very much, though he couldn't quite say why. Just one of those vibes he sometimes got with people.

"Look, Bobby, I'm here because Leah's asked me to help figure out what happened to her brother, and as far as anyone knows, you're the last person to have seen Samuel alive before he disappeared. So I was hoping you could tell me exactly what happened that day, answer any questions I might have, and then I'll be out of your way and let you get back to your television."

Bobby said nothing. Took another sip from his bottle, eyes never leaving Lance's, narrowed to slits as he contemplated what Lance had said.

"Leah wants me to tell you about that day with Samuel?" he asked.

Is he going to make me repeat everything?

"That's correct, sir."

Bobby nodded. "Why? That was years ago."

Lance didn't like that answer. "Does that make it any less important?"

Bobby didn't say anything to this, and Lance hoped the guy was kicking himself for coming off so nonchalant about a missing person—a former teammate and friend, for goodness sake.

"Look," Lance tried again, still waiting for his invitation to come inside and make his attempt to get to the meat and potatoes of the conversation, "Leah told me you and Samuel were good friends, and she told me what a great guy you are, and how wonderful your family was to hers after her brother went missing." Then he laid it on a little thick, hoping a small ego stroke might get Bobby talking. "She told me that if anybody in Westhaven other than her and her father cared about figuring out what happened to Samuel, it'd be you, and that you'd do anything you could to help us out, because that was the kind of stand-up guy you were."

Bobby listened, rubbed the back of his neck with his free hand. "I always liked Leah," he said. "Hell, if she wasn't Samuel's sister, I might have made a move. Tried to, anyway." He laughed the way guys laugh with each other when they talk about women, and Lance wanted to kick him in the teeth.

Lance took a deep breath and said, "So, can we talk? Just for a few minutes?"

Bobby Strang took one more long look at Lance and then his face changed. He offered a small smile and stepped aside, motioning for Lance to come in. "Sure," he said. "If Leah thinks it'll help."

Lance heard the rustling of the treetops behind the houses as a breeze blew through, the leaves dancing and branches swaying and sounding almost like a steady rainfall. Then there was an odd aroma in the air, something not unpleasant, but out of place. Sweet, but surprising. And then, as he stepped into Bobby Strang's house, he heard the faintest of voices among the sounds, a whisper, calling to him from somewhere far away.

It was the voice of Annabelle Winters.

"*Careful*," she said.

Then he figured out what the aroma was. It was the mixture of cinnamon and sugar and fruit. Apple pie.

Lance turned around as soon as he heard Bobby Strang close and lock the front door. Then Bobby reached behind his back, quickly, skillfully, and brought his hand back around, pointing the barrel of a pistol directly at Lance's chest.

Leah, Lance thought. *Bobby is not such a nice guy.*

[29]

LANCE STARED AT THE GUN BOBBY STRANG WAS POINTING at Lance's chest. It was matte black in color, smooth and flawless and brand-new in appearance. Bobby Strang wasn't into sport shooting—not with the weapon he was holding, that was for sure. No, Lance figured this gun had been purchased specifically for protection, for home intruders, which Lance didn't technically think he was since Bobby had invited him inside. Which was a point that seemed irrelevant should Lance be shot dead. Hard to win a court case from the grave.

Bobby Strang stood still, silently staring at Lance and keeping the gun trained directly at Lance's center mass. He looked unsure, as if he were expecting Lance to make some sort of play for the weapon, some sort of attempt to fight back. He appeared hesitant, though not incapable of pulling the trigger.

Lance replayed the moment in his head when Bobby had reached behind his back and pulled out the weapon, likely tucked into the waistband of his pants for easy access.

No way he was carrying that at the school, Lance thought. *He slid that into his pants when he got home.*

Which meant ...

"She said you might come," Bobby Strang said, his voice suddenly full of contempt.

Which meant he was expecting me.

The gun wobbled a bit as Bobby spoke, but Lance saw him tighten his grip to get it under control.

Bobby thrust the gun forward one time. "She told me you were here to ruin it all."

"Did she?" Lance asked. Bobby had unwittingly confirmed what Lance and Leah had grown to seriously suspect. There was a woman in Westhaven who was either directly or indirectly responsible for the football players' disappearances.

Bobby nodded. "She said you thought you were here to save them all," he said, "but really you were just making it that much easier."

Lance nodded this time. "Of course. I like to do what I can to help."

Bobby Strang gave Lance a funny look, digesting the sarcasm. Once it hit, he jerked the gun forward again and spoke louder. "You think this is a joke? You think she's just going to let you walk away from all this? Uh-uh. You're toast pal. I hate to say it, but you're a dead man."

Lance had no idea what exactly was going on, but he did know that the longer he could keep Bobby talking, the more time he would have to figure out what he was going to do in order not to die. Which seemed like a top priority at the moment.

"How did she know I was here?" Lance asked.

Bobby shrugged, laughed. "Fuck if I know, man. She just ... how does she do any of the stuff she does? My dad calls her the Voodoo Bitch Doctor, but we don't understand any of it. We just ... she's always—"

There was a loud blast of music from Bobby's pants pocket, startling both men. The tune was "Eye of the Tiger" by

212

Survivor, and Lance tapped his foot to the beat as Bobby cursed, nearly dropped the beer bottle to the floor to free up a hand, and struggled to pull the phone free from his pocket. The other hand made a point to keep the gun aimed at Lance. Lance had always liked the song.

Bobby Strang's iPhone screen was lit up bright when he pulled it from his pocket, but Lance didn't get a chance to see the name or number on the screen. Bobby answered directly. No greeting, no small talk, just, "I've got him."

Bobby was quiet for a minute, listening to the voice on the other end, which Lance could not hear at all. At that point he wished Bobby had some sort of hearing impairment requiring the volume on the phone to be turned up much louder. Darn his youthfulness. While Lance waited, he considered something else Bobby Strang had told him—again, likely unwittingly—which was that his father, Glenn Strang, was also fully aware of what was happening in town. Maybe.

(*My dad calls her the Voodoo Bitch Doctor...*)

Which again confirmed another suspicion, though this one had been less certain, which was that Glenn Strang had had a hand in the boys' disappearances as well. Again, either directly or indirectly.

So far, two of the three Strang family members were guilty.

And the third member of the family just happened to be an extremely attractive woman.

Lance looked at Bobby Strang's face, which had seemed to drain of most its color. He looked afraid; he looked worried. "Okay," Bobby said. "Okay, yes, if you're sure."

This time Lance did hear something from the phone's speaker. A loud burst of noise that was a human voice but impossible to pick any words from. Bobby's face reddened. "Yes, I know, I'm sorry." There was a beat, and then Bobby pulled the phone from his face and stuffed it back into his pocket. He looked at Lance.

"Wrong number?" Lance asked, wishing the ghost of Annabelle Winters would show up and drop the world's largest apple pie on top of Bobby Strang's head, crushing him to the floor and giving Lance the exit he needed. Lance figured the odds of that happening were slim.

Bobby Strang didn't even smile at the joke. Lance, realizing his soft and humorous attempts to disarm Bobby were falling short, decided to try a new offensive. A more aggressive one.

"You realize she's been trying to either kill me or scare me out of town from the moment I arrived, right?"

Bobby said nothing.

"Yeah, that's right," Lance said. "Hard to believe I'm still here, right? I've already survived a hurricane gust of wind and a fatal car accident, and I didn't tuck tail and run when she tried to murder Leah with that scoreboard tonight."

Bobby Strang's eyes lit up then, and his face grew surprised. "Wait ... that was—that was her that did that?"

Lance rolled his eyes. "Come on, Bobby. You're not that slow, are you? I thought you were on her team. How do you not see that was her threatening me? She went after Leah because she thought it would make me back off. You know, since Leah and I are ... well ..." He left it at that, would let Bobby's imagination take care of the rest. "So, you've got to ask yourself a question here, Bobby. If she's failed three times, why do you think *you* are going to be able to stop me?"

Bobby Strang stared at Lance for a long time, long enough for Lance to get bored and begin to whistle "Eye of the Tiger." But he'd only made it a few notes in when Bobby suddenly snapped, "Shut up! Shut up now!"

Lance stopped whistling.

Bobby said, "I'm not. She'll finish you off. All I have to do is get you there." He took a step forward, the gun still raised. "And the way I see it, right now I've got a pretty solid advantage. Wouldn't you agree?"

Lance glanced to the gun, then back to Bobby's eyes. "I would."

"Thought so. So do me a favor and turn around and walk forward, hands up, into the kitchen."

Lance waited a few more seconds, just in case the giant pie was going to fall, then resigned himself to being temporarily out of options and turned around. He put his hands up, as directed, and walked down a wide hallway past a living room with the television on and tuned to the local news, no doubt in anticipation of catching the local sports highlights from the night. After the living room was a closed door, behind which Lance assumed was some sort of coat closet or half bath, and then the hallway spilled into a large kitchen. Expansive, mostly empty countertops and expensive-looking stainless-steel appliances. Very nice. Lance reached a kitchen island, and Bobby said, "Okay, that's far enough."

Lance stopped and waited, eyes flickering across the kitchen, looking for anything that might serve as some sort of weapon.

There was, predictably, a butcher block full of knives sitting atop the counter next to the stove stop. Too far away to grab, and too ineffective against a firearm unless you were right on top of the person you were trying to attack. No good. There was a fancy coffeemaker with a stainless-steel carafe next to the sink, which might be good for slamming into a temple, or across the bridge of the nose, but again, the distance thing was a problem. Unfortunately for Lance, there was no spare pistol lying on a counter nearby. Nothing within reach at all, actually, except a stack of mail and some loose change and a bottle cap, presumably from the bottle Bobby had been holding on Lance's arrival.

Lance had his own fists to fight with, plus his large feet, but he wasn't trained in the way of fighting techniques, and a bullet would easily go through his skin and muscle and tendons and bone if he was merely a second too slow.

Guns sucked. *Thanks, NRA.*

In Lance's mind, he started to hear one of his mother's anti-gun rants—a topic she was vehemently outspoken on, especially after every mass shooting that seemed to increasingly plague the United States of America—but Bobby Strang spoke from just behind him, bringing him back to his own ever-increasingly unfortunate situation.

"Don't move," Bobby said.

Lance didn't move.

Bobby slid in behind him and then sidestepped to the left. Lance turned his head and saw Bobby grab a key ring off a hook by a door that must lead to the garage. Bobby kept the gun trained on Lance and used his other hand to open the door, then reached inside and felt along the wall until Lance heard the click of a light switch, and then the interior of the garage lit up with bright overhead lighting. Bobby stepped backward through the door and down a small flight of two steps, then took another step back and motioned with the gun for Lance to come out. "This way," he said. "We're going for a ride."

Lance took a couple slow steps toward the door. It swung outward, into the garage, as opposed as inward toward the kitchen. Another unfortunate thing. Lance could have tried to quickly duck and slam the door shut and then race himself back out the house and maybe make it to Renee's car, or possibly disappear into the woods for the second time in one day.

"Would it be easier if I just followed you in my own car?" Lance asked, stepping out onto the first step. "Then I can just head on home after we're finished."

For a moment, a brief, hilarious moment, it looked like

Bobby Strang was actually weighing the option, deciding if what Lance had suggested might indeed make things simpler. Then his simple brain registered the sarcasm and he snapped, "Just get the fuck down here, would ya? *Slowly*."

Lance stepped down from the remaining step and stood on the large garage's concrete floor. The right half of the garage—the half in which Lance was standing—had been converted into some sort of workshop. To Lance's right, a large tool chest and workbench were pressed against the wall. Power tools and random unidentifiable bits and parts of machinery and wood and paint cans littered the benchtop and floor around it. A row of brooms and rakes and shovels hung from neatly aligned hooks along the wall directly behind Lance, and he suddenly remembered that scene at the end of the first *Home Alone* movie where the old guy knocks the Wet Bandits out with his snow shovel. It was something Lance would love to try and recreate at the moment, though, much like the knives in the kitchen, he knew he'd never pull off the maneuver in time if Bobby Strang did truly plan on using the gun to incapacitate him if need be.

There was a pair of dirty black flip-flops on the floor by the stairs. Less-than-ideal weaponry.

There was a creaking noise, and Lance's gaze turned back to Bobby, who'd just lowered the tailgate on the massive Tundra parked on the opposite side of the garage.

"Come over here," Bobby said, always motioning with the pistol. "Stand right here." He pointed to the ground directly behind the truck.

"Am I going to ride in the back like a dog? That's not really the safest, you know. Would probably be better if—"

"Didn't I tell you to shut up?"

Lance shut up. Figured he'd probably pressed his luck enough for one potentially deadly encounter.

Lance walked, his eyes never leaving the direction Bobby

had the gun trained, which was always Lance's chest. Lance had a few inches on Bobby, so the man literally just had to hold his arm straight out to be aligned perfectly with Lance's heart. Lance walked around to the back of the truck, Bobby turning in a small semicircle as he did so, and then stopped directly behind the truck's opened tailgate.

"Good boy," Bobby said.

I'm pretty sure I'm older than him. How disrespectful.

"Now, stay put for a second. You got it?"

Lance said nothing.

"I said, do you have it?" Bobby asked.

Lance raised his hand, as if to ask a question in class. Bobby's eyes followed it, stepped back as if braced for an attack, the gun thrust out further than before. Lance didn't move, just stood with his hand raised. Bobby stared for two seconds, then three, then he got it. "Yes?"

Lance cleared his throat. "You told me to shut up. If you want me to answer, well ... just make up your mind, okay?"

Bobby Strang's face turned a deep shade of red, and then he sighed and spoke in a voice that said he was clearly tired of playing the game. "Just don't fucking move, okay? Don't move and I won't shoot you. Those are the rules. Got it?"

Lance said he got it.

Bobby nodded and stared at Lance for another five seconds before he reached forward with his free hand and slid a large duffle bag toward him, pulling it down the truck's bed toward the tailgate. He raised his gun-wielding arm up, keeping the barrel of the pistol perfectly positioned. One-handed, he struggled to unzip the bag, cursing as it slid away from him on the first two tries. He finally got it open on the third, and his hand disappeared inside, fishing around for a moment before coming back into view holding a slightly used roll of good old-fashioned duct tape.

Lance knew where this was going, and in the same instant, he looked at his surroundings, tried to predict the next few moments' worth of events, and thought he might have found a potential opportunity to turn the tables on his captor.

He took one small step forward. A shuffle, really, just a slight readjustment of his stance. But he figured it would be enough.

Bobby Strang forewent zipping the bag closed and slid it away, back toward the front of the truck. He put the roll of tape in front of his own face and used his teeth to pry loose the end and then unspool six inches of tape, just enough to get it started.

"Hold out your wrists," he said. "Together, like this." He held out his own wrists to demonstrate the position he wanted Lance to mimic, and Lance could hardly believe his luck. Bobby Strang couldn't have made himself any more vulnerable to Lance's plan if Lance had given him verbal instructions and a diagram to follow.

Lance was standing facing the bed of the truck, and Bobby Strang was beside him, standing just to the side of the tailgate. When he held out his arms, one hand holding the roll of duct tape, the other hand holding the gun, he held them out directly over the truck's opened tailgate, his forearms right in line with the hinge.

Lance knew there was the possibility of the gun going off during his next move, but he also knew if he didn't act now, he might not get another chance. He figured his odds were fifty-fifty. Not the greatest, but clear-cut all the same.

Lance had always been quick. It was one of the reasons he'd been such a great basketball player. Folks always assumed it was because he was tall. And, yeah, that certainly helped, but it was the quickness that sold it.

In the blink of an eye, Lance dipped down, reached his hands under the tailgate, and then flung it up with all the strength he could summon. There was a soft, dull resistance at impact, and a high-pitched yelp escaped Bobby Strang's lips before being followed by a harsh and violent scream as his arms were completely smashed between the tailgate and the end of the truck. Despite the human noise, Lance heard the gun clatter out of Bobby's hands, could make out the sound of the steel against the truck bed.

He didn't waste any time looking for it. Instead he moved in to end it all.

Bobby Strang was dumbstruck, staring down at his bloody arms. Lance took one step forward and grabbed Bobby's head in both his hands and

(*Oh my God!*)

smashed the man's face into the side of the truck. Bobby Strang's body went instantly limp and crumpled to the floor.

Lance stood, his heart racing and his mind reeling from what he'd just seen.

[30]

Lance didn't look for the gun, but he did quickly stick his hand into Bobby Strang's front pants pocket and pull out his iPhone and car keys. Then he bolted back up the two steps, into the kitchen, and out the front door. He ran as fast as he could back down the street, filling his lungs with the cool night air. It tasted sweet and intoxicating. It tasted like freedom. How close had he come to meeting his end? Too close.

He pushed the thought away and kept running, reaching Renee's Honda and flinging Bobby Strang's car keys overhand into the woods at the end of the cul de sac. Lance didn't feel like being chased right now. He kept the cell phone, though, sliding it into the same pocket as his own flip phone and folding himself into the driver's seat. He cranked the engine and, in a moment of clarity and caution, managed to calm himself enough to slowly pull the car off the grass and gently accelerate up the street, back past Bobby's house, and then turn right. Only then did Lance risk stepping on the gas a little to put as much distance between himself and Bobby Strang as he could.

He replayed the original trip in his mind and managed to reverse the course and replicate the correct turns, and then he found himself back on the main road, heading back toward the direction of Westhaven High School, back toward the Route 19 intersection, which would lead left into town or right toward the motel.

His heart was still pounding in his chest, but he'd gotten his breathing under control. He gripped the steering wheel tightly, sitting up as straight as he could in the seat without his head hitting the ceiling, eyes straining to see out into the night with only the help of the weak headlight beams. He was on alert, terrified that whoever had been on the other end of the phone with Bobby Strang would somehow instantly know that things had not gone as planned, and that Lance was on the loose. Therefore, Lance had a very large target on his back, and from what he'd seen thus far in Westhaven, a new threat could take any shape, could be any person. Heck, at this point he wouldn't be too surprised if the Honda he was driving suddenly did its best *Christine* impression and drove off the road, slamming headfirst into a tree.

As the car ate up a few miles of road without incident, Lance slouched a little and took a deep breath. He was approaching the high school, the bright lights no longer burning and the gates to the parking lot closed. The fun was over. Lance took stock of how much new information he now possessed since the last time he'd been in this very same spot. What had initially been a gaping-hole mystery now had quite a bit filled in.

Lance now knew for certain that there was a woman involved who seemed to be giving the orders and was probably directly responsible for the boys' disappearances. Lance wasn't sure how the power to control the weather and possess police officers played into things, but he was certain that if he found this woman, he'd figure out the rest whether he wanted to or not.

Bobby and Glenn Strang were also key players somehow.

Okay, maybe not key players, but they had a hand in the mess, and both seemed to be held in some sort of grip by the woman in charge.

Which, without the last bit of information Lance had accidentally gained, would have been enough to suspect Allison Strang. But ... with what Lance had just seen, he was positive Allison Strang was the woman running the show. She was the danger. She was the reason Westhaven had suffered so much loss. She was the reason families had been devastated and torn apart and uprooted.

Lance had never planned on getting the visions, and he could never figure out why some people's lives flooded into him like a rushing river and others didn't show him a single thing; not their favorite color or middle name or even their current thought. But when Lance had grabbed Bobby Strang's head to slam it into the side of the truck, he'd seen something so shocking and disgusting it made his stomach turn.

It had happened in an instant, as if, at the single second Lance and Bobby Strang's bodies had connected, Lance had received a file upload of Bobby's memory at the fastest bandwidth known to man. Faster, even. A single touch, instant knowledge.

Lance shuddered as he remembered the scene. The bedroom, the ruffled sheets, the backside of her naked torso, the long blond hair sticking to her shoulders that were slick with sweat, the gentle moan as she rocked back and forth atop Bobby Strang's—

There was a vibration in Lance's pocket, and he jerked back to reality. He'd not passed a single car on the road and was about to approach the stop sign at the Route 19 intersection. He slowed the car and flipped on his right turn signal. With the car stopped, he reached into his pocket and pulled out his flip phone, for one fearful moment thinking that it might be Bobby's phone ringing instead, with *her* on the other end, wondering what was taking so long, or worse, calling specifically to speak to Lance because she knew what he had done. Lance knew he'd have to confront her eventually, but he wanted it to be on his own terms.

But then Lance realized he didn't hear "Eye of the Tiger" playing, and he knew it was his own phone ringing. He saw Leah's name and quickly answered, hoping he hadn't taken too long.

"Leah?"

"Hey, I'm back at the motel. Susan dropped me off after I finally convinced Daddy I was fine to be on my own. Where are you? How'd it go with Bobby?"

Lance thought about how to answer this. He made the right turn and drove the Honda toward the motel, toward Leah.

"It didn't go so great for me for a while. But it ended up worse for Bobby."

She paused for a second, then said, "Okay. What does that mean?"

"It means Bobby's probably going to need a good dentist, and I got us a lot of information without trying too hard."

Apprehensively, Leah said, "Why does Bobby need a dentist?"

"Because I slammed his face into the side of that expensive truck he drives."

"Lance! Why?"

"Well, for starters, he pulled a gun on me."

Silence.

Lance could see the lights from the motel up the road. Thirty seconds away now.

"But, Bobby's got bigger problems than some busted teeth," Lance said. "Like the fact he's sleeping with his mother."

LANCE PULLED THE BATTERED HONDA INTO THE MOTEL'S parking lot and parked it in front of the office door. He killed the headlights and the engine and sat in the darkened car's interior, resting his head against the headrest.

He was tired. His body ached—his head, his wrist, every muscle—and he felt like he could fall asleep right there in the driver's seat and sleep through the night and most of the next day.

You can have playtime when your chores are done, mister.

His mother's voice, dug up from another memory he'd stored away. He'd heard her say this a thousand times during his youth, and while it didn't exactly apply to his current situation, he caught the drift. He pushed himself away from the seat, grabbed his backpack from the back and got out of the car. The air was still cool, but there was no breeze. Lance stood next to the Civic and scanned the parking lot. There was one pickup truck parked at the far end of the lot, right in front of the last room on the row. A guest, Lance figured. Not a threat.

He walked up to the sidewalk and pulled on the office door. It moved maybe an eighth of an inch before coming to a sudden, violent stop, shaking and rattling in the frame and causing more noise than even seemed possible in the still night. Lance jumped, shocked at the sound and the vibration up his arm, and then took a step back. The door was locked.

A small tendril of panic swirled up his spine.

She knows what happened, Lance thought. *The woman— Allison Strang—knows what I did to her son, and she came straight for Leah. Or, at least, she sent someone straight for Leah.*

Lance had just started to dart his eyes around the lot again, looking for something he could use to smash the glass pane out of the office door and make his way in, when Renee's face peeked from between the blinds, and then the noise of a dead-bolt clicking out of place found Lance's ears.

Renee pushed the door open and stepped outside. She was wearing a dirty zip-up parka, as if it were winter and not a crisp fall night, and her hair hung down around her face in untidy strands. She looked tired. But Lance thought that Renee might be a woman who always looked tired, no matter what hour of the day. Probably rolled-out-of-bed tired.

"She's inside," Renee said, her voice soft. "She's resting in bed. She wants you to come back and lock the door behind you."

Lance nodded. "Thank you for the car. It ... well, it probably saved my life."

If Renee heard him, she didn't seem to care. She asked, "Can you help me carry the boys to the car? They're sleeping, and they've gotten so *heavy*."

Lance stood on the sidewalk, his body pleading for rest. But he knew his mother would have slapped him to next Wednesday if she ever found out he'd refused to help a kind, tired single mother of two. "Of course," Lance said. "Where are they?"

The boys had been sleeping in the room next to Lance's. The room was identical to Lance's except for the Star Wars nightlight that had been plugged into the outlet along the outer wall. Renee unplugged it and stuck it into the pocket of her parka. "I'm glad I remembered this. I'd have never gotten them down otherwise."

The boys looked so small in the bed, but they'd managed to splay their limbs over and across each other in a way that made it appear that they'd had an impromptu game of Twister before falling off to sleep. Lance approached the bed and gently untangled the first boy's legs from the other's and lifted him gently up. The boy's head fell to Lance's shoulder, and his arms instinctively wrapped around his neck. Lance smelled the scent of a no-tears baby shampoo and flashed back to his youth. His mother had used the same brand on him. He'd never forget the smell.

He walked carefully back to the car and deposited the first boy into the backseat, buckling him in before heading back for boy number two. With the same routine repeated, Renee closed the room's door and stood by the car next to Lance, who was more winded than he should have been after carrying two small boys a total of maybe twenty-five yards. Lance and Renee looked at each other for a moment, an odd calmness and comfort somehow hovering over them, as if the endeavor of getting the boys into the car had sealed some sort of bond between them.

Lance was about to thank Renee again for the car and head inside, but she asked, "Why are you here?"

Lance stared at her, saw the inquisition in her eyes. It was as if she knew he was something more than what he appeared to be, as if she recognized something brighter burning inside him.

Lance wasn't sure what to say.

(*Do you, a person with your gifts, honestly believe things could be so random?*)

"Honestly," he said, "I'm here because right now I think this is just where I'm supposed to be."

Renee nodded, as if this made all the sense in the world. Then she took a step forward and kissed Lance on the cheek. "Thank you," she said. She got in the car, started the engine with a sputter, and drove away.

Lance watched her drive out of sight, then turned and went into the office.

———

The motel's office was brightly lit, as usual, but empty. The television was off. Whatever traces of Renee's two young children there'd been earlier were now cleaned up and tucked away, and things were as they should be. Lance thumbed the deadbolt behind him, then switched on the NO VACANCY sign for good measure. He didn't think Leah would mind.

He adjusted his backpack over one shoulder and crossed the room, the floorboards creaking under his weight.

"Lance, is that you?" Leah's voice called out from behind her closed bedroom door at the far end of the office.

"It is I, young maiden! Your valiant knight, back from an adventure in the deepest, darkest corner of the kingdom."

He reached the door and turned the handle and cracked the door a bit, peered in. Leah was sitting up in bed, her ankle propped up on a pillow. The television was on, muted, a late-night talk show host sitting behind a desk with a celebrity Lance recognized but could not name talking animatedly from the guest's chair.

Leah looked at Lance blankly. "You're weird."

Then she smiled, and Lance smiled and pushed the door completely open and stepped in. "I know," he said. "But you gotta admit it's better than being boring."

Leah was wearing a baggy Westhaven sweatshirt and matching sweatpants. Her right foot was clad in a bright pink sock, her left foot encased in a cast, only the tips of her toes poking out the top. Lance sat gingerly on the bed, and they looked at each other for a silent moment. Then he leaned forward and kissed her forehead, then her lips. When their lips parted and he pulled away, Leah smiled up at him.

"I'm glad you're okay," he said. "You have no idea. I'm so sorry."

She pushed him away and laughed and said, "I'm *fine*. Don't worry about me. Tell me what the hell you were talking about on the phone! You think Bobby Strang is sleeping with his mother?"

Lance took a deep breath and adjusted himself on the bed, pulling one leg up under him and facing Leah.

Then he told her everything that had happened. From the moment he'd left the high school parking lot to the moment he'd escaped from Bobby Strang's house and driven back to the motel. The whole story, no detail avoided—except one.

Leah sat slack-jawed, shaking her head the more Lance talked. When he was finished, Leah was quiet for a minute, digesting his story. She shook her head and said, "Unbelievable. I just ... they've always been so ... so *nice*."

Lance said nothing. He'd long known that some of the purest of evil could hide behind the widest of grins.

Then anger fumed from Leah's face. "And all this time, he's been lying! Lying to the police, lying to my family! He knows what happened to Samuel and he fucking lied about it!"

Lance said nothing. He let her vent.

"And the timing makes perfect sense, doesn't it? The year the Strangs came into town was the same year the first boy went missing. Samuel."

Lance said nothing.

Then Leah perked up. "Hey! None of what you told me explains how you know Bobby is having sex with his mother. He didn't ... I mean, of course he didn't come right out and say that, did he?"

And here was the moment Lance had known was coming. He knew he couldn't avoid it, and he didn't want to. He was compelled to tell Leah, craved telling her, in fact. But unleashing the full truth of what he was, what he could do, onto somebody was something he was always apprehensive about. It was the final judgment, the last true test of whether the person sitting across from him would stand by his side or run away laughing, recommending Lance book a room in a nuthouse.

He looked at Leah, and in her eyes he saw something. Was it curiosity, or was it trust? Was it compassion, or was it concern?

"In order for me to tell you how I know," he said, "I have to tell you everything. Everything about me and who I am. The best I can, anyway. You already know some of it, but there's more."

She didn't even hesitate. "Okay."

So Lance told her.

[32]

LANCE HAD STARTED WITH A RECAP OF SOME OF THE things he'd already told her, earlier, on his first night in West-haven. Then he worked his way up to the crazier stuff, like the visions he sometimes got—those snapshots of life—when he touched somebody. And of course—and he hesitated here, even though he knew of all the people he'd met in his life recently, Leah was the most likely to take it all in stride—his ability to communicate with the dead. He phrased it this way, "communicate with the dead," because that was a lot easier to swallow than blurting out, "I see dead people." Thanks to Shyamalan's *The Sixth Sense*, Lance could never use that phrase without it being tainted.

Leah had been quiet through all his explanation, never saying a word, just staring up at him with wide-eyed fascination and nodding from time to time as if she completely understood everything Lance was saying. It wasn't until he got to the communicating with the dead part that she finally spoke up to ask a question. Lance couldn't blame her.

"Wait, what do you mean you can communicate with them?

Like, you hold a séance or something? You can speak to them across dimensions, or ... what?"

Lance shook his head. "That's movie stuff. Well, yeah, maybe some people do it that way. Who am I to say what's phony and what's not? But for me it's a lot simpler. Sometimes they visit me in my dreams. Sometimes they whisper things to me in my head, show me things. But often..." He sighed. *Here we go.* "Often they just show up next to me and start talking. Though it's never for very long, and usually not frequently. I think it takes a lot of ... energy, I guess, to show themselves like that. Like I said, I can't explain this stuff, but I've long since had to accept it."

"Since when?" Leah asked, and it was the simplest of questions she could have chosen, and Lance loved her for it.

"Birth, basically."

Leah was quiet again for a while. Lance sat on the bed and took her hand in his and held it while she thought, secretly hoping to maybe pick up some of her wavelengths to see if she thought he was off his rocker, and she was contemplating the best way to tell him to get the heck out of her room. He picked up nothing. It never worked when he wanted it to.

"Do you see bad things, too?" Leah asked.

Lance's stomach dropped.

"You know," Leah said, "if you can see dead people, can you see, like, demons or something?"

Lance felt a chill up his spine as he remembered events from his past. "Yes," he said, and that was all.

Leah must have heard the coldness in his voice, or maybe she didn't want any further verification that spirits of the damned walked among them, because she dropped the subject.

With the summary of Lance's gifts complete, he went on to explain the vision he'd had when he'd grabbed Bobby Strang's head in the garage. Leah listened with a disgusted look on her face, shaking her head. "How ...?" she started. "How is that even possible? Like ... how can they even ... oh God, that's so gross!"

Lance agreed. "It is gross. But I think it's incredibly significant. Allison Strang has some sort of power, that's for sure, and she's got a hold on Bobby and Glenn Strang as well. She has to. Blackmail, maybe. Heck, maybe she's basically raping her own son and using some sort of guilt trip, some threat of embarrassment and a destroyed reputation to force him to go along with everything that's happening. Forcing him to help her."

"And Glenn?" Leah asked. "Why him?"

Lance thought, then shook his head. "I'm not sure yet."

"The Eye of the Tiger" blasted from Lance's pocket, and he jumped again and bumped Leah's ankle with his elbow. "I'm so sorry!" he said, pulling the phone out.

She laughed and said, "Please, between the cast and painkillers, I don't feel a thing down there. When did you change your ringtone? Oh, wait, when did you get an iPhone?"

Lance sat on the bed and looked at the screen, the music loop starting to repeat. The caller ID simply said UNKNOWN. Lance used his thumb to slide across the screen and answer the call, then put the speaker to his ear and said, "Hello?"

There was a hiss of static from the other end, then silence. Lance pulled the phone away from his face and looked at the screen. The call had been ended.

Then a terrible thought hit him. She (it) had to know by now that Lance had escaped Bobby, so she (it) would be hunting Lance down. And if they knew Lance had Bobby's phone, then they could use it somehow to...

"We have to go," Lance said. "We have to go now."

Leah's eyes lit up with worry. "Why, what's wrong?"

"This is Bobby's phone, and just now, that call ... I think something's going to come for us."

Leah slid her legs over the side of the bed, sitting up. "I don't have a car. I ride my bike everywhere."

"Crap!" Lance said. "Any ideas?"

Leah looked down at the carpet for a second, thinking, then back up to Lance. "Yeah, I do have one, actually. But you're going to have to trust me."

"Of course I trust you," he said.

"I can call Daddy."

"Oh."

[33]

LEAH USED HER CELL PHONE AND MADE THE CALL. LANCE listened, half-worried and half-curious as to how she'd play it. She kept things simple and to the point.

"I've changed my mind, Daddy. Can you come pick me up?" A beat, then, "Thanks, Daddy. I'm sorry I didn't just go with you from the hospital. I ... I thought I'd be okay on my own." Leah listened to her father's closing remarks and then ended the call. "He's on his way. Five minutes, probably. He was in town."

"Should we go wait in the office? I suspect he'll attempt some sort of bodily harm to me if he catches me in your bedroom."

"Yes, he would," Leah said. "But no, you stay here."

"Makes sense," Lance said.

They were quiet then, Leah hopping over to the pair of crutches leaning against the wall by her bed. Lance helped her get situated on them, and then she made her way to the bedroom door, opened it a crack and stood by, waiting. Lance studied her, the way she was trying to act too casual. She was mulling something over, and though he didn't know exactly what, he assumed it was about him.

"Something on your mind?"

She turned and looked at him, met his eyes and held his gaze. "You've seen more in Westhaven than you're telling me, haven't you?"

Lance knew he could no longer withhold the truth from her. He'd told her too much already.

"Yes."

"You know what happened to the boys, don't you?"

Lance shook his head. "No, I don't know what happened to them. Not exactly."

"But ... you know," her voice broke and Lance saw fresh tears well up in her eyes. "You know they're dead, don't you?"

Lance hated what he had to say. "Yes."

"Have you seen them? Have you seen the dead boys?"

"Yes. A couple, but not all." He'd spare her the details of the burned boy from the diner.

She inhaled deeply, braced herself and asked, "Have you seen Samuel?"

It broke Lance's heart. "Yes," he said. "I've seen your brother. Twice. I'm so, so sorry, Leah."

She closed her eyes, and Lance wanted to go to her, wrap his arms around her and hold her tight. But something held him back. Something told him she needed her moment. Leah took two more deep breaths, and when she opened her eyes they were clearer, almost relieved, the tears drying. She nodded.

"It's okay," she said. "It's okay. At least now I know the truth. No more wondering. No more worrying." She laughed, and the noise seemed so foreign. "Is it weird to feel so happy to know your own brother is dead?"

Lance said nothing.

Leah stayed quiet for another minute, and then she looked

236

at Lance once more and asked, with a voice just above a whisper, "Lance, are you some sort of angel?"

The question floored him, caught him completely off guard. Never had this idea been proposed to him, and never had he thought of it himself. It was preposterous, but now was not the time to say so.

"No," he said, shaking his head. "I'm pretty sure I'm not an angel. I'm just a normal guy, who occasionally gets a hunch and hangs out with ghosts. No big deal."

Leah laughed, wiping the last remnants of tears from her cheeks. She smiled at him, and he was about to go across the room and kiss her when they both heard the low rumble of a muffler, getting louder and louder with each passing second.

At the sound of the truck, Lance suddenly became very uneasy. He trusted Leah had a plan, but being confined to the bedroom, if her father came in and ignored Leah's attempts at palaver, Lance would have nowhere to run and would likely stand little chance in a brawl with the man.

The hum of muffler and roar of motor continued to crescendo and then reached its peak, stationary outside the motel's walls. Then the noise died and there was the slam of a car door. Some heavy footfalls on the asphalt and then the sidewalk. Then the office door rattled with force but did not open.

"Shit," Leah said. "I forgot to unlock the door."

A fist pounded on the door hard enough to rattle the glasses atop the entertainment center. "Leah! Leah, are you okay!"

Lance heard the panic in the man's voice. This wasn't starting off well.

Leah was moving then, making her way across the office as quickly as she could on her crutches. Lance stayed put in the bedroom and tried to figure out where to wait. He chose to lean against the dresser along the far wall, mainly because it put him as far away as possible from the bed, which was the last place he wanted to be caught by a father of a girl he'd gotten involved with.

Lance heard the deadbolt slide and then the door open. "I'm fine, Daddy. It's okay, I promise."

Samuel Senior didn't answer right away, and Lance imagined him standing in the doorway, the man's thick neck practically creaking with muscles as he scanned the office and looked for threats, searched for something wrong. Finally, the man spoke cheerfully.

"You ready to go, sweetie? Don't you want to bring a bag, or something? You don't have much at the house anymore. It's been a while since—"

"Daddy, I need to tell you something. I need your help, but you have to promise me you can stay calm, and promise me you'll believe me and not lose your temper."

There were a few seconds of silence between them before the man said, "What's going on, Leah? What's this all about?"

Lance could tell the man had been almost expecting something like this to happen. A parent's intuition was strong, no doubt about it.

"You have to promise me, Daddy. I'm going to show you something and tell you some things, and whether you believe me, or trust me, or ... or anything, you have to promise me, as my father, that you won't yell and you won't hurt anybody. Can you promise me that?"

Lance silently thanked Leah for the bit about not hurting anybody.

"Baby girl, you know I'll do anything I can for you."

"Daddy, I'm serious! I don't just want words, I want action. I have to know I can trust you on this!"

Leah's sudden outburst seemed to resonate with the man, because the next time he spoke, he was somber, quiet. "I promise, Leah. I haven't even had anything to drink tonight."

"Okay," Leah said. "Lock the door again and then follow me."

Lance heard the deadbolt slide again, followed by the unsteady rhythm of Leah's crutches and her father's heavy boots coming across the office floor and getting closer. Leah came into view in the bedroom doorway, and she moved forward, coming toward Lance. Her father, wide and tired-looking, filled the doorway and stopped. He saw Lance at once, and the sudden shift in his eyes made Lance very grateful Leah was standing between them.

Samuel Senior was wearing the same outfit as earlier in the diner, and the hospital parking lot—the dark and worn blue jeans and white undershirt. Lance once again took notice of the labor-born muscles of the man's arms and shoulders. One solid blow to the head from a fist connected to that torso and Lance would be down for the count.

The rage in Samuel's eyes flared and then, miraculously, softened to an exasperated, desperate pleading. He looked at Leah, his expression one of disappointment.

"Leah, I want the truth, and I want it now. Who. Is. This. Guy? And your answer better be good, because from the timing of things, he's the suspicious guy that's been spotted all over town, and was seen with you at the football game, and he's the one who crawled out of the fucking ambulance with you after you got hurt. And now, despite my best efforts, he's still here, standing in my daughter's bedroom—the last place on earth I'd ever want to see him."

Lance couldn't disagree with that last part. At least he and Samuel Senior saw eye to eye about something.

"So," Leah's daddy continued, "What's the explanation? Tell me why I shouldn't kick his ass right now and then drag him to the sheriff's office." The man folded his arms across his broad chest and leaned against the door frame, putting his muscles on display.

Lance said nothing.

Leah said, "Remember your promise, Daddy."

Samuel Senior nodded, never taking his eyes off Lance. "If there's no problem, there's no problem."

It wasn't much in the way of a philosophical mindset, but Lance figured he understood the man's point. It was up to Leah now to convince her father that there was, in fact, no problem. At least in regard to Lance being alive and well and in their presence.

"Daddy," Leah started, "this is Lance. He's a new friend of mine, and, well ... he's not like other people."

Samuel Senior had no comment.

"He's got special gifts, Daddy. He can hear things, and feel things, and see ... things that other people can't."

With still no sense of response from her father, Leah blurted, "He's helping me figure out what happened to Samuel and the rest of the boys, Daddy! He's here to help us! And now some things have happened and we need your help. I can explain more later, but right now we have to go. So please, *please*, can you take us in your truck? We'll figure out where once we get on the road."

Leah stopped talking then, and Lance knew how frustrating it must be for her to try and squeeze so much information into a rush of a speech, trying to keep her daddy from boiling over and disregarding her. Lance knew his story didn't make any sense and was near impossible to fully explain, even with unlimited time and with the most open-minded of listeners.

Samuel Senior was quiet for a long time. So long that Lance thought maybe Leah had caused some sort of temporary shut-down in the man's head, that of all the possible explanations Leah could have given her father as to why Lance was there, the honest truth was so far beyond comprehension that the man was shocked into silence.

Lance was wrong.

Leah's father uncrossed his arms and straightened himself. He spoke softly to his daughter. "Your brother disappeared nearly three years ago."

"I know, but—"

"The whole town looked for him. The sheriff's office did everything they could. And when the other boys started to go missing, the state police started workin' on it, too. And you know what they found? Not a goddamn thing."

"Daddy, I know all this, but—"

"So you know what I think? You know what I think, Leah?" The man took a step forward, and Lance took a step backward, bumping the dresser. "I think this guy here, this *new friend* of yours, I think he's using the memory of your brother to get into your pants."

"Daddy!"

Another step forward, but Lance had nowhere to back up further.

"He's duping you, sweetie. He's saying whatever it is he thinks you want to hear. Guys do that, Leah. That's *all* guys do with pretty young ladies like yourself." He turned his head and spoke directly to his daughter. "I'm not surprised. Not with him, that is. But I am surprised you fell for whatever bullshit he's been feeding you. I thought you were smarter than that, baby girl. In fact, I know you're smarter than that. Which must mean this guy here is one *slick dick.*"

Lance saw a flicker of something to his left and turned his head ever so slightly to see that the television screen had changed from the muted late-night show and was now filled with nothing but snowy static.

Leah stepped forward on her crutches and yelled at her

father. "It's not like that, Daddy! You don't understand. Tell him, Lance. Tell him what you can do."

Lance said nothing, glanced between the television screen and Leah and her father.

"He can talk to the dead, Daddy! He can ..." Even Leah had to pause here. It simply wasn't something you could easily tell someone. "He can even *see* them."

Samuel Senior's face lit up at this, like he'd just heard a funny joke. "Oh, he can *see* them, can he? Well, my God. That changes everything! Why didn't you tell me that at the start? I suppose next you're going to tell me he's seen the boys who disappeared, right? I bet he even told you he saw your brother, didn't he?"

Leah hesitated, knowing her father was being sarcastic, but also knowing she was going to tell him the truth. "Yes."

Lance knew it was going to happen just a fraction of a second before it did. He saw Leah's father's muscles tense, poised for action, and then the man gently used his left hand to push Leah to the side, where she took one and a half hops before toppling over to her bed, her crutches clattering to the floor. And then the man was coming straight at Lance with the reignited fire in his eyes.

"You goddam son of a bitch!" He already had his fist cocked back, his body twisted and locked and loaded to deliver a single devastating blow to Lance's face.

Lance wasn't incredibly strong, but he was quick. He ducked and darted to the left, Samuel Senior's fist flying over his head in a wide, upward-swooping arc that hit nothing but air and nearly spun the man around with force. Lance popped back up, backed himself away, his butt knocking into the television. Samuel Senior regained his footing and turned back around, facing Lance with a face red enough to stop traffic. Veins stood out on his bald head, and his eyes were narrowed to slits.

He growled, "You've got nowhere to run, slick dick!"

But Lance didn't hear him. Didn't even register the fact that the man was pivoting off his heels and rushing at Lance with a speed and force that would knock Lance through the drywall. For Lance, time had slowed to nearly a freeze frame. His vision blurred and his head was filled not with the noise from the room, but with a low, staticky buzz that sounded like somebody trying to tune an old AM radio. The imaginary dials turned and twisted, the static popping and cracking and whining, and then from somewhere deep down in the static came a voice, calling out. It was so faint Lance made out nothing the first time except a foreign sound. But the second time the voice called out, Lance recognized it as human, and recognized the pleading urgency in the words.

Louder, Lance thought, willing his subconscious to reach the other voice.

The voice tried again.

Ace Bandage? Lance thought. *No, that's not right.*

And then, with a final burst of sound and energy, the spirit of Samuel Junior—the lost son and brother—broke through the static and rang true in Lance's mind.

"Bait sandwich!" Lance yelled. He was back in the real world, eyes focusing to see Samuel Senior charging at him. "Bait sandwich! Bait sandwich!"

Samuel Senior heard the words, his eyes clearing and looking at Lance with a startled realization. But he was coming too hard and too fast, and despite slowing himself slightly, when his body collided with Lance's, both men went toppling hard to the ground. The back of Lance's head bumped the edge of the dresser, sending a white flash of pain and light across his vision, but otherwise, he was unhurt.

Samuel Senior spun away from Lance, sitting up on the

floor with wide-eyed disbelief. He was breathing hard now, and sweat glistened from his brow. "What did you just say?"

Lance sat up, leaned against the dresser and felt the back of his head, where a new knot was forming. "Bait sandwich." And it was then that Lance realized he'd not only been delivered the phrase from Leah's brother's spirit, but the entire memory. Another instant upload.

"Samuel was eight," Lance said. "It was summer, and the two of you went fishing out on King's Pond. There was a little rowboat out there you could use, and the two of you packed a lunch and took your rods and went out early one morning."

Samuel Senior said nothing. Just looked once to Leah, who was now sitting on the edge of the bed, her eyes glued to Lance, and then back to Lance.

"You were out there all morning, and by twelve thirty you hadn't caught a single thing. You figured the pond needed to be restocked, but you didn't really mind. You were happy to be spending some time with your son.

"But Samuel got frustrated, thought he was doing something wrong for not catching any fish. You tried to calm him down, but he was stubborn about it and started to ignore you. And then you made a joke to try and lighten the mood. You told him not to worry. You said that even if the two of you didn't catch any fish, you had plenty of worms left and you could just have bait sandwiches for dinner."

Lance smiled. "Samuel nearly fell out of the boat laughing. I think ... I think that was one of your son's favorite memories."

The next time Lance looked at Samuel Senior's eyes, they were red and fresh with tears. He held them back as best he could, but as tears do, they eventually fell. He sniffled and wiped his cheeks and turned to Leah and said, "I never told your mother that story."

Leah's eyes spilled fresh tears as well, but she was smiling big and brightly. "And Samuel never told me, either."

Samuel Senior pushed himself off the floor and rushed to his daughter, sitting next to her on the bed and wrapping her in his strong arms. Leah buried her face into her father's chest and cried, and her father stroked her hair and said soft things to soothe her and cried his own cry, his tears dripping on top her head like raindrops on a roof.

Lance said nothing. Just watched as a father and daughter who'd been apart for so long took the first step in coming back together.

When they were able to compose themselves, Samuel Senior pulled away and stood from the bed, walking toward Lance. He stuck out a calloused hand and Lance took it, allowing himself to be pulled up.

"I normally don't believe in this sort of stuff," Samuel Senior said. "I mean, who really does?"

"Not many people," Lance said. "Why would they?"

"But there's no other way on earth you could possibly know about that day on King's Pond. No other way except ..." He trailed off, wanting Lance to say what he was too unsure to say himself.

"Your son told me, sir," Lance said. "Right before you speared me to the ground. I think he was trying to help me stop you, help me show you what I really am."

"And what are you?" Samuel Senior asked, nothing but curiosity in his voice.

"A friend," Lance said. "I'm a friend."

Samuel Senior looked Lance in the eye for what felt like a full minute, then nodded. "Can you look me in the eye right now and tell me man-to-man that my boy is dead?"

Lance stood tall, looked the man in the eye. "I'm sorry, sir. But, yes, he is."

Samuel Senior nodded again, and Lance saw the flash of

pain cross his face. But the man repressed whatever he had briefly felt and said, "I figured as much. I mean, all this time ... but still, to finally know, to have a God's honest answer. I just ... thank you."

Lance said nothing.

"And you think you can figure out what happened to him?" Samuel Senior asked.

Lance nodded to Leah. "We've learned a lot today, and we think we know the next step to take, but, with all due respect, sir, I'll have to fill you in later. Right now, we've got to go. I think whoever murdered your son is coming here, or sending somebody here to stop us from stopping them."

Samuel Senior's eyes began to boil again. "Then I'll stand right goddamn here and wait for them. They'll be sorry they ever decided to—"

"Sir, again, with all due respect, what's coming for us might not be exactly human. And in that case, I think it best we tuck tail and run, at least for now. At least till we come up with a plan."

Samuel Senior didn't have much of a response for this. But Lance's story about King's Pond had instilled enough of a trust in Lance's words that he didn't argue. He thought for a moment and then said, "Okay, let's go. Leah, the shotgun still behind the counter?"

"Of course," she said, getting up and adjusting her crutches under her arms.

"Lance," the man said. "Go grab it. I'll meet the two of you in the truck, and then you can tell me what you know and how I can help."

"Yes, sir," Lance said. And when Samuel Senior left the room, Lance turned around and looked at the small television. The snowy static was gone. Back in its place was the late-night show.

[34]

LEAH'S DADDY'S TRUCK WAS BLACK, BLENDING SEAMLESSLY in with the night sky. It was at least ten years old and had a regular cab with a simple bench seat. Samuel Senior was sitting behind the wheel when Lance and Leah made their way out of the office, Lance with the shotgun held sheepishly in his hands, and Leah turning to lock the deadbolt with a key she quickly shoved back into the pocket of her sweatpants. Crutches under arms, she made her way quickly but somewhat clumsily to the truck, and Lance opened the passenger door for her. She tossed her crutches into the bed of the truck and then the two of them climbed in, one after the other, Leah the middle of a very awkward sandwich between the two men.

Lance adjusted the shotgun at an angle across his lap, the barrel pointing directly at the floorboard. Any mishap would hopefully only blow a hole in the bottom of the old truck, or maybe take a toe or two from Lance. With his new weapon in place, Lance pulled the door closed and said, "Okay, let's go." His skin suddenly prickled with gooseflesh. He looked out the window and saw nothing, but still he repeated, "Let's go."

Samuel Senior cranked the engine, and the truck roared to

life with a near-deafening assault on the ears. The muffler hummed and the seats vibrated, and Lance felt as though he was about to be launched from a rocket. But then Samuel Senior shifted into reverse and everything quieted down a little, and once they started driving down Route 19, the vibrating and rumbling dulled and Lance could hear himself think again.

"Know how to use one of those?" Samuel Senior asked.

Lance glanced over and saw the man eyeing him, pointing to the shotgun.

"No, sir. Never fired anything other than a slingshot in my life. And my mother took that away from me when she found out."

"Some sort of pacifist, your mother?"

Lance thought for a moment. "You could say that," he said.

Leah's daddy nodded once. "S'okay." Then, "Loaded, Leah?"

"Of course," Leah said. "Always is."

"Good girl."

There was silence then, and Lance figured Samuel Senior had assumed Lance was smart enough to figure out the mechanics of shooting the shotgun on his own without much trouble. If it came to it—and Lance certainly hoped it wouldn't —Lance would aim, pull the trigger, and see what happened.

Leah's daddy turned down a side road Lance had passed earlier in his walks, a desolate-looking jut from Route 19 that had been nothing but high grass and trees as far as Lance could see. The truck hit a bump in the road, and the three of them bounced in their seats with soft grunts. Lance glanced nervously at the shotgun, suddenly very fond of his toes.

The headlights cut cones of light down the dark road. The asphalt was cracked and chipped and dotted with holes. The truck's suspension practically screamed, but the ride was tolerable, once you braced for it. The high grass grew higher and higher, becoming trees. Branches began to encroach on the road, creeping toward the truck.

"You were at the motel last night, weren't you?" Samuel Senior asked, swerving the truck to avoid a large hole. A calm, practiced maneuver he must have made frequently.

Lance looked at Leah. She nodded.

"Yes, sir," Lance said. "I was hiding in Leah's bathroom when you stopped by." Lance wasn't sure why he'd insisted on divulging such a level of detail, but at this point, he felt honesty was the best course of action. Even if it was beyond usefulness.

Samuel Senior spoke again, this time turning to Leah. "And you knew what he was then? When you were hiding him from me? Lying to me?"

Leah put a hand on her father's forearm, tenderly. "Not completely, but ... I knew he was special. And something ... something bigger than I can understand felt like it was compelling me to trust him. Even if just long enough to figure out why he'd come through the motel door."

Lance thought again of how he'd felt something coming off Leah, something wonderful and warm and all the good things in life. Something that made him return the trust she'd shown him without question. Whatever gifts Lance possessed, Leah possessed a small bit of something similar herself. Heck, maybe everybody had a tiny bit of it, if only they could open their minds enough to use it.

Lance heard Samuel Senior sigh, then caught what he thought might have been a sniffle. "You always had a way of reading people, baby girl. Your mother ..." He paused, cleared his throat. "Your mother was the same way."

Leah smiled, and Lance's memory jolted him back to the previous night, when he'd been fearing for his life in Leah's bathroom. Remembered the conversation he'd overheard.

"Sir," Lance started, "when you came to the motel last night, you said you'd been sent home because of a scheduling error. You said your boss had forgotten to call and had been in a meeting with Mr. Strang about some sort of fundraiser?"

Samuel Senior avoided another pothole. Rubbed the side of his face and said. "Yep. That's what happened. It was the damnedest thing. Spur-of-the-moment shit you don't usually see 'round work."

Lance thought about the timing, how it coincided with his showing up in town. Thought about Glenn Strang and the word "fundraiser." He looked at Leah. "What are the odds it had something to do with Westhaven athletics? A sports booster meeting, or something like that?"

Samuel Senior answered. "Oh, I bet that's pretty likely," he said. "Strang gives all sorts of money to the football team and such. Kenny McGuire's always poking around the place, going out to lunch with the big man. Having meetings up in the big conference room none of us are allowed to go near."

Lance asked one more question. "Do they ever bring their wives to the meetings?"

Samuel Senior laughed, shook his head. "Oh, sure. You should see all the heads turn when Allison Strang's within the line of sight. Doesn't seem to bother her, though. Always real nice, she is. Coach brings his wife from time to time, too. Makes sense I guess, being she's vice principal now." He paused, then added, "She's not too bad looking herself, in my opinion."

Leah gave off an embarrassed groan. Lance looked at her and said, "If Allison Strang was there last night, she already knew—somehow—that I was in town, and she knew where I was. She convinced her husband to get your father to leave and come to the motel." Lance paused, looked cautiously at Samuel Senior before saying, "I guess she could expect him not to welcome me with open arms if he found us together."

Samuel Senior grunted. "She was right."

Leah nodded as she processed Lance's theory. Her daddy switched on the left blinker, an action Lance found incredibly odd considering they were on a desolate road with no sign of traffic—vehicular, pedestrian, or even animal. But at the same time, Lance commended the man's commitment to safe driving habits. More people should follow his example.

The man slowed the truck, and a gap in the trees presented itself, along with a large aluminum mailbox and a thick wooden post. Samuel Senior turned, splitting the gap with the truck, and the tires rumbled over a gravel driveway. A quarter mile later, the trees opened into a wide clearing, in the middle of which sat an old two-story farmhouse illuminated only by the truck's headlights.

The house might have been old, but it was well maintained. Even in the light of the headlamps, Lance thought the paint on the front porch bannisters and railings and shutters looked fresh. The grass was neatly trimmed, and an American flag jutted from the house next to the front door. It danced lazily in the night breeze.

Samuel Senior pulled the truck alongside the house, parking it next to two large metal trash cans. Behind the trash cans was a large object covered in a plastic tarp. Lance studied it for a moment, guessed it to be a tractor. A large air-conditioning unit protruded from a window on the second story. A bedroom, Lance thought.

Samuel Senior killed the truck's engine, and the night was suddenly very quiet. The driver's-side door was opened and the song of crickets permeated the night. Samuel Senior got out and said, "Come on, then. We'll talk inside, and you can explain to me what the hell you think is going on."

As Samuel Senior walked around the rear of the truck, Leah pointed to the covered object behind the trash cans, looking toward it almost longingly. "That's my mom's car," she said quietly. "Just an old VW Beetle, but she always loved it. Always kept it clean, inside and out." Then Leah paused, smiled at a memory. "Daddy still takes care of it. Keeps it nice. That's why it's covered. I don't think he's driven it anywhere but the driveway since she passed. Nobody has."

Lance pondered the complexity of the human mind, human emotions. He ached for this broken family.

Lance opened his own door, mindful of the shotgun. He got out and then extended his hand to help Leah out. She hopped up and down until she got her crutches situated, and then they rounded the house and took the three steps up the front porch and went inside, where they found Leah's daddy sitting at a kitchen table with two cans of light beer in front of him. One was already cracked open, and Samuel Senior slid the other across the table's worn surface toward Lance. Lance caught the can and stared at it, his mother's opinion of alcohol weighing heavy on his mind. Plus, Lance generally disliked the taste.

But, in this particular situation, Lance figured it would be extremely rude to decline the friendly offer, especially from a man who'd attacked him only a couple hours ago and was the father of a girl he'd kissed multiple times today.

Lance rested the shotgun on the floor next to the table, terrified that if he simply leaned it against the wall, it would accidentally fall over and blow the brains out of him or one of his companions, which, aside from the certain death, would make an awful mess to clean up. He sat in one of the empty chairs and took the beer, popped the top and took a small but respectable sip.

The taste was bitter and sour and awful. He swallowed and tried his best not to grimace. With the duty done, he set the can back on the table, wiped his mouth with the back of his hand and said, "Long story short, sir, we think Allison Strang is murdering the boys."

Samuel Senior shifted in his chair, the old wooden boards of the flooring creaking under his weight. He stared at the table, sliding the beer can back and forth between his workman's fingers. Lance looked around the kitchen, saw creamy white appliances along with chipped but clean countertops. The kind of things that would have been new and modern and the latest style twenty years ago but now looked dated, yet respectable. Well kept, like the front of the house. Leah's daddy took pride in what was his, that was certain. There weren't even any cobwebs or dust on the overhead light fixture above the table.

Samuel Senior lifted the beer can to his mouth and took a long gulp. Burped under his breath and looked at Leah, then at Lance, eyes narrowed. "Look, I'm trusting you only because of the thing you knew about my son. The bait sandwich. But this ... you're going to have to explain."

Lance nodded, hating the time they were losing by having to recap again what he and Leah had figured out. There was no deadline, so to speak, but the longer they waited to take some sort of action, the higher the chance Lance would be stopped, or worse, others would be hurt.

Lance told Samuel Senior everything he knew. Started with the gust of wind that had knocked him out the night before, worked through the possessed sheriff's deputy and car accident, the conversation with Susan Goodman, the incident at the football game, his somewhat of an abduction by Bobby Strang and the conversation he'd overheard and the vision he'd gotten when he made his escape, finally ending with the phone call on Bobby's phone at the motel and Leah's daddy himself showing up.

When Lance had finished the story, he took another sip of his own beer—a *small* one—because all the talking had made his throat dry.

Samuel Senior was quiet for another moment. He finished

his beer and then stood from the table and tossed the empty can into a small trash can by the sink. He stood there, crossing his arms and leaning against the counter. "So you're saying that Allison Strang can ... what? Control the weather? Can control people? Like some sort of, I don't know, witch?"

(*My dad calls her the Voodoo Bitch Doctor, but we don't understand any of it.*)

Lance formed his answer carefully. "Yes and no, sir. I think Allison Strang is calling the shots, somehow, but I think she's being ... used. Used as some sort of vessel for something else. Something ... not of this earth."

Samuel Senior frowned. "And you can tell me for certain that things like this—these *things not of this earth*—actually exist. You've seen them?"

"Yes, sir."

If Leah's daddy was waiting for more, he wasn't going to get it. Not then and not there.

To the man's credit, he was moving the conversation along without questioning Lance's credibility. "And how exactly is Allison Strang managing to get these boys off somewhere alone, and then managing to overtake and murder them? She might be pretty, but there's no way she's strong enough or quick enough to outdo most of the boys on that football team."

"Biology, sir."

"What?"

"Sex, sir. She's using sex. At least, that's what I think."

Samuel Senior grimaced and then made a face as though he'd be sick. "God, and you're positive she's sleeping with her son? Her own goddamn son?"

"It appears that way, sir."

Samuel Senior ran a hand over his closely shaved scalp, blew out a big breath of air. "So, what exactly do we do about any of this? Assuming it's all true," he added.

Lance looked at Leah and took a deep breath of his own. "At this point, I think it's best everybody stay out of it as much as they can, and I'll go find Allison Strang."

Leah's eyes widened. "Nope, no way. We're going to help you. From what we know, the entire Strang family is working together in this. There's no way you can fight off all three of them. They'll kill you for sure."

Lance shrugged. "Maybe. But maybe not. They might let me go with a warning."

"This isn't funny, Lance!"

"No, it's not," he said. "But it's also something that none of you can help with. This is coming down to me versus her, or it, or whatever."

"And I don't suppose the police would be any help?" Samuel Senior said, opening the refrigerator and popping the top of another beer. "Haven't been up until this point."

"Correct, sir. I don't think this is something they'll be of use to us with until we can present them with solid evidence. Also, I was seen fleeing the car accident earlier by the truck driver who called in the wreck. If the gossip mill in town was already concerned about my showing up, the police are definitely looking for me now. Especially with one of their own dead."

And then, as if waiting for their stage cue, the blue lights of a police cruiser danced off the kitchen walls, followed by the sound of tires crunching on the gravel outside.

[35]

"WHAT THE HELL?"

Samuel Senior stood up from the kitchen table and mumbled more obscenities. He looked at the beer can on the table, still half-full. "I'm not drunk," he said. "I'm not drunk, right?" He looked at Leah, his eyes pleading. Lance again felt sorrow for the man, a man who'd been broken by life and was holding things together the best he knew how. Flaws and all.

"No, Daddy," Leah said, hopping up from the table. "No, you're not drunk. I can always tell when you're drunk. Plus, you're in your own home. They can't give you grief for drinking in your own home."

Samuel Senior's demeanor changed. He stood up taller, more confident. "Then why the hell are they here?"

Lance was the last to stand from the table. "Me," he said. "They're here because of me."

"They can't know you're here," Leah said. "Maybe because of the call on Bobby's phone they—Allison Strang ... whoever— maybe they knew we were at the motel. But how would they end up here? Everybody in town knows ..." She paused, looked at her father and shrugged in a half-apologetic sort of way.

"They know I never come here anymore. I *live* at the motel, for goodness' sake."

And then Lance wanted to kick himself in the head. "You just said it," he told her. "Bobby's phone. I bet they tracked it. It's an iPhone, so he could have just used that, what's it called, Track My Phone app thingy?"

"You need to upgrade and get with the times," Leah said. Then she thought for a moment. "But damn, you may be right. But would Bobby really call the cops, given what happened? What he's been hiding? All over a cell phone?"

There was a knock on the door. Three hard bangs meant to be loud and disturbing and get people's attention. Lance glanced around the kitchen. Looked down a small hallway to a living room, then found a closed door halfway between. He'd have to head toward the front door to get there, but it looked to be his only place to hide.

"Go, Lance," Samuel Senior said. "The window in that room faces the backyard. If you think you need to get out, just go. Straight through the woods about a mile and you'll come out on the ass-end of town. You do whatever you need to do from that point on. You've already given me more closure than I've ever had before."

Lance looked at the man, saw the sincere thanks in his eyes, then looked at Leah. He could tell she wanted him to stay, but also that she knew he had to go. "Text me the Strangs' address," he said. Then he took a step forward, gave her a quick kiss, and quietly walked down the hall toward the closed door and slipped inside.

Three more loud knocks.

"I'm coming," Samuel Senior hollered. "You guys know what time it is?"

Lance turned, and in the darkness, he found himself in a sort of home office. A worn couch pushed up against one wall, a cheap computer desk against another. A large and ancient Dell computer sat atop it with what looked like nearly an inch of dust encasing it. The monitor was bulky and deep, not like the new flat-screens you saw today. For a brief moment, Lance imagined Leah sitting in this room and using the computer to type a paper, or do research for project for school, back when she still living at home and her brother was still alive and everything was still picture-perfect. Before the tragedies that would dictate her life going forward. Lance wished he could send her back to that time. Her father, too.

Between the couch and desk, in the middle wall, was a window with the blinds down. Lance made his way to it and gently pulled the string, the blinds rising in what sounded like a deafening noise. Then he thumbed the lock on the window and eased it up, a cool night breeze blowing in.

Lance heard a knob turn and the front door open.

"Jesus, Ricky, what the hell you doing here at this hour? It's after one in the morning!"

"Can I come in, Sam?" A new voice, higher-pitched than Samuel Senior's, and a little nervous.

Samuel Senior sighed, "Sure. Sure, might as well. You're lettin' the bugs in anyway."

Lance heard the sound of two sets of heavy boots in the hall-way, then the door shut.

"All right, you're in. Now why are you here?"

Lance heard the soft rubber scuffling of Leah's crutches coming across the floor.

"Leah?" the new voice said. "Oh, thank God you're here."

This statement confused Lance. Why would the officer be glad Leah was at her own family home? Did they think Lance had abducted her and taken off?

"Goddammit, Ricky. Tell me what the hell's going on." Samuel Senior raised his voice but did not shout. Then he got quieter and said, "Ah, Jesus, this isn't about the thing at the hospital, is it? Look, I told Roger it was just a little misunderstanding. Nobody got hurt and—"

"I don't know anything about that, Sam."

There was a small moment of pregnant silence. All of them —Lance included—waiting for whatever news was coming.

"Your motel is burning down, Sam. The whole damned thing is ablaze right now. The crews are there, workin' it hard, but ... but I think it's gone, Sam. Most of it, anyway."

Again, silence.

"We were scared to death Leah was in there. We were worried she'd been asleep and ..."

He didn't have to finish.

Because of me, Lance thought. *All because of me.*

"How?" That was all Samuel Senior could seem to muster.

"Don't know yet," the man named Ricky said. "Fire guys mentioned something about electrical. Since the building's so old. Makes sense, I guess. We won't know more for a while, though. Like I said, the crews are still—"

"Thank you, Ricky," Samuel Senior cut him off. "Thanks for coming to tell me. You have a good night, now."

A hesitation. "Um, Sam, I think ... I think you should come back with me."

"Why?"

"Well, um, I guess some folks want to talk to you. There's some questions that need to be answered, and I guess insurance details need to start being worked out."

"I can drive myself," Samuel Senior said.

Another pause. "You sure?" the man named Ricky asked. "You haven't had too much, um, you know?"

"I've had one and a half beers, Ricky, you asshole. You and I both know it's going to take a hell of a lot more than that to impair me."

The man named Ricky sighed. "Sam, do an old pal a favor and just let me drive you. Please?"

Samuel Senior started to protest again, annoyance lacing his words, but then he cut himself off, suddenly choked back his retort and paused before sighing again and saying, "You know what, fuck it. Why not? It'll save me some gas. Can you give me a sec with my girl before I go?"

"Uh, yeah, Sam. Of course."

The front door opened and closed, and Lance waited a beat before cracking the office's door a tiny bit and peering out. He found Samuel Senior and Leah standing in the hallway, staring back at him through the tiny slit.

He's leaving us the truck. He thinks we'll need it. Lance silently thanked Leah's daddy for being a lot smarter than the town might have given him credit for.

"This is part of it, isn't it?" Samuel Senior asked. "This is because they know you're getting close?"

Lance stepped into the he hall and nodded. "I think so, sir."

Samuel Senior took one deep breath and then nodded once. There was a jangling noise as he pulled his key ring from his pocket and worked to free the key to the truck. He held it out and pressed it into Lance's hand. "I've got to go, Lance." He gripped Lance's shoulder with a strong hand. "You do what you got to do, but dammit, keep my baby girl safe. If you can find out what happened to my son, I'll owe you everything. But don't let me lose the only child I have left."

Lance swallowed. "Yes, sir."

Samuel Senior hugged his daughter and kissed her on the top of the head, and then he left. Lance and Leah waited for the tires to crunch over the gravel as the police car drove away, then turned and met back in the kitchen.

"What now?" Leah asked.

261

Lance swung his backpack over his shoulders. "Now I go try to end this. Even if it kills me."

The look on her face told Lance she didn't like his choice of words, didn't care for his mindset. But another part of her, the one that understood the situation they were facing was bigger than just her and him, asked, "And me?"

Lance picked up the shotgun and set it gently on the kitchen table. "You stay right here, and put holes in anybody that comes through that door that's not me or your father."

He didn't give her time to argue. Just kissed her one more time and left out the front door without looking back.

[36]

THE TRUCK ROARED TO LIFE, SHAKING LANCE'S BRAIN around in his skull for a moment before he slipped the motor into gear, made a three-point turn, and drove slowly down the driveway. Away from the house, away from Leah. He glanced in the rearview as he went, begging the girl not to be standing in the doorway watching him leave. It'd been hard to walk away from her in the kitchen, but if he saw her standing there now, it would be even harder not to turn the rumbling truck around and go back for another kiss.

He kept his eyes glued to the gravel road, squinting into the headlights slicing through the darkness. He slowed, then stopped at the mailbox, flicked on his right turn signal because it was what he felt Samuel Senior would have done, and then pulled out onto the pothole-speckled road and drove cautiously back toward Route 19, back toward town, back toward the Strangs. It was an odd feeling to know you were directly seeking out evil, walking into danger. It wasn't the first time for Lance. Didn't mean it got any easier.

His phone vibrated in his pocket. Since he was still on the desolate road, he came to a full stop before fishing it out and reading the message from Leah. He very well might die later. No sense in expediting the process by hitting a pothole, swerving, overcorrecting, and then slamming into one of the encroaching trees. He probably wasn't going fast enough to do any serious bodily harm, but the way the day'd been going, he wasn't going to take the additional risk.

Leah had sent him the Strangs' address, and then, probably assuming Lance's relic of a phone lacked a GPS feature, had given him some crude directions, which he scanned through and figured he could follow easily enough. He'd followed the Strangs from the high school earlier when he was tailing Bobby, so he could get at least that far by himself.

"You're very brave, do you know that?"

Lance jumped, his foot slipping off the truck's brake before finding it again and stamping down hard. He swung his head around and found Annabelle Winters sitting in the passenger seat. She was ramrod straight, looking ahead out the windshield. Lance followed her legs down from the seat and saw them passing right through his backpack on the floorboard.

"You know," he said, regaining his composure, "you could give me a little bit of a warning. What if I'd been driving? I could have wrecked."

Annabelle Winters shrugged her bony shoulders. "Don't suspect it would bother me much." Then she turned toward him and offered Lance the tiniest of grins.

He shook his head. "You're hilarious."

"I tried to warn you about the boy earlier. Sorry I couldn't sooner. It's funny how it works on my end. I know things ... but sometimes I don't know things. And other times, it's like ... it's like I only get a whiff of the smell right before everybody else. That was one of those times."

Lance leaned back in his seat, rubbed his eyes. He was so tired. "Why are you here?"

"You don't like the company?" she asked.

Lance chuckled, exhaustion pouring over him. "No, I mean ... I mean why are you *here*? Why are you still in our world, instead of moving on to ... whatever is out there? Like most others."

Annabelle Winters smiled. "You know, I've been asking myself that question since the day I died." She looked out the window into the darkness and trees. "I've gone over every aspect of my life. Every decision, every choice. I've thought about all my good days and my bad days, and I analyzed my life until there was absolutely nothing left to ponder."

"And?"

"Nothing. For the longest time I just sort of assumed I was living in my version of hell and was damned to never understand why."

"You say that like something's changed."

She grinned again. "It did."

"What?"

"You showed up."

"You're kidding."

Annabelle Winters shook her head. "No. Like I said, sometimes I just know things. And the moment I saw you in the diner the other day, it was like the locked box of information in my head snapped open, and it all flooded out and it all made sense. I've been here waiting for you. Because something knew what would happen to Westhaven. And something knew you would come to save us. And I'm the lucky one who gets to help."

"Something?" Lance asked.

Annabelle Winters sighed and used a wrinkled index finger to point up toward the roof of the truck's cabin, toward the sky. "Whatever's in charge. The big guy upstairs, so to speak."

"God?"

"Call it whatever you want."

Lance rubbed his eyes again. Said nothing.

"You're missing something," Annabelle Winters said.

Lance forced another chuckle. "I know. I can't figure out why Allison Strang is doing this. What's her endgame, and what's really in charge?"

Annabelle Winters shook her head. "No. No, I think ... I think it's more than that. Something else."

Lance looked over at her. "But you don't know what?"

She shook her head. "If I can get close enough and it comes to me, I'll let you know the best I can. I promise. But until then, be careful, Lance. I think you're meant for bigger things than Westhaven."

He nodded. Said nothing.

"She loves you, and misses you. And she understands why you had to leave her."

Lance thought of Leah and felt that small tingle of excitement coupled with turmoil. "It'll never work, will it? Leah and I can't be together."

"Not her, Lance," Annabelle said. "I'm talking about your mother."

Lance looked at her with the widest of eyes, his mouth gaping.

Annabelle Winters smiled. "I told you. Sometimes I just know things. Be careful, Lance."

And then she was gone.

Lance sat in the cab of the truck, his foot still pressed hard to the brake for another full minute, the road and trees behind him bathed in the red glow of the brake lights. He thought about Annabelle Winters's words about his mother.

Can she really know that?

Of course she could. She'd have to. Lance had told Annabelle Winters nothing of his mother, or the night he'd had to leave his home.

Leave her to die.

For the briefest of moments, Lance felt the idea of tears begin to build in his brain, but he slaughtered the thought and relished the idea that his mother's spirit was still burning somewhere. Some form of her was strong enough to offer him a tiny bit of reassurance.

And that was enough for Lance. It eased his mind just the right amount to feel the warmth of his mother's love inside him again, gave him a renewed and focused strength to deal with what was at hand.

He was about to let off the brake and start forward, but his phone buzzed again in his hand. He looked down. Another text from Leah.

I know you like to wing it, and I know you've got all these hidden talents, but thought you might like to know Daddy keeps a gun under the driver's seat. Daddy's got a saying. Doesn't matter how big you are when somebody else can pull a trigger. XOXO

Lance reached down with his left hand and felt—gently!—around the bottom of the truck's bench. First it was all smooth, and then his hand found some sort of holster and mount attached to the bottom, directly under his butt. It was a smallish pistol, nothing like the shotgun he'd left with Leah. In this case, he didn't imagine the size would make much of a difference.

He used his thumb and texted back: *Thanks. Your father is a smart man.*

He thought about using his own set of Xs and Os, but decided against it. If his phone had been newer and more modern, he might have considered one of those red heart icons. What were they called? Emojis? But maybe it was too soon for that, too. Plus ... like he'd told Annabelle Winters ...

He pulled up the previous message containing the directions to the Strangs' house, memorized them, and then released the brake and drove forward, headed toward Route 19.

As he approached the intersection where he could turn right toward town or keep straight to head toward the high school, which was where he needed to go, his eyes were drawn left, toward the bright orange glow flickering in the dark night sky. Flashes and bounces of amber light glowed from atop the tree line, accompanied by the shadowy presence of billowing smoke.

The motel on fire.

Part of Leah and her daddy's livelihood, reducing itself to ash and rubble.

All my fault.

He ignored the guilt and drove on, fueled partially by anger and partially by an overwhelming feeling that this would be the end. Whatever waited for him at the Strangs' house, it would all be over soon. The only question he didn't know the answer to was whether good or evil would prevail. Fifty/fifty weren't the worst odds, but certainly not the best.

He checked that the road was clear and then drove straight. He crossed Route 19 and was maybe a quarter mile from the high school when something streaked across the sky, causing him to jump on the brake again. The truck skidded to a stop and Lance ducked down and then craned his neck to peer out the windshield and up at the sky, his heart stuck somewhere between his chest and throat, slowly sliding back down.

Something had just flown by overhead. Something there, but not. It seemed to blend with the black of night, but still, Lance had caught a glimpse, just long enough to see the shape of a head ... and the wings and the tail.

A dragon?

He shook his head, nearly laughed at the thought. *Really, Lance? A Dragon?*

He'd never even seen an episode of *Game of Thrones*.

He stared up, looked around him. Nothing but the faint outline of clouds scattered and the dancing of treetops in the breeze.

Tired, he thought. *I'm too tired.*

But as he drove on, he couldn't quite convince himself that was the case.

He recalled Leah's directions and watched the truck's odometer closely. He needed to go three miles from the school and then turn right.

He'd only made it a mile when his cell phone vibrated in the seat next to him. He took a quick glance down and saw it was Leah calling. But just as he reached over to answer the call, the sky split open like a paper bag ripped in half, and down came a thunderous downpour of golf ball–sized hail.

Lance jumped at the sudden noise and assault against the truck, his visibility reduced nearly to zero. He pumped the brakes hard enough to send his cell phone sliding across the truck's bench seat, unable to hear it clatter to the floorboard.

He never heard the buzz for the voicemail.

Never heard the buzz of the incoming text message.

The only sound was that of the hail, pummeling the truck from all sides as Lance drove slowly along the road, steering wheel gripped tightly in his hands, eyes squinting, peering intently out the windshield through the manic whooshing of the wipers.

This, he thought, *is not a coincidence.*

37

THE HAIL DID NOT LET UP, A PHENOMENON OF A STORM that Lance knew was meant for him in some twisted cosmic way. It didn't stop him, but it certainly succeeded in slowing him down. Samuel Senior's truck had big tires with deep treads, meant to churn through the toughest of weather, and they did their job well, gripping the road and keeping the truck true to its course. It was seeing where he was going that was the problem. Calculating what he could from his memorized directions, Lance figured the trip from the Route 19 intersection to the Strangs' house should have taken roughly fifteen minutes. It was thirty minutes later when Lance finally found the last turn on his list and guided the truck into it.

And just as suddenly as it had started, the hail stopped, a few stray pebbles of ice clink-clanking off the roof of the cabin for good measure before finally ceasing completely.

Lance stared through the windshield at the fully visible outside world. The cabin sounded deathly silent after all the staccato tinkering of the hail. "Well, that's not weird at all."

Ahead, on a small hilltop surrounded by a white privacy fence, was the largest house Lance had seen in Westhaven. It was easily twice the size of Bobby Strang's home, and despite the upscale feel of Bobby's neighborhood, the house on the hill made those houses look like secondhand gifts.

The road was freshly paved, and Lance had to wonder if the Strangs had built this home when they'd moved to Westhaven and created this road as a lengthy driveway. There were no other homes on it, as far as Lance could see, just what looked like a half mile of blacktop with a slight curve up the hill, leading to a gate.

Two porch lights burned at the house's front door, and another by the gate, but otherwise, Lance saw no lights anywhere in the house. No movement.

He sat another minute and stared at the house, tried to reach into it with his mind and feel the people inside. He closed his eyes, breathed deeply and focused.

He got nothing.

Never works when I want it to.

He sighed, then drove forward slowly. The truck climbed the hill with ease, requiring little more than a feather's touch on the gas pedal, and as Lance rounded the corner and approached the fence, the entry gate slid sideways on a motorized track, disappearing behind the rest of the fence's wall and leaving a wide and inviting mouth for Lance to enter through. He looked at the tall lamppost mounted by the gate, searching for a camera or speaker box or anything else. He saw nothing. One of two things were happening: either the gate was activated by a motion sensor, or somebody knew he was here and couldn't wait to meet him.

You know what you have to do, Lance. Drive the darn truck.

He drove forward, hating himself for being so vulnerable to his self-motivation. *This could be suicide*, he thought.

But, maybe not. Fifty-fifty, remember?

As he drove the next fifty yards to the front of the house, the gate began to close behind him. He glanced in the rearview and hoped the symbolism of what he was seeing wasn't as foreboding as it appeared. If this had been a horror movie, that shot of the gate closing him in would have all but sealed his character's fate.

The truck's engine rumbled once thrown into park, and Lance killed it by turning off the ignition switch and sliding out the key. He bounced the key up and down in his palm, checking his surroundings, seeing if he could get a feel for things.

He'd parked directly in front of a two-car garage that was attached to the main house by what appeared to be some sort of breezeway. The house was all stone and brick and was essentially a towering, beautifully designed masterpiece of home architecture. A winding concrete walkway wove along a garden path in front of the home, approaching a large front porch on which sat two large rocking chairs. Lance's eyes shifted from the rocking chairs and followed the line of sight away from the house. From up on the hilltop, he was sure the view would be spectacular. The two porch lights still burned with a comfortable glow, but otherwise the house was dark and still. Lifeless.

Lance got out of the truck, thought for a moment, then reached under the truck's bench and fumbled with disengaging the pistol from its holster until he was holding the gun in his own hand.

Lance wasn't afraid of guns—until they were in the hands of the wrong people—but he'd never had reason to handle firearms before and therefore felt almost as uncomfortable holding this handgun as he had when he'd been entrusted with the family shotgun earlier. The pistol he was holding looked a lot like the weapon Bobby Strang had used. Sleek, compact, and surely powerful enough to get the job done. He found a latch that he was certain was the safety, checked it was on, and then—while saying a silent prayer he wouldn't maim himself, tucked the weapon into the waistband of his shorts and pulled his shirt over it.

As Lance made his way through the garden path in the darkness, a tingle at the base of his skull told him the gun wouldn't matter. The outcome would be the same with or without it.

But still, it definitely didn't hurt his confidence to feel its cool surface against his skin. And plus, he'd been wrong before.

He reached the porch, stepped up and then was directly beneath the two lamps on either side of the door. They were wrought-iron and meant to resemble hanging lanterns. Elegant. A few bugs buzzed around the bulbs. A breeze rocked the chairs in a slow, ghostly show.

What's your plan, Lance?

He watched his right hand rise up, watched his index finger point itself out, and then felt the cool plastic of the doorbell's button and heard a soft, soothing chime come from behind the large wooden door.

I don't have one, he thought. *I usually never do.*

The chimes faded away in a decrescendo, and then there was silence. A few creaks from the house as a gust of wind whipped by and then vanished.

Lance waited.

One full minute. Then two.

He'd been expecting to be expected, anticipating a "so we meet at last" moment to take place as the door swung open to reveal the villain, unmasked and ready to battle.

He'd been expecting *something*!

He pressed the bell again. Again the chimes followed and faded, and Lance stood on the porch like a man being stood up on a date.

He felt confusion, and disappointment. Disappointment in himself for getting it wrong. He'd been certain this was where he was supposed to be. He and Leah had pieced it together and Lance had had the vision with Bobby, and ... it was supposed to be here. It knew he was here, and it knew Lance had found it out.

He felt in his pocket for his cell phone, intent on texting Leah. His pocket was empty, and he suddenly recalled some flicker of memory of his cell phone sliding off the truck's bench as he'd braked for the hail. He turned, ready to walk back, and that was when he heard the deadbolt disengage.

Lance froze, his heart suddenly hammering. *This is it*, he thought. *Now we face the Devil.*

The front door opened slowly, first just a crack, and then all the way.

Allison Strang stood in the open doorway, wrapped in a large plush robe with her hair falling around her shoulders. A vast atrium of a foyer was visible in the background. A tasteful lamp on a small table by a massive staircase backlit her with a soft glow. Otherwise, the house was dark.

Lance stared into her eyes, stared into the eyes of a killer, a murderer of four innocent boys. The reason Deputy Miller's family was mourning tonight and so many nights to come. The reason Leah and her daddy's motel was burning to the ground. The reason Leah had almost been killed at the football game. Lance had blamed himself for most of the latter, but now, staring into the face of his foe, he cast all his blame outward toward the woman before him.

And as their gazes met, Lance took a step backward, nearly toppling from the porch. He regained his balance and looked hard into Allison Strang's eyes. He breathed in deeply, one quick gasp of air, and nearly fell to his knees with the overwhelming surge of love and happiness and compassion he felt coming from the woman in the doorway.

"You're the boy who was with Leah at the game," Allison

Strang said, her voice pleasant and warm. "What on earth are you doing all the way out here so late? Are you all right? Do you need to come inside?"

Something propelled Lance to nod and step over the threshold as Allison Strang stepped aside and motioned him in. And as she closed the door behind him, Annabelle Winters's voice echoed in his head.

You're missing something.

38

SHE REMINDS ME OF MY MOTHER.

This thought solidified as Lance watched Allison Strang turn the deadbolt, locking him inside the Strangs' home.

It wasn't the way Allison Strang looked—Lance's mother had never been one for excessive beauty products or fancy clothing, and she'd had the same hairstyle Lance's entire life—and it wasn't the way she talked. It was the vibe she gave off. That aura of happiness and kindness. It was so strong Lance could nearly reach out and touch it, grab it, as if it were tangible and his for the taking.

A kind soul. That was the best way to describe it. Folks used that term all the time, but Lance was blessed (or cursed) to truly know when it was an appropriate saying. His mother had had one, and Allison Strang's soul was nearly as pure and as light. But, just like snowflakes, no two souls were alike. They each had their own unique fingerprint, their own pattern. And Lance's mother's had been the most exquisite he'd ever seen.

Leah had one too—a kind soul—but hers had been tarnished, scarred. The loss of her brother, the situation with her father, and the town's tragedy had whittled away some of the purity and replaced it with a strong contempt. A deep sense of caution and skepticism. She glowed outwardly, but inside she was complicated. Lance found the combination intoxicating.

"Is everything all right?"

Lance focused his gaze, found Allison Strang still standing by the door. She tightened the belt of her robe and then fussed with her hair, as if suddenly aware she was in the presence of company. Her feet were bare. French pedicure. The small lamp on the table cast its warm glow, and Lance's shadow looked like a monster on the wall behind Allison Strang. He looked at her, and she smiled back at him. Her teeth were white and perfect, the result of expensive dental work or a lifetime of personal hygiene.

Lance seesawed between the idea of having being completely wrong about Allison Strang and the notion that he was currently walking into a well-laid, well-executed trap. He didn't know if it was possible for something—*it*—to be powerful enough to pull a mask over its true self, to blot out the evil and replace it with the purity Lance felt from Allison Strang. Deceiving normal people was easy, but deceiving somebody with Lance's gifts would be much harder. Lance figured as much, anyway. Though he always admitted he didn't fully understand his own gifts.

"I'm missing something."

He said it out loud without meaning to, and Allison Strang cocked her head to the side, interpreting his words. "You've lost something?" she asked. She crinkled her brow. "And you think it's here?"

Lance searched for a response. Was at a complete loss as to how to proceed. *Well, you see, ma'am, I came here because I thought you were in cahoots with an evil spirit, riding your son in his own bed, and murdering innocent high school football play-*

ers. But clearly I was mistaken. Sorry to bother you. I'll see myself out. Lovely home, by the way.

Allison Strang took three steps forward and then side-stepped Lance. She entered the hallway behind him, and as she did so, the recessed lighting turned on and followed her as she walked.

Motion sensors, Lance thought. *Not supernatural powers.*

When she reached the end of the hall, a much brighter light lit up, and Lance saw an expansive kitchen behind her. She turned and said, "I don't know why you're here, but you seem troubled. And ... a friend of Leah's is a friend of the Strangs. Such a lovely young girl she is. I called the hospital to check on her and they assured me she'd be fine. I was so relieved. That family's gone through so much, you know."

She turned and walked deeper into the kitchen, disappearing from sight. She called out, "I'm going to make some tea. Why don't you join me, and we'll see if we can figure out why you're here? Unless you'd prefer coffee. I don't like the stuff, but Glenn's got one of those Keurig things."

Lance walked slowly down the hall over expensive wood flooring and glanced at the framed art on the walls. Modern stuff you'd find in a gallery exhibit in a large city. Not the type of thing you'd pick up in town along with your groceries.

As he got closer to the kitchen, the feel of his concealed weapon against his skin seemed to grow with each step. Allison Strang had been kind and polite—*too* kind and polite to live on the same planet Lance did—and Lance was nearly convinced she wasn't putting on an act. He'd nearly accepted he'd been completely wrong about her. But, whether genuine small-town hospitality or an enemy lying in wait, a glimpse of Lance's gun—a gun he didn't even want to be carrying—would surely escalate the situation in a direction Lance didn't want.

He entered the kitchen and marveled at the size of it. There was a sea of granite countertops and commercial-sized stainless-steel appliances that looked like they belonged more in an upscale restaurant or on one of those cooking shows on TV. Allison Strang turned on a large gas burner and set a teakettle atop it. Then she reached over along the counter and powered on the Keurig for Lance. "You look like a coffee guy," she said. "Tell me I'm wrong."

Again, a flash of the perfect teeth. Another brush of hair out of her eyes. A slight adjustment of the robe across her chest. Lance hated the term MILF, but he could definitely admit when it was applicable. Up close, Lance could see the woman's face appeared older than the rest of her, despite any work or makeup, but she was still an attractive older woman. Lance found himself wondering how she and Glenn Strang had met. Was it during his days playing football, or was it after, or...?

And then it struck Lance that there was something terribly wrong about his situation. He glanced at the Keurig on the counter, its blue lights aglow and waiting for somebody to feed it a pod. *Glenn's got one of those Keurig things.*

"Mrs. Strang," Lance said, trying to find his voice. "Where is your husband?"

Because of the surprise Lance had been blasted with when Allison Strang had opened the door and greeted him, because of the sudden table flip of his non-plan of attack when he'd quickly had to come to terms with the possibility that Allison Strang was not the monster he'd come here to accuse her of being, Lance had taken entirely too long to stop and wonder why, at what had to be approaching two in the morning, the woman of the house would be the one to answer a stranger's nighttime knock at their door. That was the man's job. The odd noise after bed, the sudden recollection that maybe the oven had been left on, and definitely a knock or ring at the door well past midnight, these were things that fell on the husband's shoulders to take care of.

Call it protection, call it pride, call it simple husband duty, Glenn Strang should have been the one to answer the door when Lance arrived.

Allison Strang laughed and pulled a box of tea bags down from a cabinet. She had to stretch up on her tiptoes to reach them, and Lance couldn't help watching her silky-smooth calves flex as she did so. "Oh, you know. Glenn's over at his boyfriend's house, doing boy things." She giggled at her own joke. Lance didn't follow.

She saw his confusion and said, "Glenn goes over to the McGuires' almost every night after a home game. They drink a couple beers and watch the local news stations talk about the game, then they camp out in Ken's man cave and do whatever two middle-aged guys do to entertain themselves on a Friday night. Sometimes they analyze the game film—Ken has always valued Glenn's opinion. But, I like to pretend they eat Doritos and play Xbox games." She shrugged. "He usually just spends the night there on their sleeper couch. He and Ken are so close I'm almost jealous. I don't even have a girlfriend that close."

"Why don't you go with him? To the McGuires' house. I mean... you and Mrs. McGuire are close, right? I saw you sitting together at the game tonight."

Allison Strang smiled. Nodded her head. "Melissa and I get along, and she really is a lovely woman, but our friendship is really just a byproduct of our husbands' relationship. Does that make sense?"

"Sure," Lance said. For what felt like the first time since he'd stepped off the bus into Westhaven, he had somebody—a live human being—answering questions and talking to him without raising an eyebrow or giving him the cold shoulder. He figured it was time to make himself comfortable, act like this wasn't as strange of an event as it was. He found a row of tall barstools along an island counter and sat down, making sure to keep his back facing away from Allison Strang. Didn't want a slip of his shirt to show he was packing heat. "You're saying you and Mrs. McGuire wouldn't have sought each other out organically. You get along, but you don't have that much in common."

Allison Strang said, "Exactly," and then pulled open a small metal drawer next to the Keurig, plucked a coffee pod from it and stuck it in the machine. Then she grabbed a ceramic mug from another cabinet and pressed a button, and in thirty seconds, Lance had a steaming-hot cup of black coffee in front of him.

"Cream and sugar?"

Lance shook his head. "Black is perfect."

The teakettle boiled, and Allison Strang filled her mug and dipped the tea bag and then joined Lance at the island, resting her elbows on the opposite side of the counter instead of taking a stool. Lance turned to face her. Took a sip of his coffee. It was okay. He'd never really cared for those little coffee pods. But the caffeine would be useful, would help him think.

"I actually didn't believe it, at first," Allison Strang said. She dipped her tea bag again and then raised her mug for a sip. Lance watched the way her lips curled over the edge of cup.

"Didn't believe what?"

She grinned and gave off an embarrassed sort of laugh. "I was just being silly, is all. I mean, it was hard when Glenn was playing ball, always traveling and always having women at the hotels. It wasn't like it is for players today, don't get me wrong, but the temptation was always there for him. It was hard to trust him. But ..." She smiled and took another sip of tea. "I did. And he always came home happy to see me, and he'd swoop me up in his arms and kiss me and tell me how much he missed me and ... well, it just didn't seem like the sort of thing he could fake. Glenn might have been a decent football player, but he's a terrible actor."

282

Lance said nothing.

"But after a few weeks of these late-night McGuire house sleepovers, I noticed that sometimes when he'd come home, he'd act a little off. A little distant. After all these years of marriage, you become pretty in tune with your spouse. You learn their tics and their quirks, and you can instantly tell when they aren't themselves." She was quiet for a moment. "And then one day, when I was doing his laundry, I noticed that his clothes smelled of perfume."

Lance sat up straight, the hairs on the back of his neck standing up and his ears prickling.

"Perfume?"

She nodded. "I passed it off as a fluke the first time, just somebody he'd maybe hugged at the football game, or something stupid, you know? But then the next week when he got back from the McGuires'—he hadn't spent the night that night, I do remember that—I waited till he fell asleep and then went to the hamper, and sure enough, the same perfume smell was on his shirt."

Lance instantly remembered Susan Goodman's story about her brother smelling like perfume when he'd come home late one night, shortly before he'd gone missing. His heart pumped quicker in his chest. He took another swig of the mediocre coffee and asked, "Did you ask him about it?"

Off to the right of the kitchen was a breakfast nook with a small four-top table. A pair of French doors stood behind it, and outside, bright lights suddenly flashed on and illuminated an elegant outdoor patio set, complete with industrial-sized grill and smoker. Allison Strang's eyes flitted to the doors and said, "Deer. Sometimes they get close enough to trigger the lights. Had a bear one time. Boy, what a sight that was."

Lance looked from the woman and then back to the doors. When they'd flashed on, in that instant millisecond between full dark and full light, he could have sworn he had seen something. And it hadn't been a deer. It had been black, like a shadow, and it had had a tail.

He drank more coffee, his nerves beginning to feel on edge. He was getting close.

"So ... the perfume?"

Allison Strang laughed and then reached out and gently grabbed his wrist. "Why am I telling you all this? I don't even know you."

Lance smiled and shrugged and prayed to any god that would listen that she wouldn't stop the story now, not when he might actually gain a shred of actual information. "People have always said I'm a good listener."

She laughed again and said, "Fine. But then it's your turn. You have to tell me what you're doing here and explain why I haven't already called the police to tell them that the man they've been looking for, the suspicious boy who's been walking all over town, is right here in my kitchen."

Lance's heart sank to the pit of his stomach. He nearly knocked his coffee mug over as he moved to leave.

But Allison Strang gripped his wrist tighter and held her other hand up in a *calm down* gesture. "Relax," she said. "I'm not calling them. I don't think you're any trouble. I hope not, anyway. The folks in this town, not to mention the police, they're all just a little ... wary. You know, especially since all the disappearances."

"And you're not?" Lance said, willing himself to sit back down on the stool.

"Oh, I am. It's terrible what this town's been through. Those young men, all missing, all probably dead—yes, I'm a realist, honey," she said when Lance looked at her, surprised. "I suppose it's possible they ran away, off to find a better life and escape whatever was haunting them here. But ... I don't buy it."

"So why aren't you suspicious of me like everybody else?"

Because she's got some of it. Just a drop, but enough to know you're one of the good ones.

"Because I know you had breakfast with Leah at the diner, and I know you had dinner with her at Sonic, and I know you were with her at the football game. You two are obviously close —I don't know in what capacity, but you are—and that girl is probably the best judge of character in this entire town. Head-strong, no-nonsense, rational, and the last person on earth who would fall in with the wrong crowd. If she's cool with you, I'm cool with you."

Leah, you are amazing. You're saving my butt and you're not even here. Lance reminded himself to kiss her extra long when he saw her again.

"Well, I appreciate your support," Lance said, sounding like a politician on the campaign trail.

She waved him off. "Anyway, no, I didn't ask Glenn about the perfume." Lance felt his disappointment creep up. "I decided to—and I'm not proud of this—I decided to spy a bit. The next home game after he dropped me back here at home, I waited fifteen minutes and then jumped in my car and drove over to the McGuires'. And sure enough, Glenn's car was right there in the driveway. I turned around and drove home, but the next morning when I checked his clothes, there was that scent again."

"And then you asked him about it?"

She shook her head. "Nope. Instead, I forced his hand a bit. Next home game, I asked Melissa if she'd maybe want some girl company while the boys did their thing. She agreed, and I rode with Glenn to their house right after the game. I was only there ten minutes before I realized what was going on."

"Which was?" Lance was practically standing up in his seat.

"It wasn't perfume," Allison Strang said. "It was definitely a womanly, floral-type scent I kept smelling on Glenn's clothes, but it wasn't perfume." She laughed, clearly amused by her own mistake and mistrust. "It was incense! Turns out Melissa McGuire burns the stuff in the evenings to help her relax. She's big into herbs and holistic-type remedies. You should see her den. She's got all sorts of fragrances and little burners and candles and"—she chuckled again—"I told her that her setup looked like some sort of witch's supply closet." The chuckle became a full-on belly laugh. "I asked her if she had eye of newt!"

Lance froze. His mind raced.

(*My dad calls her the Voodoo Bitch Doctor.*)

He pulled up the image of Melissa McGuire from earlier at the school, and then again at the football game later that evening. *Her hair was in a bun! I thought it was Allison Strang because the hair was longer, but Melissa's been wearing hers in a bun!*

Lance replayed the vision he'd gotten from Bobby Strang when he'd attacked him in the garage. Watched the woman arching her back as she rode the boy on the bed beneath her, her hair sweaty and splayed across her shoulders.

The hair.

I was wrong, he thought. *Darn it, Leah, I was completely wrong. It's not Allison Strang who's behind the boys' disappearances, it's Melissa McGuire! It's the coach's wife!*

Lance shouted, "I've got to go!" as he stood from the counter and turned to head down the hall, and he couldn't help but think that maybe he wasn't being baited to the Strangs' house to confront the monster, but maybe whatever goodness there was left in the town—Annabelle Winters and whatever forces she rolled with—maybe whatever was on *his* side was pushing him toward Allison Strang so he'd be able to uncover the truth.

He heard Allison Strang scramble after him as he fled down

the hall and out into the foyer. He nearly collided with the door as she called out, "Whatever you're doing, be careful!"

Lance fumbled with the deadbolt and ripped open the heavy door.

He took two steps onto the porch before something hard and heavy slammed into the back of his head, and everything went dark.

39

LANCE'S EYES FLICKERED, COULDN'T STAY OPEN. HIS BODY jostled, and he could hear and feel the rumbling of tires over road beneath him. He strained, trying to open his eyes again, but it was like trying to wake yourself from a dream. It was as if his eyelids had been glued shut. His head pounded and pulsed.

I've had enough head injuries for the week, thank you.

He tried to speak, to force any words from his mouth, just to reaffirm he was still alive. He couldn't, but that was only because there was something over his mouth. Tape, probably. He tried to reach up and pull it away, but his hands wouldn't obey. They were bound together behind his back. More tape. The tape had gotten to him after all.

A man's voice up ahead of him, sounding very far away, yet perfectly clear, said, "Yes, I've got him. I'm on the way."

A pause.

"She won't say anything."

A pause.

"Because she's my wife and we can trust her. I'll ... look, I'll figure it out."

There was another pause and a heavy sigh and then, "This has to end tonight. You see that, right? No more. It's done."

A pause.

"You know what? Maybe I don't care anymore."

There was a large bump in the road, and Lance heard the man mumble a curse word under his breath before Lance went under again, swallowed by the darkness. Taken back into the dream.

40

THERE WAS A SUDDEN JOLT, AND THEN THE DARKNESS gained a faint gleam of light, like the early-morning sun rising behind closed bedroom curtains. Lance's eyes opened this time, slowly, and he found himself in the rear cargo area of an SUV. The rear hatch had been opened, and Glenn Strang stood in its mouth, staring down at Lance with a look not of anger or hate or frustration, but of a man who'd been broken and was fulfilling an obligation. He wore the same clothes Lance had seen him in earlier at the football game, but his face held none of the enthusiasm.

Lance was just regaining his full consciousness, the dull ache at the back of his head growing in intensity the closer he swam back to the surface, but even in his weakened state, he could pick up the slow trickle of sorrow from Glenn Strang.

Lance recalled the voice he'd heard earlier when he'd briefly come up for air. The one-sided conversation.

(*This has to end tonight. You see that, right? No more. It's done.*)

And from earlier....

(*My dad calls her the Voodoo Bitch Doctor.*)

It became even clearer to Lance than before. Melissa McGuire was running the show. She was in charge—at least among the mortals. Glenn Strang was only a pawn in a game he wanted no part of. Bobby, likely the same.

(*She won't say anything ... Because she's my wife and we can trust her.*)

Allison Strang had been oblivious to her husband's role in the town's tragedy. She'd thought at first he'd been having an affair and had then debunked the theory, failing to ever consider he was a part of something much, much worse. She was innocent and had ended up being a gift to Lance, the town's only way of pointing him toward the truth he'd been searching for. Lance smiled, the tape over his mouth pulling at his skin, as he remembered the warmth and happiness he'd felt from her, the way her soul had been so closely aligned with his own mother's. However things turned out for Lance—and right now things weren't looking so good—he hoped Allison Strang would walk away unscathed. He hoped she always burned as brightly as she had when Lance had met her.

But the reality was, a line had been crossed for her tonight, more than likely. She was now on a side she could not turn away from, whether it had been voluntary or not.

Lance looked up and focused his vision on what was behind Glenn Strang. It was the back of a house. Dark brick. A walkout basement with steps leading up to a rear deck. Beneath the deck was a slab of concrete forming a patio, a respectable John Deere parked there along with a set of wicker furniture. There was a door leading inside. Behind it, the light was on, and Lance knew it was waiting.

Glenn Strang lifted his right hand, and Lance saw the baseball bat. Wooden, scuffed and well worn with use. The back of Lance's head thump-thump-thumped with his heartbeat.

"You shouldn't have come here," Glenn said, his voice dripping with empathy. Then he motioned with his free hand for Lance to get out. "Slowly and carefully," he said. "I don't want to make this worse than it'll already be. Just get out, and walk straight toward the door over there." He nodded over his shoulder to the basement door. "You look like an athlete, so I don't have to tell you how damaging a blow from this bat to one of your knees will be. Don't make me do it, okay? Please ... just don't."

Lance tried to speak, his voice muffled behind the tape.

Glenn just looked at him.

Lance tried again.

Glenn Strang sighed. "If you scream, I'll bash you." Then, more to himself than Lance, "God, I just want this all to be over."

Lance nodded, and Glenn reached down with his free hand and peeled the tape away from Lance's lips, a quick rip with only minimal pain.

"Thank you," Lance said. "Why are you doing this for her?"

Glenn Strang said nothing, just stood back and again motioned for Lance to step out of the back of the SUV. Lance struggled to sit up, his bound hands behind his back making the task difficult and awkward, his sprained wrist perking up and making itself known. Glenn Strang smacked at a bug buzzing around his head.

"I can help you stop her," Lance said. "We don't have to do it like this. I'm on your side."

Glenn looked at the ground, then back to the house, back to the light burning inside the basement door. He looked at it for what felt like a very long time, then shook his head. "She'll ruin my son. She'll ruin Bobby's life if I don't do what she says. It'll ruin our whole family."

Glenn Strang's head jerked up to the darkened sky, startled.

His eyes darted around briefly, then he shook his head and looked back to Lance. "Come on, let's go."

Lance tried again. "What happened with Bobby?" Though he thought he already knew, the picture was now becoming clearer. Another misinterpretation realigning itself with the truth.

Glenn Strang thumped the rear of the SUV with the bat, just to the right of Lance's knee. "*Enough*. Get out. Now."

Lance threw his legs over the edge and hopped out. Standing straight, looking down on Glenn Strang and feeling sorry for the man. Lance didn't believe Glenn Strang was a bad person. Just a man who'd been trapped in a bad situation.

"Walk," Glenn said, pointing with the bat toward the basement door.

Lance walked, his long strides carrying him quickly across the grass and then the concrete patio until he was inches from the door. He heard Glenn walking quickly to keep up behind him.

Lance stared at the small pane of glass in the basement door, the light burning behind it blurring out all chances of seeing in. Lance only looked in on his own reflection, and the image of Glenn Strang standing behind him. Glenn looked much more afraid than Lance did.

Lance stood tall and waited for further instructions, wondering if he stood any sort of chance with what waited behind the door. He tried to adjust his hands behind his back and was greeted by a pleasant surprise. Something jagged and rough digging into the small of his back. Samuel Senior's pistol. Glenn Strang—ex-football player, successful businessman, respected philanthropist, proud father and husband—was no expert in apprehending another human being. He'd done a rough job of knocking Lance out and then quickly securing him with the tape, but he'd never stopped to check for any weapons. Lance was suddenly very thankful his pants fit him correctly.

But if he was being honest with himself, his opinion on the weapon hadn't changed much since the moment he'd grabbed it in the Strangs' driveway. It probably wasn't going to do him much good. Especially with his hands taped behind his back.

"I'll open the door, and I want you to walk straight ahead," Glenn said.

Lance met the man's eyes in the reflection. He thought about trying to reach him again and quickly decided it wasn't worth it. Glenn's eyes said it all. He was numb; he was spaced out. He was going through the motions in hopes of getting the task at hand over with as quickly as possible so that he could maybe return to a normal life.

Lance said, "Okay."

Glenn reached cautiously around Lance, as if Lance were a viper that would suddenly strike out with a poisonous bite. He grabbed the doorknob and turned it quickly, shoving the door open.

Lance stepped inside. One step, then two. He heard Glenn bring up the rear and close the door.

Lance's eyes adjusted, and he found himself in what he assumed was the man cave Allison Strang had alluded to earlier. There were a large leather sofa and recliner facing a moderate-sized flat-screen mounted on the wall. Surround sound speakers and lots of cords and electronic boxes stashed in a cabinet beneath the TV. Movie posters hung on the wall—*Hoosiers*, and *Rudy*, and *Miracle*, and *Remember the Titans*—all sports films. There was a small wet bar to the side, just beneath a set of stairs that must have led to the first floor. A Westhaven pennant hung on the wall by the stairs.

But in a room you'd expect to smell of beer or whisky and peanuts and maybe cigars, Lance was practically nauseated with the wave of flowery perfume that hung thickly in the air. It made his eyes water, and he tried to breathe only through his mouth.

Coach Kenny McGuire was asleep on the couch. He was fully clothed and stretched out with his feet dangling over one end. A pair of Bose wireless headphones were on his head. His chest rose and fell in slow, deep breaths.

"Poor bastard," Glenn said. "I don't know what she does to him, but it works. He's oblivious."

Lance's head started to swim, just a small bit, but enough for him to notice something was off. He shook his head, trying to clear the cobwebs.

"Through there," Glenn said, nudging Lance with the end of the baseball bat. Lance looked to his left and saw another door, slightly ajar. More dim light seeped through the crack.

If you go in there, you're going to die.

He stared at the door and wondered where he'd gone wrong. Wondered why he'd been so arrogant. Why had he come here alone? Why had he thought he could win? Did he truly believe he could beat an evil force that had already killed three boys simply by sitting down and having a chat?

You've overestimated yourself, Lance. You were stupid, and now this is the end.

You've failed.

Glenn nudged him again with the bat. "Hurry up. I've got to get out of here before this smell makes me yak up my dinner."

Lance looked once more around the room, searching for anything, any sign, any help, any warning. In return, he got nothing but a choked-off snore from Kenny McGuire on the sofa.

How fitting, Lance thought. *I'm going to die just over forty-eight hours after my mother. How very* Where the Red Fern Grows. *Or maybe* The Notebook.

He smiled, thinking how much his mother would have hated that joke. She loathed Nicholas Sparks.

Lance walked forward, his head held high. He supposed he'd always known that because of his gifts, his life, he would likely die by very unusual means. He just hadn't woken this morning expecting today to be the day. And really, who does? Death is an illusion to most, until the day it shows up at your doorstep and rings the bell.

Lance pushed the door open and stepped across the threshold.

[41]

THE ROOM WAS UNFINISHED, A LARGE OPEN STORAGE SPACE with studs showing and electrical wires snaking through them. Two banks of overhead fluorescents hummed, echoing off the concrete floor. Boxes were piled everywhere, some labeled auspicious titles such as KITCHENWARE and CHRISTMAS ORNAMENTS. Others were more vague and mysterious, like KENNY'S STUFF or KNICKKNACKS.

But what drew Lance's attention was the heat. He felt as if he'd just stepped outside the airport in Phoenix after flying in from Maine, a shock of heat slamming into him like a wave in choppy waters.

The source of the heat was a large wood stove burning near the rear of the room, a black cast-iron thing with a grated front door for feeding wood and stoking the flames. Orange and yellow light flickered and bounced from inside the stove's belly. A large pipe went up from the top of the stove and into the ceiling. Another, smaller pipe came out of back and went halfway up the wall before making a hard right angle and feeding into the wall. A pile of cut wood was neatly stacked next to the stove,

299

a pair of gloves tossed atop it, a black fire poker resting against the wall.

All around the stove and along the edges of the walls were what seemed like hundreds of candles and incense burners glowing. The heat, combined with the nearly knockout strength of the perfume aroma, caused Lance's head to do another jiggle, his vision blurring and his knees weakening. He shook his head again, breathed in deeply through his mouth. He squeezed his eyes shut and tried to focus. When he opened them, Melissa McGuire was standing directly in front of him.

Like Allison Strang, Melissa McGuire was wearing a robe, only hers wasn't heavy and plush and meant for comfort. Hers was thin and silky and short. It fell just to the middle of her thighs, and the sash was cinched loosely, the robe falling open around her neck and midway down her chest, her bare breasts just barely concealed. Her hair was up in a ponytail, the same golden hair that Lance had seen in his vision from Bobby Strang and had mistaken for Allison Strang's. Up close, Melissa McGuire's face was smooth and appeared much more natural than Allison Strang's, but this didn't equate to beauty. Up close, Melissa McGuire's face was plain, normal. But her body ... Lance glanced down to the open robe, the slim legs ... her body was a surprise.

She was staring directly at Lance, and he met her gaze with a conviction to stay strong till the very end. He would not give this woman, this *thing*, the satisfaction of making him cower. When Lance looked into her eyes, he felt...

Nothing.

He reached out, bored deeper into her unflinching stare, searched for any feeling. He found an emptiness that rocked him, confused him. He knew he wasn't always able to reach into people and get a sense of them—one of the many things about his gifts he could not explain—but previously it had always been

300

a very binary result. It was either ON or it was OFF. It worked, or it didn't. In Melissa McGuire's case, the switch was ON, he was able to see inside, could feel himself poking around in the drawers of her consciousness, but all he found was cobwebs.

It was as if she were empty, not even alive. Her soul was made of stone, impenetrable and dark and hard and cold. There was no emotion, no feeling. No sense of being human. She carried with her zero sense of meaning.

(*I'm keeping you out.*)

Lance flinched, Melissa McGuire's voice booming in his head as if through a megaphone.

(*You've never been rejected before, have you? How does it feel? How does it feel to know you're not as special as you thought you were? You're nothing, Lance. You're puny compared to what I am, what I'm doing.*)

Lance looked into the woman's face, feeling true terror for the first time. She grinned at him, and suddenly the heat and the smell and the realization of just how scared Lance truly was collided in his mind, and the room began to spin again and stars peppered his vision and blackness crept in from the sides.

"Glenn," Melissa McGuire said, "get him in place, please. Then get the hell out of here. I'll call you when I'm ready."

Lance felt himself shoved forward as his vision continued to darken. He stumbled, felt his left knee hit one of the boxes. The heavy aroma in the room seemed to be seeping into him through his pores. He tried to hold his breath but felt as if the scent was still making its way in, still doing its job.

He was certain he was going to vomit. He blacked out before he could.

He snapped back to consciousness, jerking his head up and taking in a gasping breath. The storage room was darkened, the fluorescents turned off, and only the light from the candles and burners and wood stove lit the place. It had a cozy appearance, soothing and relaxing. He breathed in deeply again and found the flowery aroma had dissipated some, or maybe his body had just adjusted to it.

The problem was no longer the aroma. Lance's arms were no longer bound behind his back. Instead, he was standing upright against one of the exposed studs along the wall, his arms raised above his head and secured by a set of handcuffs to a hook that'd been drilled into the wooden beam. He tugged once, twice, and instantly knew he wasn't getting out of this.

To his left, a piece of wood popped in the stove, the sound resembling a gunshot. Lance jumped, his back rubbing uncomfortably against the stud. And that was when another realization hit him: his gun was gone.

"Did you really think it would do you any good?"

Melissa McGuire appeared from the shadows on his right. Her robe was gone, and she padded barefoot and naked across the room to him. She must have seen Lance's surprise. "Don't you see, Lance? I'm in your head now. I'm buried deep and you'll never get rid of me." She laughed, and the sound was like nails on a chalkboard. "You're weak, Lance. I think the good ones almost always are, in the end."

Lance said nothing.

The golden light from the fire bounced off Melissa McGuire's flesh. Her skin appeared warm, reddened. Her breasts swayed as she walked, her nipples hard despite the heat. Lance felt a stirring in his groin and was instantly disgusted with himself.

Melissa laughed again. "Oh, come now, Lance. Enjoy it while you can." She reached up and grabbed her own left breast, gave it a small squeeze and laughed again when Lance looked away. "None of the others have been able to resist me. Why should you be any different?"

She took a step closer.

"All but one were virgins. Can you believe that, in this day and age? It was so easy. A little flirting at first, then a little teasing. Eighteen-year-old boys care about one thing and one thing only. And here's a hint: it ain't football." She laughed again. "And let me tell you, I love my husband, but he just can't compete with an eighteen-year-old's cock anymore. Eager and hard as oak." She shook her head. "It's almost a shame they all had to die. I was quite enjoying myself."

Lance felt his stomach churn, his revulsion growing stronger the more he understood. He needed to snap out of it. He needed to steady himself. He had to fight back.

"You're lovely and all," he said, trying his best to sound confident, "but I'm saving myself for marriage."

She ignored him. "So easy," she said again. "They walked right into it."

Lance stood on his toes, creating some slack in the chain holding his arms up. "So you seduce young men and then murder them? Your parents must be so proud. But, hey, everybody needs a hobby, right?"

He was stalling, obviously, but Melissa McGuire appeared to be in no hurry. Lance couldn't blame her. She had the definitive advantage. He flexed his arms and pulled down on the chain as hard as he could without appearing to visibly struggle. His sprained wrist screamed. He thought he felt the hook give a little, but it might have been wishful thinking—his brain playing a cruel trick.

Melissa walked up to him and stroked his face with her fingertips. They were electric, fiery hot. Lance held her gaze and refused to pull away. "Big boy like you ..." She shook her head. "I'd have liked to see what you have under those shorts."

Lance felt that unwanted stirring again, but he held firm.

"Why do you do it?" Lance asked. "What's the point?"

Melissa McGuire stepped back and looked at him. She

looked uncertain, as if she weren't sure Lance was being truth-ful. "You really don't know?"

"I asked, didn't I?"

She cocked her head to the side. "You mean to tell me a man with your gifts, your ... whatever it is that I can feel pouring out of you right now, desperately trying to fight me away—you're telling me you're here, and you still don't know what I'm doing? What *we're* doing?"

Despite his bound position, Lance tried to shrug. "My good looks only get me so far."

Melissa McGuire laughed another chalkboard screech, throwing her head back and producing a sound that bordered on cackling. "You're even weaker than I thought."

Lance despised the truth in her statement. If he were half the person he'd thought he was, he wouldn't have lost this fight. He wouldn't have been so stupid.

"Don't worry, Lance," she said, taking another step closer. "You'll find out very shortly."

Lance kept pushing forward. If he was going to die, and Melissa McGuire was going to continue to talk, he might as well get some answers.

"You're blackmailing the Strangs. How?"

She smiled at him, and Lance could feel her picking through his memories. He tried to close her out, lock away the important stuff. She found what she was looking for, and her eyes lit up and focused. "Ah ... I see. You got a little sneak peek from that boneheaded hillbilly son of theirs." She walked over to the wood stove and bent over, stared into the flames through the front grate, her ass presented in the air as if waiting for a lover. Lance looked away. "*Soon*," he heard her whisper. "*Soon*."

She stood and turned. "Being a female in America doesn't come with too many benefits, I'm afraid." She brushed something from her shoulder. "But there's one thing we always win. *Always*. Do you know what that is, Lance?"

"*The Bachelor?*"

Her hand darted out and grabbed his crotch. She squeezed, and Lance went further up on his toes. "A rape accusation, Lance. When we say *rape*, the poor guy on the other end doesn't stand a chance." She gave him one more squeeze, then a gentle pat for good measure.

Lance wasn't too surprised by this. He'd pieced most of it together while trying to convince Glenn Strang to let him go.

"A hidden camera—my fucking iPhone, in this case—and an off-camera conversation about liking it rough and liking to be dominated, mixed with some well-chosen words screamed while he thought he was giving me the time of my life ... you get the picture."

Lance did. "So you show the Strangs the video and tell them they can either help you or you'll ruin Bobby's life. And the family's, by proxy? That it?"

She nodded. "See? You're not *that* dumb."

"But why involve them at all? You've got the breasts and the butt and the sex. What could the Strangs give you? Glenn's nice and all, but I don't think he's many eighteen-year-old boys' type."

The wood stove cracked and popped. A clanging noise rattled through the small pipe coming from the wall.

Melissa McGuire's eyes lit up like a firecracker. "Poor thing was a little tired after trying to slow you down earlier. I was hoping to get Glenn to stop you before even getting to speak with Allison. Believe it or not, there was a part of me that honestly hoped you'd just go away. That you'd move on from Westhaven without digging any deeper. I tried to scare you. So many times I tried to run you off. And I tried to kill you. But you're a stubborn one."

Lance thought of the falling scoreboard. His fear that Leah would be crushed. He saw the image of Deputy Miller's family. His hatred bubbled and boiled, and he gritted his teeth. He was losing his cool. And at this point, why bother trying to control it?

A thought hit him. Melissa had said it had tried to slow him down earlier. She must have meant the hail. He thought about the gusts of wind and the lightning that had broken the scoreboard.

"You're controlling the weather," Lance said. "That's a first for me. And I've seen some weird stuff."

"Not me, Lance." She stared at the wood stove's grate. "Not me."

Lance stared at the fire, too. Watching the flames sway together in the blackened oven.

The flames.

The fire.

He thought about the burned boy he'd seen at the diner.

Then his mind flashed to Samuel, the first time he'd seen him, in the mirror. The way he'd looked so blue and swollen. Almost as if he'd ... drowned.

Two victims.

Two different ways to die.

Then it clicked.

"The paper mill!" He hadn't meant to scream. But the revelation was so suddenly clear he needed to get it out before anything else could disturb it. "You're using Glenn Strang to get rid of the bodies at the mill! That's why you're blackmailing him. First his son, and now you've got him so far involved he has no choice but to continue!"

Melissa McGuire ignored Lance's breakthrough. The fire in the wood stove gave off a loud *whoosh*, and the heat and light flashed like a bomb. Wood split and popped. Something clanged in the pipe again.

"You know the funniest part, Lance? You know what just absolutely tickles me about you showing up in town and thinking you could actually stop me?"

Lance said nothing. His eyes stayed focused on the fire burning in the stove. The light seemed to be picking up a greenish tint.

"The funny thing is you made it that much easier for me! This was probably going to be the last year. Even in a dumb fuck town like Westhaven, you can only go on so long without suspicion finally knocking at your door.

"Four boys would have been the limit, I'm afraid. Even though they all had sob stories to milk to make it so easy to believe they were runaways, even a blind cop finds his nut eventually. Plus, I think poor old Bobby was about to crack."

She laughed. "But this year, I can use you! So really, I should be thanking you."

Lance was about ask a question—he had so many—but the wood stove's belly exploded in a belch of green fire. The front grate blasted open on its hinges and slammed against the stove's side. The noise was like a gunshot. The pipe coming from the wall seemed to expand and contract, heat and air again *whooshing* out of the stove's open mouth.

And then the dragon flew out with the flames.

Only it wasn't a dragon. Not really.

It looked as though it were made of pluming black smoke, sometimes airy and transparent, sometimes as thick and as black as a starless night sky. It floated through the basement, its shape first resembling a snake, then growing legs and feet, looking more like a squashed lizard. It moved slowly, as if riding the heatwave across the room, and as it neared Melissa McGuire, its neck lengthened and its tail forked, and it landed on Melissa's shoulder in a soft puff of black smoke. The world's ugliest parrot.

Lance was certain of only one thing: this was what he'd seen in the sky right before it had started to hail.

This was what he'd seen outside the Strangs' patio doors.

This ... *thing*. This was the true evil in Westhaven.

And Lance didn't have the first clue what it was.

[42]

LANCE PULLED AT HIS CHAIN AGAIN, HIS WRISTS AND forearms burning with fatigue. The hook above his head was unflinching. Solid.

The thing on Melissa McGuire's shoulder stayed put, its body of smoke swirling and floating and ever-shifting. But its form stayed mostly the same. The tail and the torso ... and the head. A head that seemed to have grown two black holes for eyes, two sockets of darkness that had the tiniest spark of jade. Those eyes stared at Lance, appraising him. Lance's stomach turned in revulsion, fear. But he kept up his charade. "I think I saw your cousin in *FernGully*," he said, looking directly at it.

Of course, it said nothing. But it did open its mouth in what looked like a yawn, spawning two rows of black teeth, gooey needles of smoke that elongated the wider its mouth opened.

"Isn't he beautiful?" Melissa McGuire said. She reached up with her right hand and appeared to stroke the thing's side, her fingers disappearing into the smoke, raking through its body and causing tendrils of black to puff into the air. "He's been in my family for generations. He's gone from woman to woman, all the way back to my great-great-grandmother in Bulgaria. That's as far back as we can trace him." She smiled and shook her head. "The Bulgarians called him a demon—a *hala*—but what a terrible name for something so grand!"

"I'm more of a dog person," Lance said.

Melissa McGuire ignored him. "The early legends said the hala would cause terrible storms and destroy farmers' crops. But, if you were respectful and gave them what they wanted, they would in turn give you good fortune, blessing you and your family."

Lance felt his stomach churn. "And what did they want?"

Melissa McGuire sighed. "Like with most myths and urban legends, the early reports were mostly in agreement that a hala ate children to survive and sustain itself."

The thing on her shoulder stood on its rear legs, standing tall and appearing to stretch, its mouth widening again to reveal the smoking teeth. Melissa McGuire made a *shhhh* sound, as if soothing it. "Soon, my love. Soon."

The heat pouring out of the wood stove was becoming overbearing. Sweat dripped down Lance's face, his shirt stuck to him as if he'd gone swimming. His head began to feel faint again. His arms tingled and burned. He was suddenly tired. Tired of everything. His mind reeled with everything he'd learned.

"You're killing the boys so ... what? Your husband can win football games?" he said, his voice sounding small.

She laughed. "Among other things, yes. The *hala* brings good fortune to us in more ways than just football. But keeping Kenny happy and respected in the community is one big way. It keeps the suspicion away, and in small towns like this, where sports are king, the perks of coaching a winning team run deep." She walked closer to Lance. "And poor Kenny. He actually thinks his coaching is what's winning games." She shook her head. "I'll never have the heart to tell him. He snoozes away every time my baby needs to feed, and then he gets to wake up and reap all the benefits. I do all the work, but I don't mind. Kenny wouldn't understand. He's like…" She glared at Lance, a sudden fierceness in her eyes. "He's like *you*. He's too kind, too good."

Lance said nothing. His mother *had* been too kind a person. But Lance had always thought himself to be healthily balanced. Polite and courteous and respectful to all, until it was time to get dirty. Then he could show his claws. Then he could fight.

Given his current predicament, he wondered if his whole bad-boy side had been an illusion. Something made up in his head.

I walked right into this. Just like the others.

You could call him a psychic, you could call him clairvoyant, you could call him strange. He could see the dead, and he could see people's lives in a flash with just a single touch. You could call him whatever you wanted, but he felt a great pang of sadness in his heart as the certainty of his fate suddenly rang true. He'd not been ready to die, but in a matter of minutes, he would have his life ended at the hands of a monster.

He wished he could have told Leah goodbye. Told her to get out of this town and start a good life for herself. He could have used one more kiss to take with him.

Do not fear death. His mother's voice came out of nowhere, trumpeting in his head with an unexpected announcement. She had told him this repeatedly over the years as he'd progressed from child to adolescent to adult. *It does not fear you.*

Lance wasn't sure he'd ever understood exactly what this philosophical quip had meant, but at that moment, he sucked in a deep breath of hot, heavy air and let it out in a relaxed rush. He straightened and said, "So, do you give everyone the history lesson before you feed them to Puff the Magic Dragon?"

The thing made of smoke uncoiled itself from Melissa

McGuire's shoulder and slithered down her torso, its head and neck covering her breasts before swirling around her like an anaconda ensnaring its dinner. Melissa McGuire threw her head back and moaned, her eyes closed and her mouth turned down in an expression of what appeared to be pleasure.

"So warm," she said. "So perfect."

Lance continued to stare at what could be the kinkiest porn he'd ever seen. What would you even call it? Smoke-on-girl action?

And then Melissa's eyes shot open again, and her head snapped forward. She looked at Lance and said, "It's time."

She walked forward, the smoke beast continuing to encircle her as she came toward Lance, its head darting around her body and stealing quick glances at Lance as it went.

It's excited, Lance thought. *That can't be good.*

Melissa McGuire held up her left index finger, and Lance saw the fingernail shimmer in the firelight. It was long and sharp, pointed like a spear.

"Kenny thinks this is because I open so many envelopes at the school." She laughed, and then she reached down to her left thigh, just below her sex, and made a tiny slit. It was less than an inch wide, but the blood flowed fast all the same. The head of the beast darted to the wound in an instant, its face appearing to sniff, a smoky tongue flicking from the mouth and tasting the cut.

"This is the worst part," Melissa McGuire said, raising her finger to Lance's neck. "One quick pinch, and then the rest is painless. It'll be like you're getting so, so tired, and then finally you'll fall asleep." She made a quick slashing motion, and Lance felt the cut and then the warm tickle of blood down his neck, dripping onto his shirt.

Melissa McGuire wiped a drop of blood from Lance's neck,

then reached down and swiped a drop of her own blood onto her finger as well, smearing and mixing them together. She held her new blood concoction out toward the black thing's head, and it caught the scent, quickly snapping its head toward her finger. Once it was close and began flicking its swirling tongue of smoke and vapor, Melissa moved her finger up and away from her body, toward Lance's neck. The carrot leading the rabbit.

And that was the first time Lance was hit with the urge to scream. The thing's head passed by his own, its jade sparkles for eyes locking on to his for just the briefest of moments, the black billows of smoke swirling around Lance's head as the thing's body got into place.

And just as Lance opened his mouth to shout, the thing shot with unearthly speed to the cut on Lance's neck, and he was shocked into silence.

The sensation was so unnerving, startling, Lance's voice was trapped in his throat. His mind floated to the time Amber Tutkus had given him a hickey his freshman year of high school. When his mother had seen it, she'd been more inquisitive about the event than upset at her son's promiscuousness. The conversation was something Lance would never forget. As was the sensation he'd experienced that night in the Tutkus family basement. The gentle amount of pressure, the suction of Amber's lips and warm tongue against his skin.

The feeling now on his neck was just like that night, only intensified by a factor of ten. The creature was weightless, seeming to have no solid form or bearing against Lance's body, yet the suction was there, the sudden rush of pressure on his neck where Melissa had cut him. And there was warmth. A warm, sticky heat, like a summer afternoon thunderstorm.

Lance's head fell involuntarily to the side, allowing the suckling beast's mouth to work its way further in. Lance's eyes looked straight ahead, seeing through the rising tendrils of black-ish-gray smoke coming off the creature's body as it seemed to pulse and swirl. In the glow of the greenish-gold light from the stove and the candles, Melissa McGuire stood still, staring as her hala did its work. She smiled a wide, sinister grin, an evil acknowledgment of the horrors she was witnessing.

And then the room started to fade.

First the smell, that strong, flowery aroma that Lance had nearly forgotten existed, began to fade from his senses, replaced by a sterile gray-smelling nothingness.

The heat of the room seemed to suddenly cool, the temperature plummeting from what must have been a hundred degrees to something like freezing, before finally there was no sense of temperature at all. It was perhaps the most definitive observation of comfort.

His legs began to buckle, his muscles slackening like melting putty.

His ears began to ring, then cleared. Sound warped in and out, like somebody quickly twisting the volume knob.

Something rumbled outside the walls. Something ... *familiar?*

Then the sound was cut and Lance felt his legs begin to fail him completely, and the room grew dim as color drained from his vision.

And then he understood he was going to die.

It's not sucking my blood, he thought, straining his eyes, his muscles, his heart, his mind, straining everything he was or could be to survive a little longer.

It's sucking my soul. It's eating the life force right out of me.

Lance's eyes slid closed, and a sleep so deep and so wonderful called to him, begged him to give in. His body slid further down the wall, his arms pulled tight by the chain.

(You're not finished yet! Get up and fight!)

Annabelle Winters's voice grabbed hold of his consciousness and slapped it across the face. Lance's eyes shot open just in time to see the woman's ghost lunge from the shadows of the room. She held a wooden rolling pin in both hands, gripped tightly by one handle, and she leapt and reared back and slammed it into the neck of the hala, an explosion of smoke billowing and puffing and clouding Lance's vision.

And all at once, the sucking sensation stopped, a fierce jerk of Lance's neck followed by a coldness where the beast's face had been buried. The thing sprang to action, snapping its needle-toothed mouth open and closed. It hit the ground on all fours and then pounced, its tail swooshing through the air in a murky cloud. It rose up in the air, high above Annabelle Winters's head, and the old woman swung her rolling pin in an upward arc and caught the creature on the chin. Its head split in two, right down the middle, the rolling pin appearing to slice it cleanly in half.

Lance felt a bit of strength returning. Was able to regain his footing and stand upright.

Melissa McGuire stood slack-jawed, her eyes following her monster as it flung itself through the air. Her eyes never left the beast, and her face told Lance everything he needed to know.

She can't see her. She can't see Annabelle. The colors and heat and sound regained their presence, and Lance chuckled. Looked like he still had one advantage over Melissa McGuire and her Bulgarian demon.

The hala's head came back together, the two smoking halves resealing and re-forming. Even in the darkness, even with the creature's vague and shifting features, Lance could make out the snarl as the beast hurled through the air and slammed itself into Annabelle Winters's chest.

The two of them toppled to the ground. The rolling pin left Annabelle's hand and vanished into nothing as she lost her grip on it. She swatted at the creature with her hands, pounding her small fists into its neck and face. Its mouth snapped and bit at her assault.

"What is happening!" Melissa McGuire yelled. Her head turned and she bored an enraged stare into Lance. "What are you doing to him? What are you doing to my baby?"

And then she was moving, coming at Lance like a defensive tackle ready to spear an opponent into the earth. He tried to shift out of the way, but with his arms bound, he could only move so much, and her weight hit him hard, his back ramming into the stud behind him. Lance let out a soft cry at the pain and was then choked off as Melissa McGuire's fiery hands wrapped around his neck and squeezed. His Adam's apple compressed and he gagged—or at least tried to. His airway was blocked and his head was slammed against the wall and his eyes felt as if they were about to pop from their sockets.

"*I'll kill you myself!*" Melissa screamed, her grip tightening further. "*And then I'll feed your girlfriend to my baby!*"

And then a shadow darkened the right side of Lance's vision, right before a fist slammed into the side of Melissa McGuire's face hard enough to send a tooth through the air, clacking on the cement floor as it landed. Her body collapsed in a naked, sweaty heap. Lance looked up toward the stove just in time to see the hala dissipate, clearing from the air like a fog evaporating, until there was nothing left at all. Its puppet master had been disarmed, rendered useless.

Annabelle Winters's ghost was gone, too, the battle over as quickly as it had started.

Lance looked to his right. Found Samuel Senior standing next to him. The man's face looked haggard, but he reached out a hand and gripped Lance's shoulder. "Are you okay? Are you with me?"

Lance's breath was rapid, irregular. But he sucked in a deep breath and nodded.

Samuel Senior said, "Let's get you down. Police'll be here soon."

Lance heard the words. Nodded again.

And then he passed out.

43

THERE WAS ONLY DARKNESS.

No dreams. No visions or visits from lingering spirits. There was nothing. It was as if Lance had been powered off, as if somebody had hit the shutdown button.

And then all at once he gasped, choking on the fresh air filling his lungs and squinting against a dull light as he opened his eyes.

He was staring straight up through treetops, gazing at the night sky, the moon large and bulbous and bright. The cloud cover had cleared away, and stars seemed to actually twinkle. Lance felt hard earth under his head and body, could feel blades of grass itching his ears.

"Thank God, you're back."

Lance jumped, was about to sit up before a gentle hand found his shoulder and pushed him down. "Easy," Susan Goodman's voice said. "Go slow at first."

Lance obeyed and sat up gingerly. Blood flooded into his head and his vision did a momentary jiggle before settling. He took three deep breaths, his fingers digging at the ground, his ears listening to what sounded like many voices speaking in rapid, official conversation.

He was alive.

He was completely and fully alive.

He looked to his left and found Susan Goodman wearing a pair of Westhaven sweatpants and an *Alf* t-shirt that was two sizes too big, even for her. Her dark makeup was gone, her face washed. She looked much younger this way, more innocent. Her medical bag was on the ground next to her, and she zipped it quickly and stood, motioning for Lance to follow. "We need to go. Something tells me you don't want to have to talk to them." She nodded over Lance's shoulder.

Lance turned and looked and found that the two of them were standing just inside the tree line that bordered the McGuires' backyard. Fifty yards ahead, policemen and para-medics rushed in and out of the McGuires' basement door. Beyond the house, Lance saw the flashing blue lights from the cruisers decorating the sky.

Samuel Senior was standing to the right of the house, halfway up a small hill that led to the front. He was talking to one of the policemen in wild, frantic gestures. But his hands were uncuffed, which Lance took to be a good sign.

"Where's Leah?" Lance asked. But Susan was already moving, her large torso squeezing through the trees with a surprising agility. Lance took one last glance at the scene near the house, scanned the skyline for traces of ... anything. Then he turned and followed.

They went maybe a hundred yards before Susan turned right and they were spat out onto a neighborhood street. Her 4Runner was parked along the sidewalk, and she hustled toward it and got in, tossing her bag into the backseat. Lance got in the passenger seat and buckled himself in.

"Cut on your neck wasn't much of anything," Susan said, starting the engine. "I put a bandage and some antiseptic on it."

Lance reached up and felt the small piece of material on his neck, shuddering at the memory of the hala sucking there. "Thank you," he said, wondering how much of him—the true, inside part of him—had been sacrificed. "Where's Leah?"

Susan drove through the neighborhood and out onto the main road, heading toward downtown. "She called and told me to find you at the McGuires'," Susan said. "Said something bad was happening and you might need help. She also said to keep it quiet and to make sure the police didn't get to you first. She sounded absolutely desperate." Susan looked over at Lance. "Are you some sort of fugitive or something?"

Lance shrugged. "Probably."

Susan kept driving.

"Where is she?" Lance asked again.

Susan made a turn. "You did it, didn't you? You figured out what happened to my brother?"

Lance stared straight ahead. "Yes."

"And he's dead?"

"Yes. I'm sorry."

From the corner of his eye, Lance saw Susan nod twice, then reach up to wipe her cheek with the back of her hand. "Thank you," she said. "It's good to finally know."

She drove through the downtown street, all the shops dark except a bakery. Lance looked at the clock on the radio and saw it was approaching five in the morning.

Up on the left, Annabelle's Apron's lights burned bright, and Lance's stomach grumbled. He could go for some pie. As they passed the diner, Lance looked in through the large windows.

He smiled.

Annabelle Winters stood inside, her head and shoulders just rising above the windowsill, looking right back at him. She raised her hand in a wave. Lance waved back, hoping the woman could finally go and find her peace. He hoped she knew how eternally grateful he'd be to her for saving his life. Saving the town.

"Who are you waving to?" Susan asked.

Lance craned his neck and looked out the back of the 4Runner, back toward the diner. Annabelle Winters was gone.

"A friend," Lance said.

Susan kept driving.

They were quiet, the two of them, nothing much more to be said. Lance knew if he closed his eyes, he'd fall asleep, so he kept them open, staring out the passenger window and watching Westhaven pass by for the last time.

He knew where Susan was taking him.

He knew it was time.

Susan kept driving.

The bus station was right where Lance had left it two days ago. Tucked away at the end of a large parking lot on the outskirts of the town. Susan turned on her blinker and entered the lot, passing what might have been ten feet from the spot on the sidewalk where Lance had stood upon his arrival, readying his search for breakfast.

The lot was mostly empty, except for a few darkened cars scattered here and there, but buses lined up near the depot, some with their lights on and engines running. A couple sat still and silent, resting before the next journey. Susan pulled her 4Runner around them and stopped at the station's main entrance. She didn't put the car into Park, just held the brake and asked, "No more boys are going to die?"

Lance thought about it and shook his head. "No. I think it's over." And though he had no evidence this was the complete truth, his gut told him it was fact. What had happened in the McGuires' basement tonight had disrupted things. Put a halt to Melissa McGuire's schemes. Hopefully forever.

Just one of those feelings of his.

One of those things he couldn't explain.

"Will Leah be able to tell me what happened? I mean, what really happened to Chuck?"

"Yes," Lance said. Another feeling. "She'll know the truth. If not now, soon. She'll know everything."

Susan Goodman nodded once more and said, "Okay, get out of here before I get arrested for aiding and abetting."

Lance forced a smile and opened the door, cool air rushing in and feeling good on his face, his neck. He got out and said, "Thank you, again. For everything."

Susan winked. "Anytime, slick. Now get going."

Lance closed the door, and Susan drove away. He watched the taillights until they were out of sight, leaving just him and the idling buses alone outside.

He turned and pulled open the door to the bus station's lobby, stepping inside to the tune of classical piano. An old-timey music choice for an old-timey mode of transportation. The ticket counter was directly to his left, across a scuffed and scarred linoleum floor that might have been attractive a decade before Lance was born.

To his right, there were three rows of benches, old wooden things that had probably held thousands of travelers over the years—businessmen, Army husbands on furlough, and drifters, like Lance, who just needed to move on.

Leah sat alone on the first bench, her crutches on the floor at her feet, Lance's backpack at her side.

At the sight of him, she leapt from her seat and hopped on one foot, covering the ten or so feet between them. Then she sprang and jumped toward him, her arms outspread and reaching. Lance lurched forward, his long arms sliding under hers and swooping her up, catching her and holding on tight.

She buried her head in his neck, and he breathed in deep the smell of her, inhaled until his lungs felt they'd explode. He never wanted that smell to go away. He wanted to bottle it and keep it safe and have it forever.

She squeezed him hard and then pulled away and kissed him on the lips, long and meaningful and full of the words *Don't let me go yet.*

He didn't. At least not then. They kissed and hugged and laughed and carried on oblivious to the rest of the world until finally, regrettably, Lance set her down, gently.

She smiled up at him, and Lance felt his heart melt.

But they knew … they both knew the unspoken truth.

"How did you know?" Lance asked, taking Leah's hand and leading her back toward the bench. She hopped alongside him and then turned and sat. Lance did the same. "How did you know it was her? Melissa McGuire?"

Leah grinned at him. "It was because of you, actually. You had the right idea the very first night."

Lance's head still felt a little scrambled. "What do you mean? What grand idea did I have and then obviously ignore?"

"When I told you about the football team suddenly having a winning record, you asked me if Coach McGuire had been successful at his previous school."

Lance nodded. "Right."

"Well, after you decided to run off and leave me alone with nothing but a shotgun and my thoughts, I got bored and started thinking and remembered you asking that. So I looked it up on my phone."

"So Kenny McGuire coached a winning football team before coming to Westhaven?"

"Nope," Leah said. "And that's what threw me at first.

When I Googled his name, the other school that came up had a terrible football team. Not as bad as Westhaven's was, but not much better."

Lance didn't understand.

"He was the *basketball* coach," Leah said, sounding proud. "And guess what?"

"They won a state title?"

"Yep!" Leah sounded almost giddy. Pleased with her sleuthing. "But just one. The McGuires came to Westhaven the next year. So I called Daddy's cell and told him what I thought and that we had to get to you."

"Why didn't you call me?"

"I did! You didn't answer."

Lance remembered the hail, the way it had appeared so suddenly. A trick from the hala. He again remembered the image of his cell phone sliding to the floorboard. He'd left it there when he'd gone into the Strangs' home.

"So," Leah said, "Daddy got the officer to bring him home, and we took my mom's car up to the Strangs'. Thank God it actually started. We saw Daddy's truck and I ran up and pounded on the front door, but nobody answered. I rang the bell and pounded some more and just as I was about to turn and run around to the back of the house, the door cracked open just the tiniest bit, and I saw Allison Strang through the slit. Her face was red and puffy. I think she'd been crying. I didn't even have to say anything. She just looked at me and said, 'He's not here.'"

Lance felt pity for Allison Strang. There was no turning back from what she'd been thrust into. Her entire life had been flipped upside down in a single night.

"I told Daddy we had to get to the McGuires', and he said he'd go. I started to beg for him to let me come—I was determined to help—but he told me he'd rather die than risk losing his last living child." She paused. "I couldn't argue with him about that. No matter what I was feeling inside." She took a breath. She'd been talking so fast Lance had trouble keeping up. "So I let him go, and then I called Susan and I came here. I've been waiting for hours, it feels like. Couldn't you have gotten here quicker?"

Lance smiled and then leaned forward and kissed her forehead. "I almost didn't get here at all."

And then he thought about the McGuires moving on after only one basketball state title. He thought about Melissa McGuire's speech in the basement. How she said four boys would probably be the number she'd stop with, before moving on to somewhere else. He remembered her talk of good fortune and keeping suspicion away. He remembered how heavily she relied on Glenn and Bobby Strang to play by her rules.

"Something happened," Lance said, more to himself than Leah. "Something must have made her vulnerable. Only reason they would have left after just the one year."

Leah looked at him, not following. "What do you mean?"

So Lance told her everything, the entire series of events from the basement. Everything he'd learned and seen and understood. He even told her about Annabelle Winters. All the way up to the moment Susan Goodman had dropped him off at the bus station. When he was finished, Leah said, "That's the most unbelievable thing I've ever heard in my entire life. I can't believe all that stuff is actually out there. Ghosts and spirits and demons." She shivered. "I'm glad I don't see it."

Lance nodded. "It's going to be hard to top, that's for sure." Then he added, "Your father was talking to the police when Susan got me out of there. I don't know exactly how this is all going to play out, but I'm pretty sure Glenn Strang will crack and confess. He'd been strung along too long, I could feel it. He was begging to tell the truth. I think it was eating him alive."

"Good," Leah said. "Bastard deserves to suffer."

Lance couldn't argue. Instead he said, "Your father saved me, you know. He kept Melissa from killing me and then must have gotten me out of there before the police showed up."

Leah nodded her head. "Daddy's not as bad as some people think. He just hasn't been himself for a long time."

Lance said, "Be sure and thank him for me."

Leah nodded and said she would and then asked the question Lance had known would come. "Lance, you said you saw Samuel, right?"

Lance nodded.

She waited a beat, as if trying to figure out how to phrase the next part. "How was he? I mean, I know he's ... I guess what I'm asking is..." She sighed in frustration. "Why was he here?"

Lance thought back to the ghost in Leah's television. He smiled. "Honestly, I think he was just keeping an eye on his little sister. If I had to guess, I'd say he's moved on now. You're safe, and he knows it."

They were quiet for a long time then, both staring ahead at the ticket counter. A large clock hung above the window, slowly ticking off the seconds as the first morning light appeared outside, peeking through the lobby's windows.

"How did you know this is where I would come?" Lance asked. "How did you know to tell Susan to take me here?"

Leah opened her mouth to speak, then stopped. Lance looked at her, and she refused to meet his gaze.

"Leah?"

Then she turned and he saw the tears. She sobbed, "Because I know you can't stay. Not after what happened, and because ..." Lance would have slit his wrists to make her crying stop; the pain inside him was almost unbearable. "Because somebody like you will always have to move on. You're too valuable to the world to stay in one place. Too many people need help."

Lance was astounded at the girl's unselfishness. He'd not known it was possible to grow to love somebody so quickly in such a short, tragic span of time.

He hated himself for being cursed with such an unfair burden, doomed to walk the earth forever knowing he would never fit in, would never be able to live the normal life he desperately wanted to embrace. He wanted to stay in Westhaven, wanted to go eat breakfast at Annabelle's Apron and have hot dogs at Sonic and see if the Westhaven basketball team would be any good this winter and decorate a Christmas tree with Leah and read books with her by the fire and watch her unwrap her gifts and spend all the time in the world together.

He wanted to live, not just be alive.

"You could come with me," he said, already knowing the answer.

She wiped tears from her face and shook her head. "I can't. Daddy will need me. Now, more than ever. With the motel damaged and all. And ... what would I do? I've done nothing my entire life except live in this dump of a town and work at a fleabag motel."

Lance pushed a stray strand of hair out of her eyes. "I didn't see any fleas."

She didn't laugh. Just said, "I can't."

Lance understood. He got up from the bench and walked to the counter. He rang an old-fashioned bell by the window, and a minute later, an elderly man wearing bib overalls and bifocals appeared. "Help you?" the man said.

"I'd like a ticket, please. The first thing out that's going anywhere but south."

The man didn't question the request, just looked down at a chart on the desk in front of him and then punched a few keys on a relic of a computer. Lance handed over money, and the man handed Lance a printed ticket. Then he disappeared back to wherever he'd come.

Leah was standing now, her crutches under her arms. Lance looked at his ticket. "Leaves in fifteen minutes. I bet there's room for one more."

She looked up at him with eyes brimming with tears, ready to spill at the slightest provocation. "Your phone's in your backpack. My number's still in it, I hope." Then she took one step toward him, the crutches loud on the linoleum, echoing in the empty lobby. She rose up on her good foot, and Lance leaned down and they kissed one last time. When their lips parted, she said, "I'm going now. I can't ... I can't watch you leave. I can't watch that bus carry you away."

Lance said nothing.

"Thank you for everything you've done for us," she said. "Thank you for being you."

She grabbed his hand and squeezed it, her fingers soft and angelic. Then she let him go and turned and headed out the door. The sound of her cries pierced Lance's soul.

44

Lance sat alone on the bench in the bus station lobby. The bus would be leaving in five minutes, but he couldn't bring himself to step outside just yet. He didn't want any extra time between the moment he took a seat and the moment the driver drove him away from Westhaven, from Leah.

He unzipped his backpack and found his phone, sitting right there on top of his clothes. He flipped it open and pressed the buttons and saw his missed call and messages from Leah, warning him about Melissa McGuire.

His life had been saved by two women tonight. One dead, one alive.

Then he saw a third message, the voicemail left by Marcus Johnston yesterday. The sight of his old friend's name caused a sickness in Lance's gut as he remembered the last time he'd seen the man, his last night in his hometown. Lance sighed, pressed the button and put the phone to his ear. Listened.

The message ended and Lance played it again, listening more carefully this time, hardly believing what he was hearing.

Marcus Johnston was calling to tell him that eventually, Lance would need to settle his mother's estate, and that there was a sizeable amount of money to be dealt with. Lance wasn't sure what to make of this. His entire life, his mother had seemingly been about as uninterested in physical possessions and money as one could be. Frugal was her middle name—one of many. She'd never so much as even mentioned a savings account to Lance, even when he was clearly old enough to be included in such conversations. She'd worked, of course, changing jobs frequently but always committed to whatever she'd taken on at the time. This revelation was a mystery.

Lance saw the time on his phone's screen and got up quickly, shoving the phone into his pocket and slinging his backpack over his shoulder. He crossed the dirty linoleum and stepped outside, the sun halfway up on the horizon, the air chilly and clean and mixed with exhaust fumes from the rattling bus waiting by the curb.

Lance looked out to the parking lot, not wanting to, but finding himself unable to stop, some part of him desperately hoping to see Leah's mother's car sitting in one of the spaces, a head of blond hair visible behind the windshield. The best smile on the prettiest face.

The lot was empty except for a red Ford van, covered in dirt.

Lance mentally said goodbye to Westhaven and turned and walked the few paces up the sidewalk to the waiting bus. The driver looked tired and impatient through the large windshield as Lance approached.

The door to the bus was open, and Lance reached in and grabbed the railing to pull himself up the steps. And as he took the first step up, he stopped, halfway in, halfway out of the open door.

He turned and looked around and sniffed the air.

He caught a whiff of lavender. A hint of honey.

His mother's favorite tea.

The sidewalk was empty.

Lance stared at the deserted walkway another ten seconds before the driver cleared his throat behind him.

Lance climbed the rest of the steps and found a seat on the mostly empty bus. The two other passengers—a couple, from the way they were huddled together in seats near the back—didn't bother to even look up as Lance boarded.

He tossed his bag onto the seat and had barely sat down before the bus jerked forward and drove away, gears grinding.

The scent of lavender and honey faded from his senses.

As the bus pulled out into the street, Lance closed his eyes and leaned his head back. For the first time in as long as he could remember, he felt the warm caress of tears spill down his face.

For all the latest info, including release dates, giveaways, and special events, you can visit the page below to sign up for the Michael Robertson, Jr. newsletter. (He promises to never spam you!)

http://mrobertsonjr.com/newsletter-sign-up

Follow On:

Facebook.com/mrobertsonjr

Twitter.com/mrobertsonjr

More from Michael Robertson Jr

LANCE BRODY SERIES

Dark Vacancy (Book 4)

Dark Shore (Book 3)

Dark Deception (Book 2.5 - Short Story)

Dark Son (Book 2)

Dark Game (Book 1)

Dark Beginnings (Book 0 - Prequel Novella)

OTHER NOVELS

Cedar Ridge

Transit

Rough Draft (A Kindle #1 Horror Bestseller!)

Regret*

Collections

Tormented Thoughts: Tales of Horror

The Teachers' Lounge*

*Writing as Dan Dawkins